Tig and Lily

Party Animals

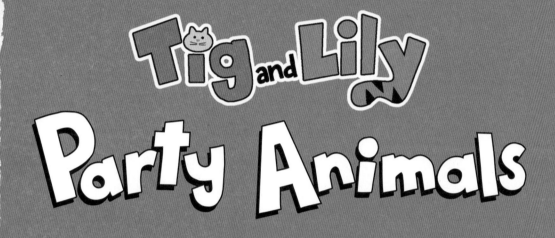

Copyright © 2023 by Dan Thompson

All rights reserved. Published in the United States by RH Graphic, an imprint of Random House Children's Books, a division of Penguin Random House LLC, New York.

RH Graphic with the book design is a trademark of Penguin Random House LLC.

Visit us on the web! RHKidsGraphic.com • @RHKidsGraphic

Educators and librarians, for a variety of teaching tools, visit us at RHTeachersLibrarians.com

Library of Congress Cataloging-in-Publication Data is available upon request.
ISBN 978-0-593-48631-3 (hardcover) — ISBN 978-0-593-48632-0 (library binding)
ISBN 978-0-593-48633-7 (ebook)

Designed by Patrick Crotty

MANUFACTURED IN CHINA
10 9 8 7 6 5 4 3 2 1
First Edition

A comic on every bookshelf.

Party Animals

Dan Thompson

For my wife,
kari

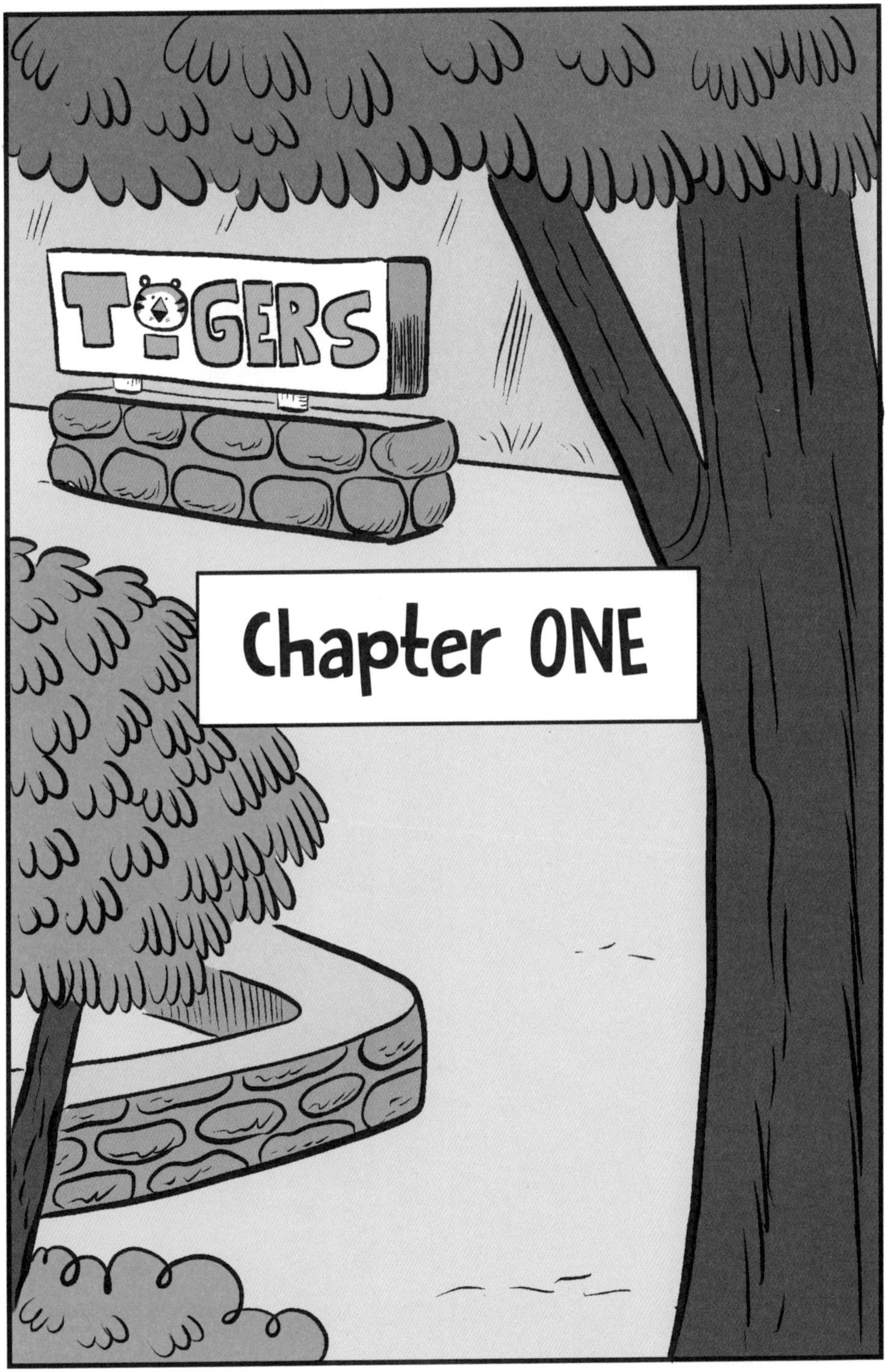
TIGERS
Chapter ONE

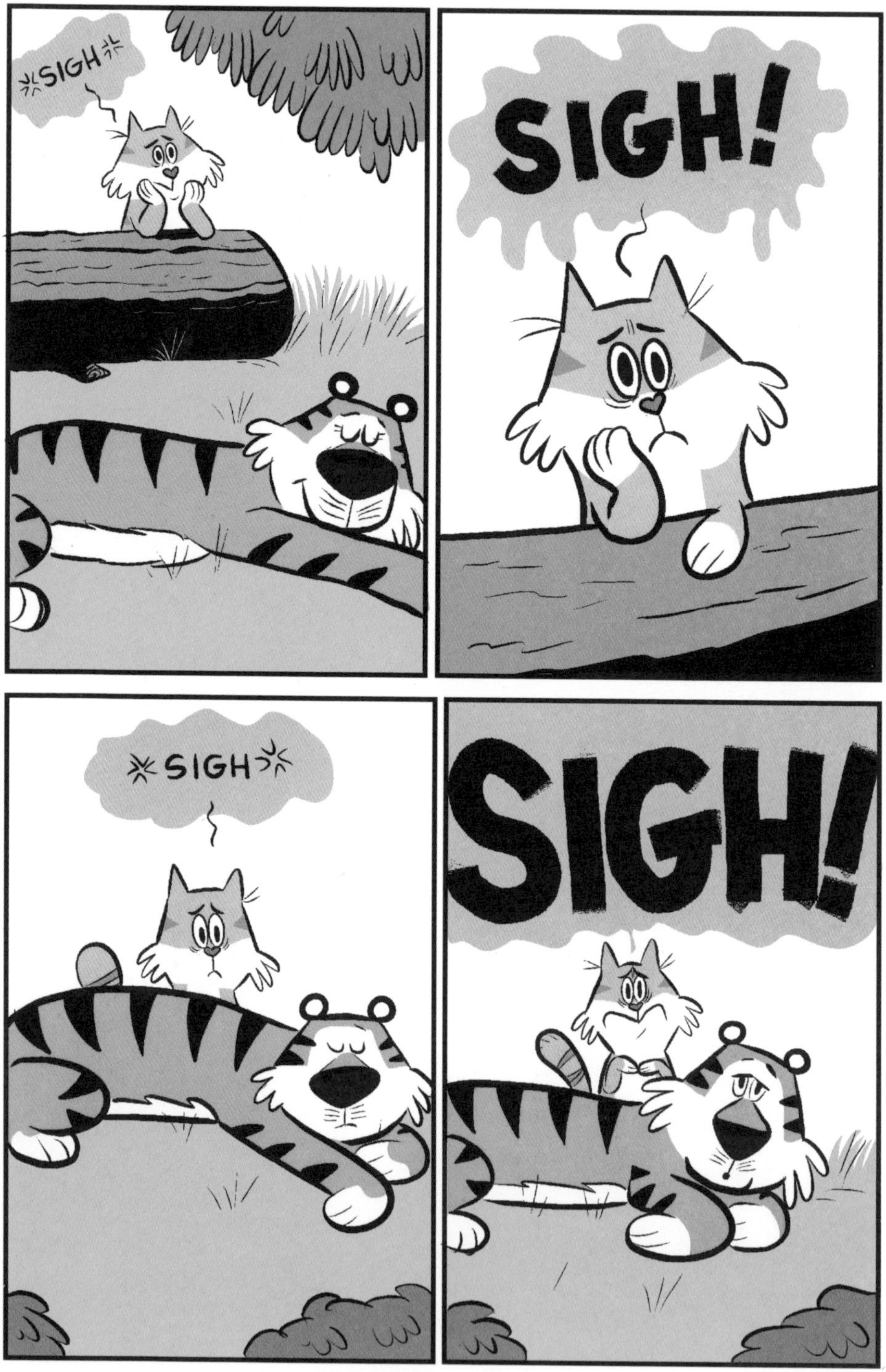
SIGH
SIGH!
SIGH
SIGH!

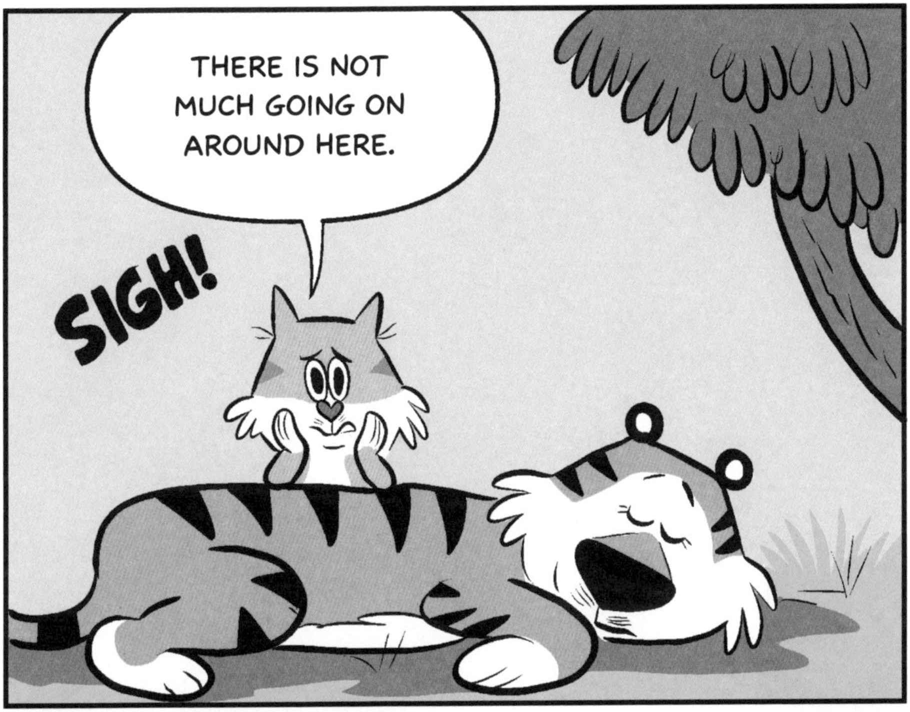
THERE IS NOT MUCH GOING ON AROUND HERE.
SIGH!

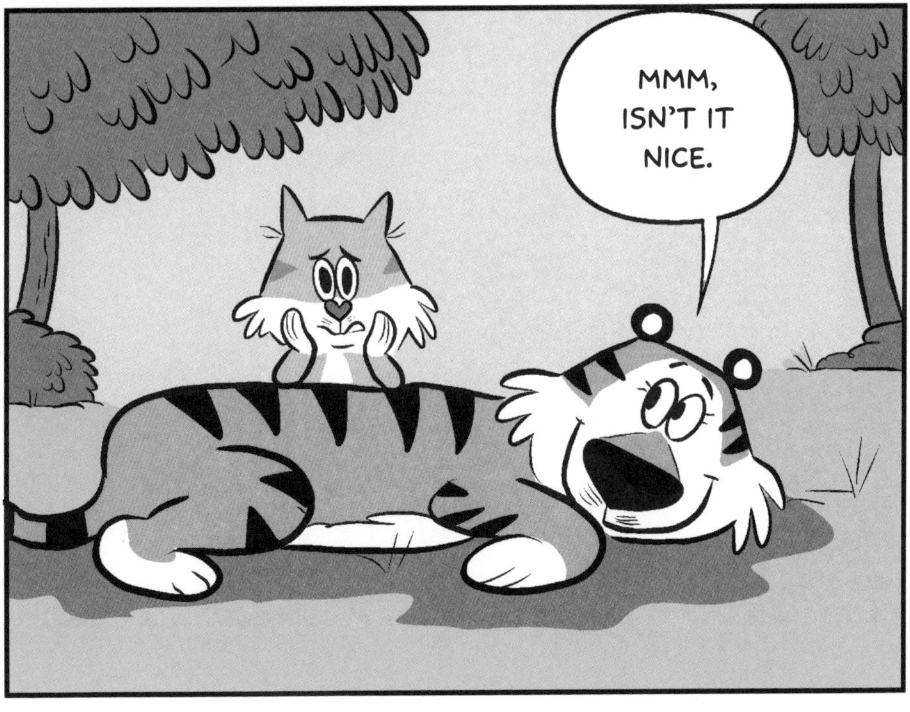
MMM, ISN'T IT NICE.

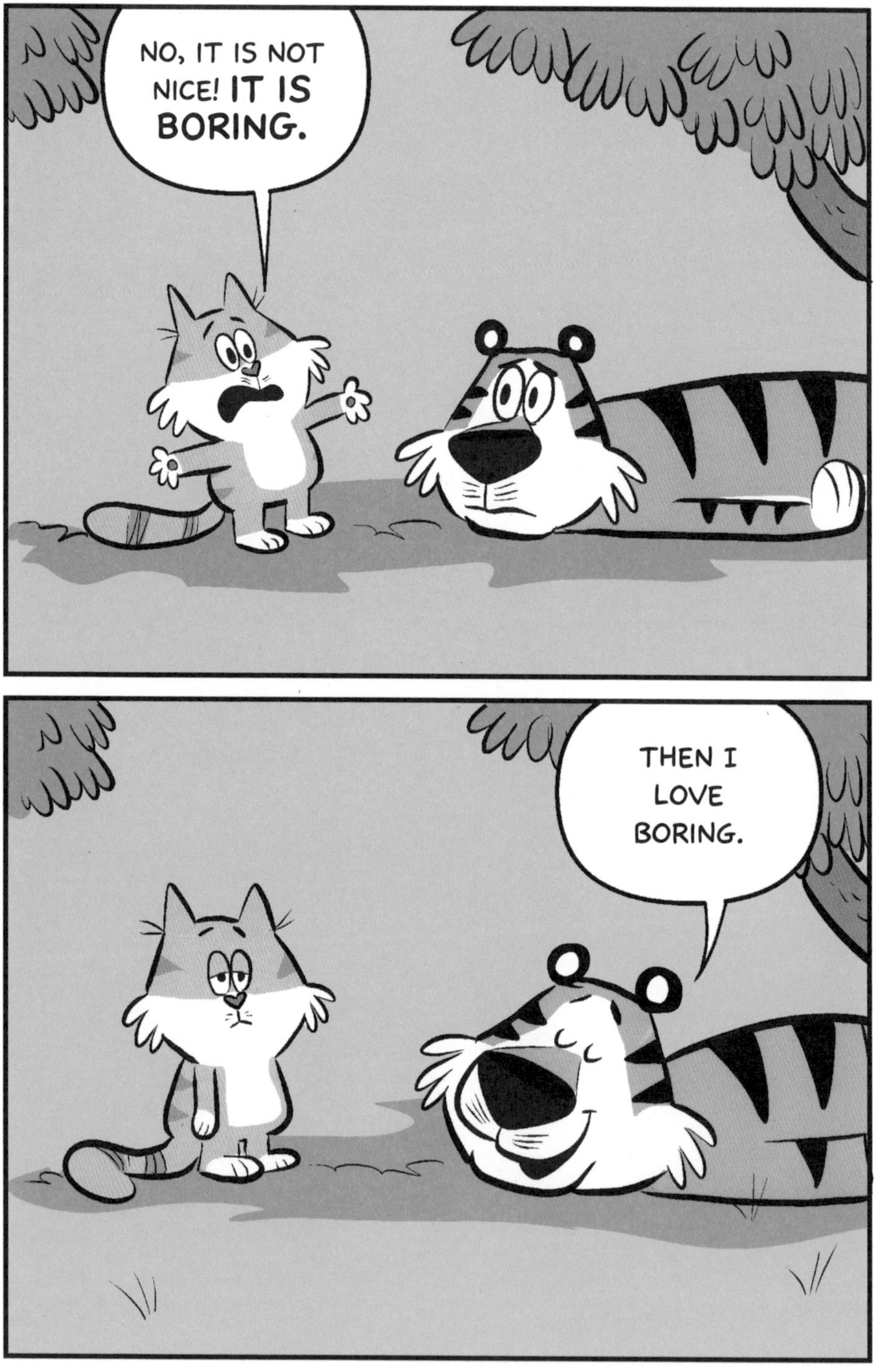
NO, IT IS NOT NICE! IT IS BORING.
THEN I LOVE BORING.

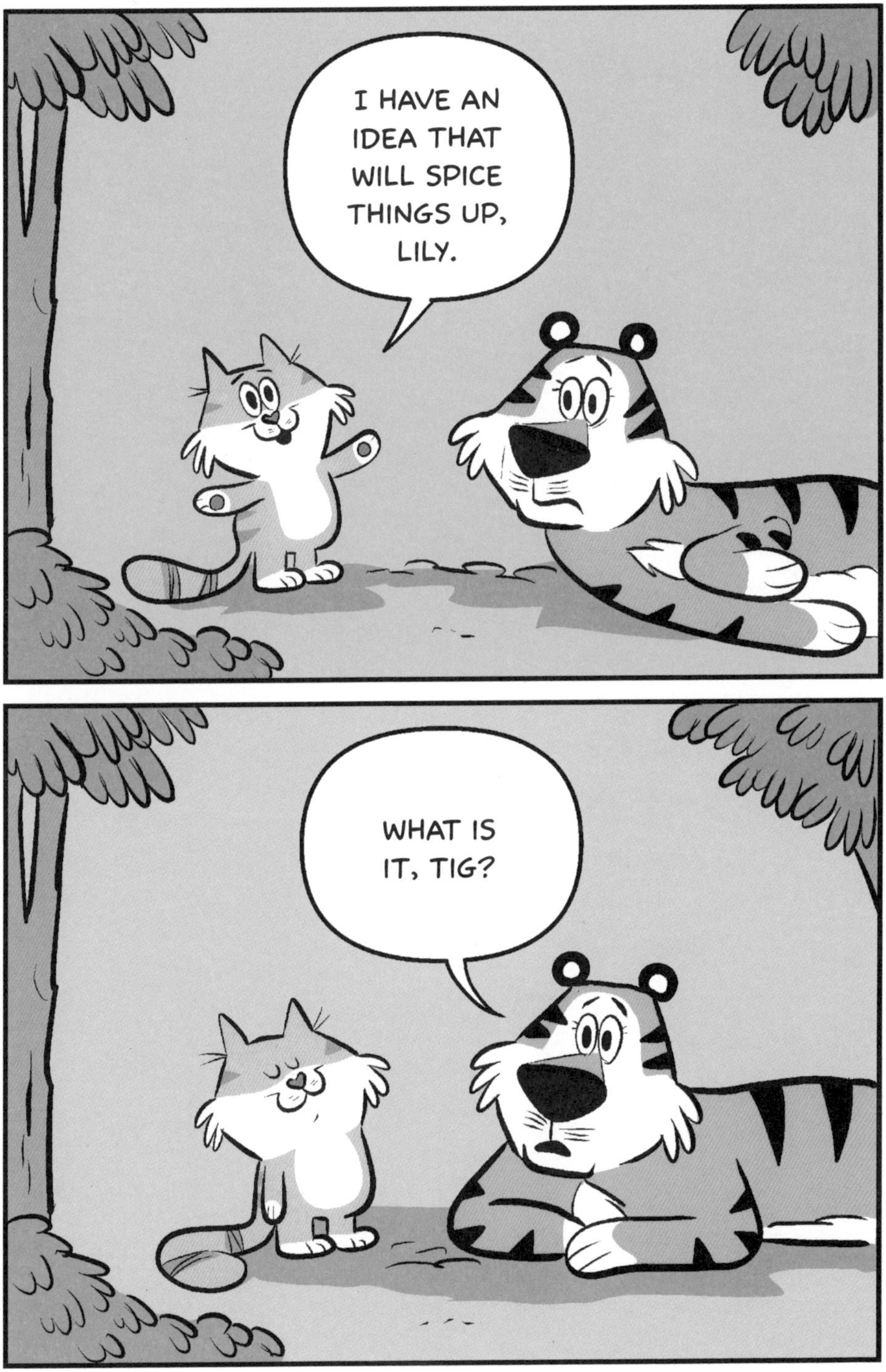
I HAVE AN IDEA THAT WILL SPICE THINGS UP, LILY.
WHAT IS IT, TIG?

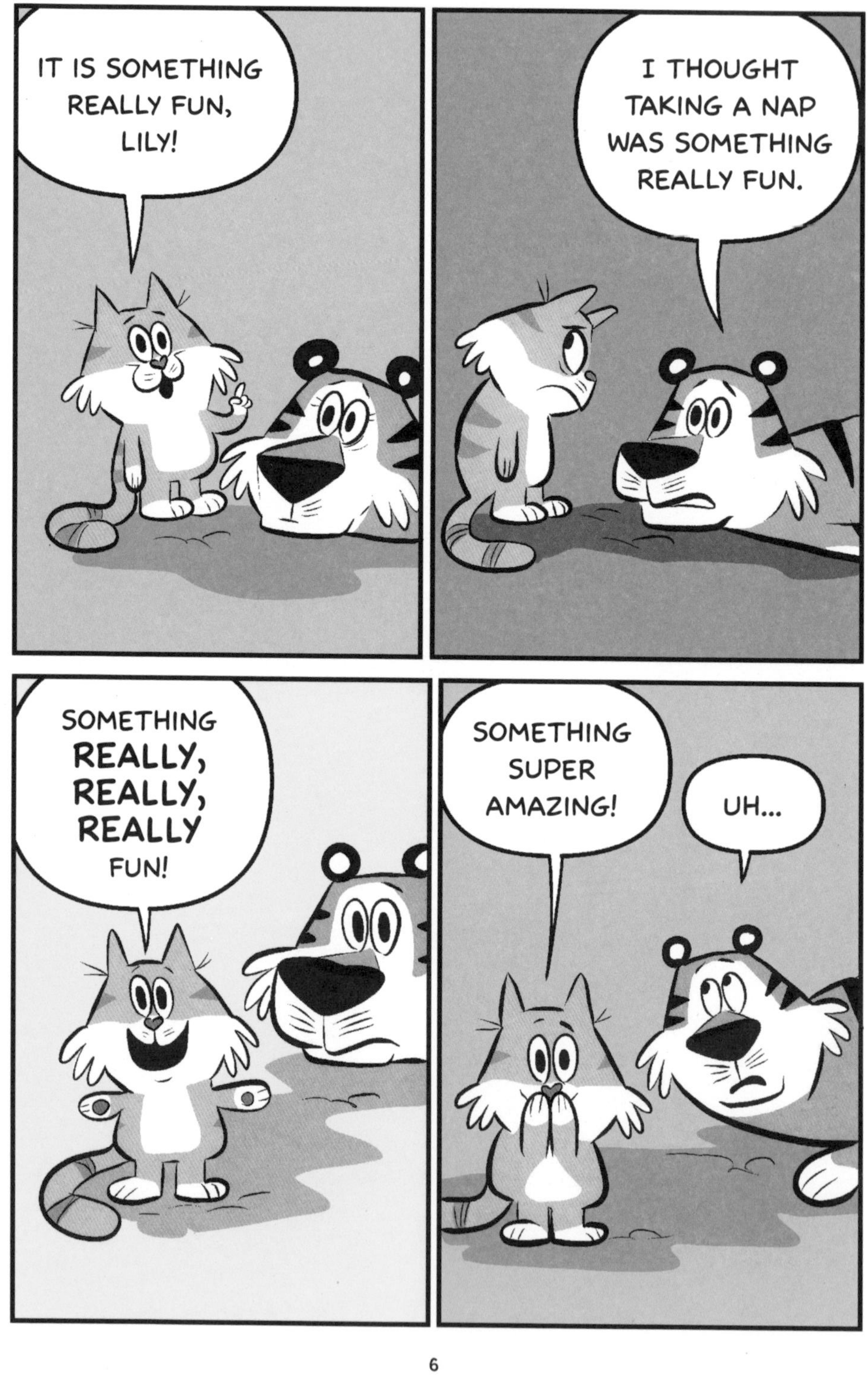
IT IS SOMETHING REALLY FUN, LILY!
I THOUGHT TAKING A NAP WAS SOMETHING REALLY FUN.
SOMETHING REALLY, REALLY, REALLY FUN!
SOMETHING SUPER AMAZING!
UH...

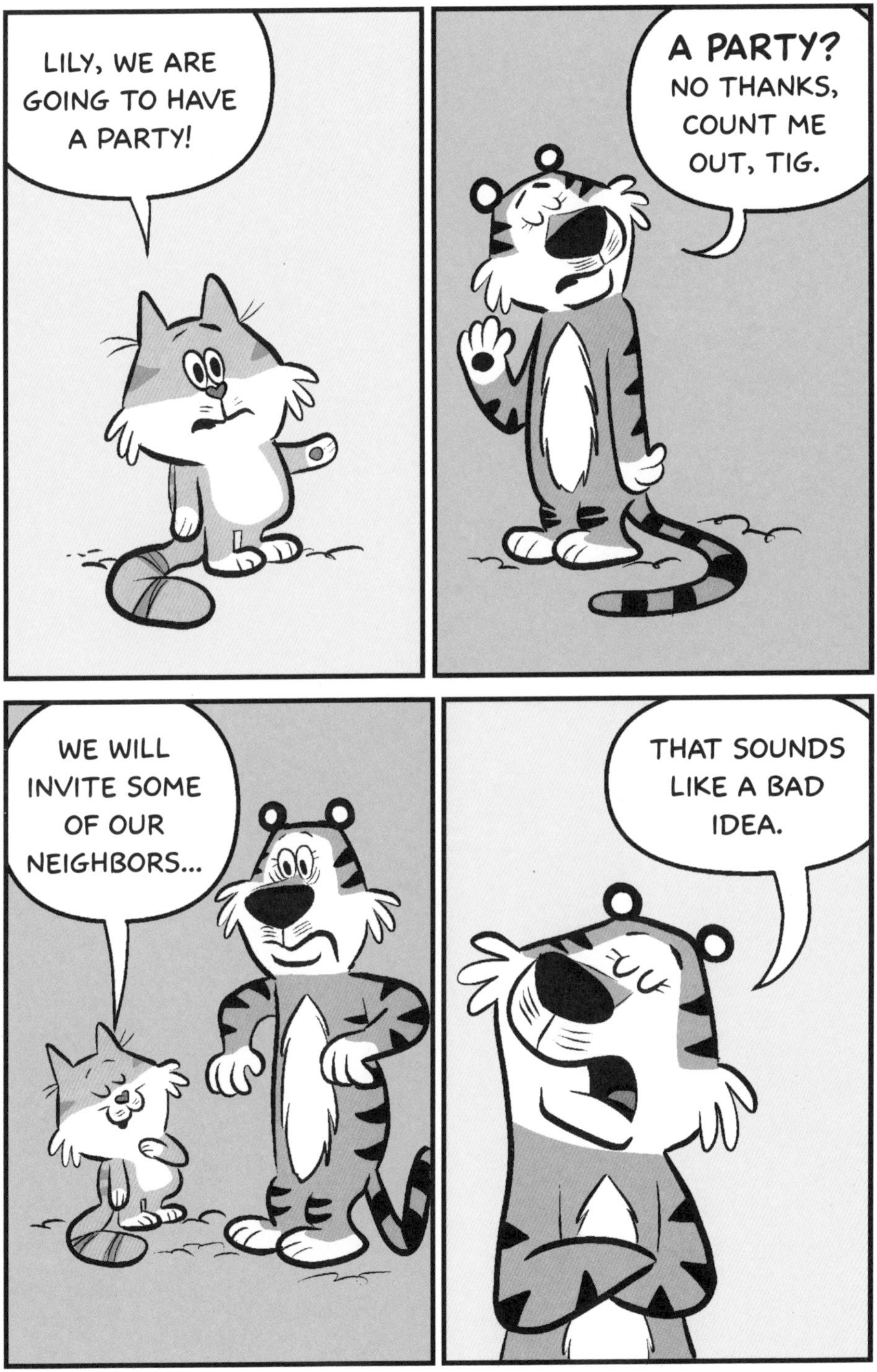
LILY, WE ARE GOING TO HAVE A PARTY!
A PARTY? NO THANKS, COUNT ME OUT, TIG.
WE WILL INVITE SOME OF OUR NEIGHBORS...
THAT SOUNDS LIKE A BAD IDEA.

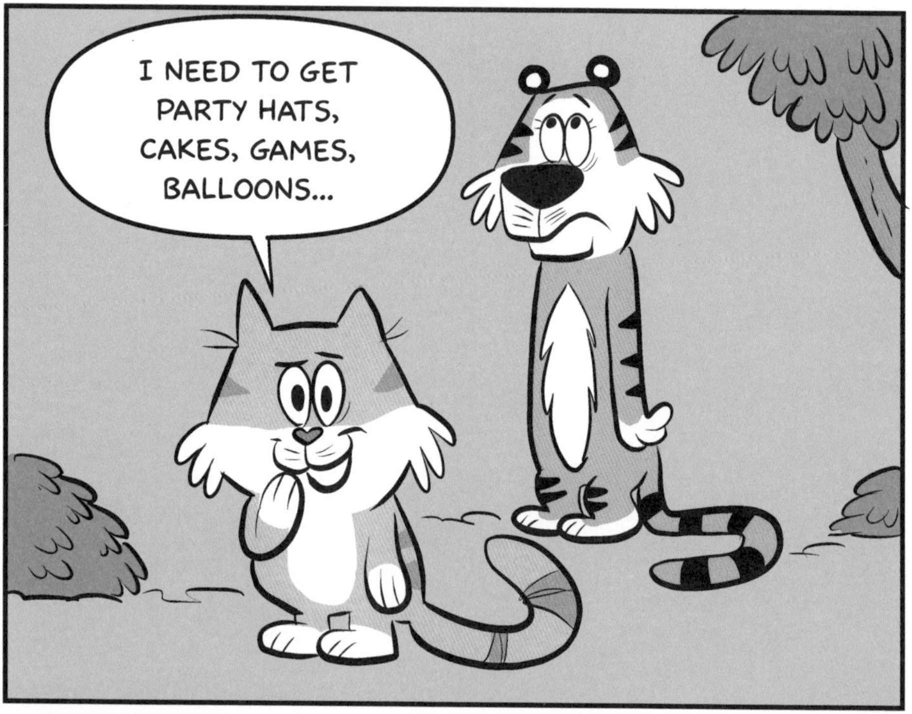
I NEED TO GET PARTY HATS, CAKES, GAMES, BALLOONS...

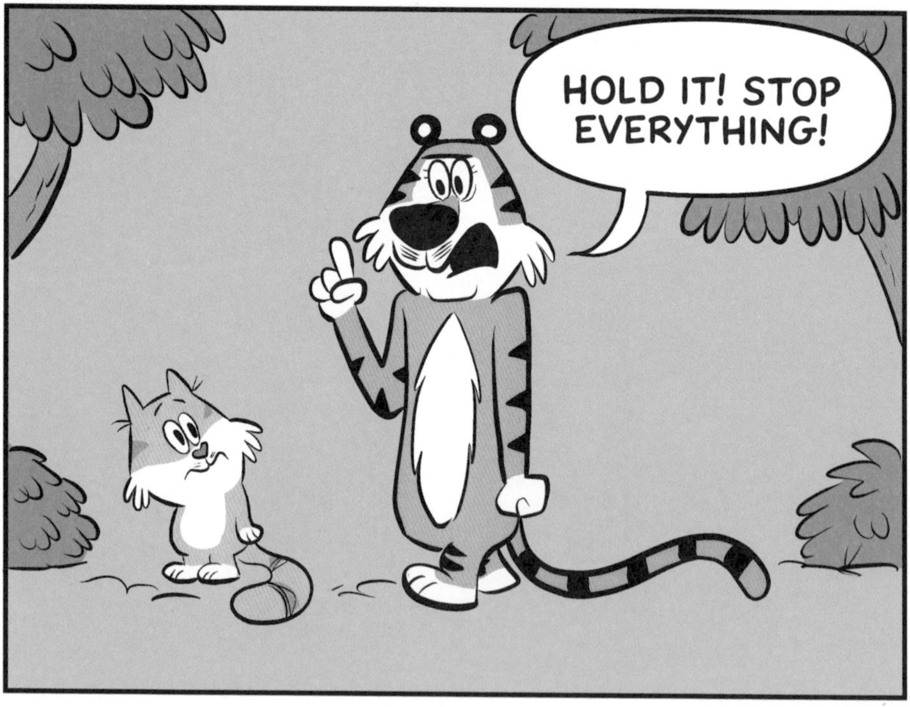
HOLD IT! STOP EVERYTHING!

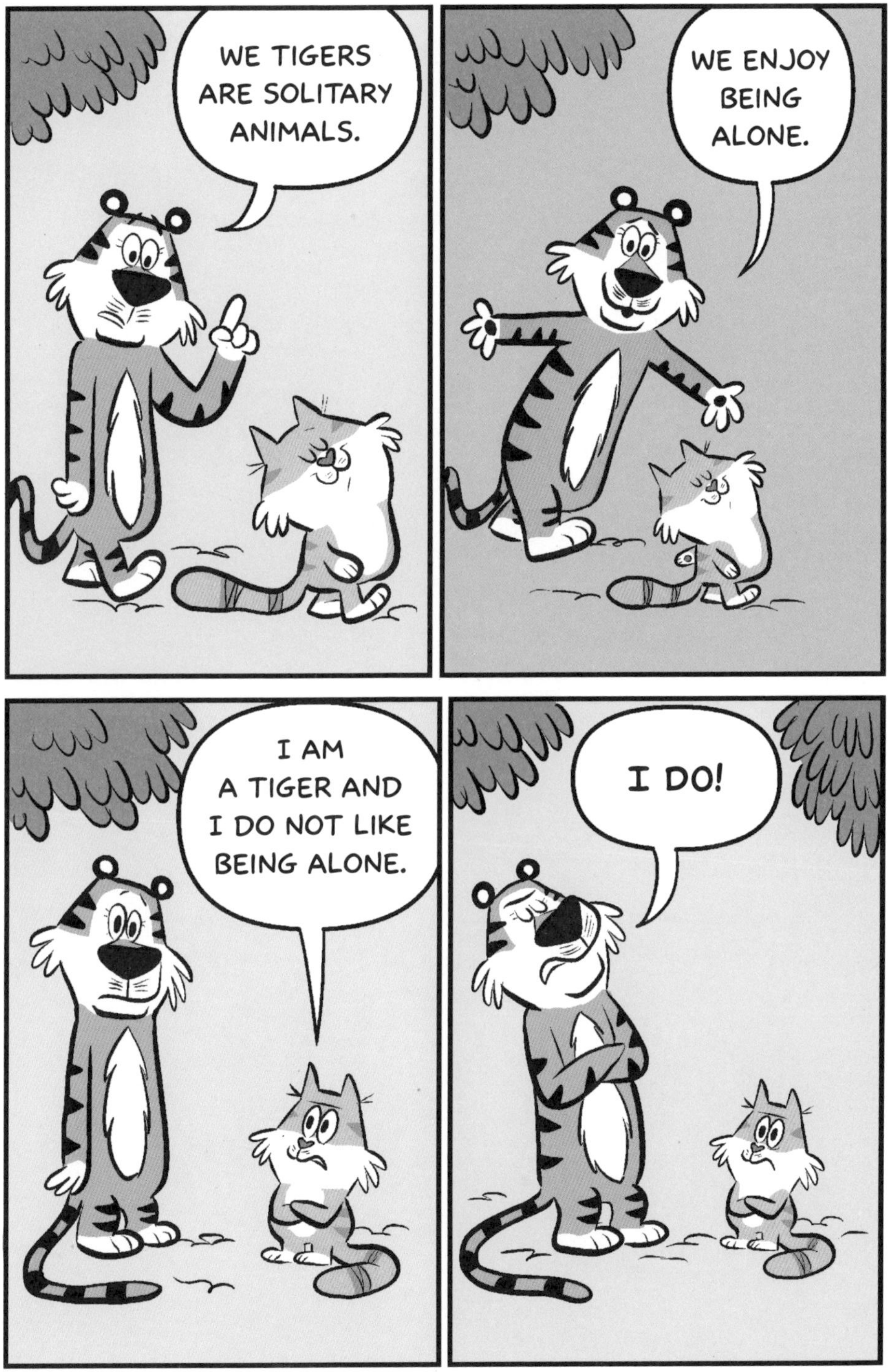
WE TIGERS ARE SOLITARY ANIMALS.
WE ENJOY BEING ALONE.
I AM A TIGER AND I DO NOT LIKE BEING ALONE.
I DO!

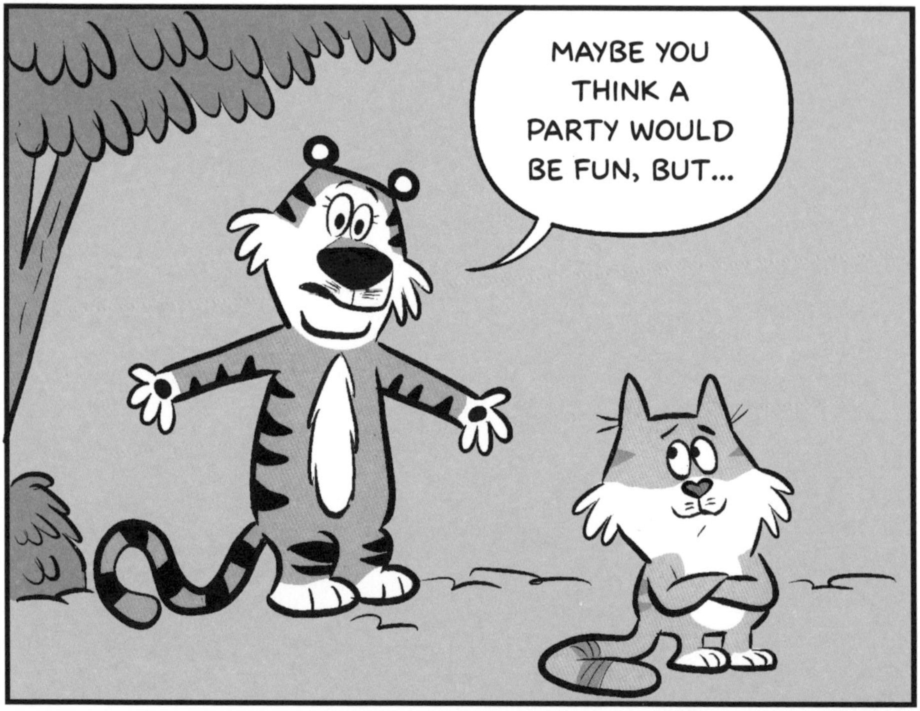
MAYBE YOU THINK A PARTY WOULD BE FUN, BUT...

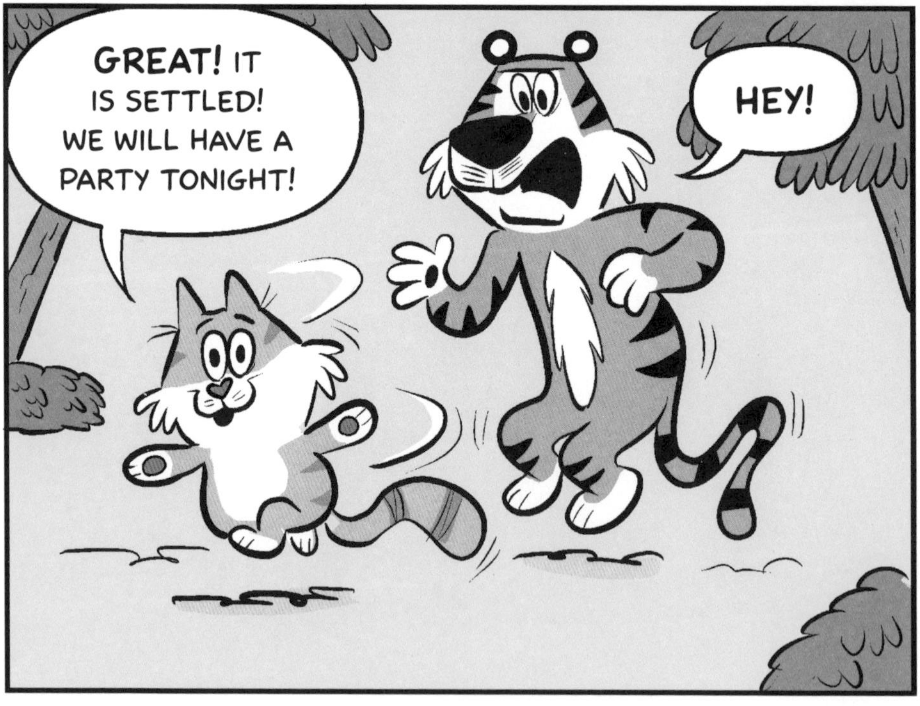
GREAT! IT IS SETTLED! WE WILL HAVE A PARTY TONIGHT!
HEY!

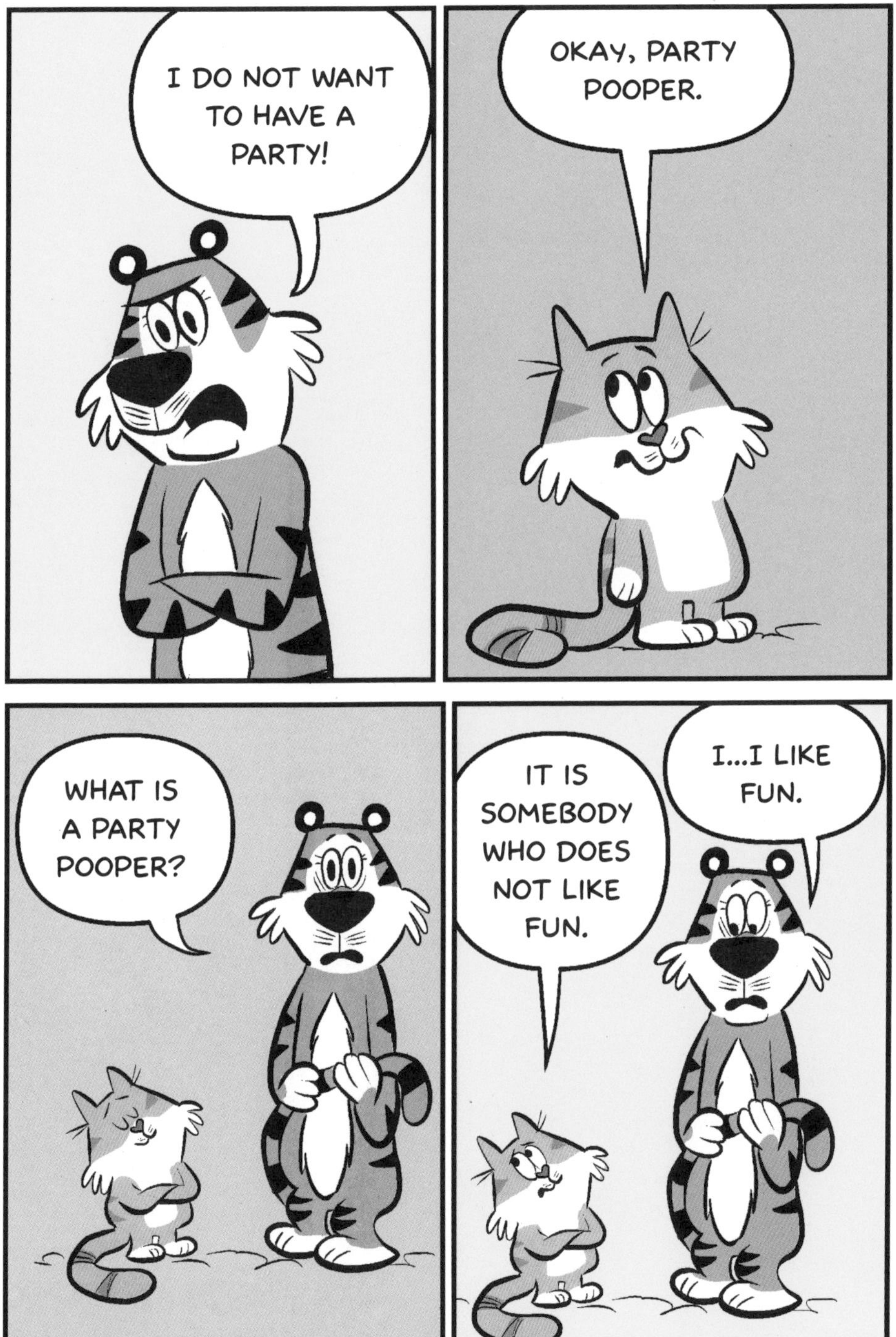
I DO NOT WANT TO HAVE A PARTY!
OKAY, PARTY POOPER.
WHAT IS A PARTY POOPER?
IT IS SOMEBODY WHO DOES NOT LIKE FUN.
I...I LIKE FUN.

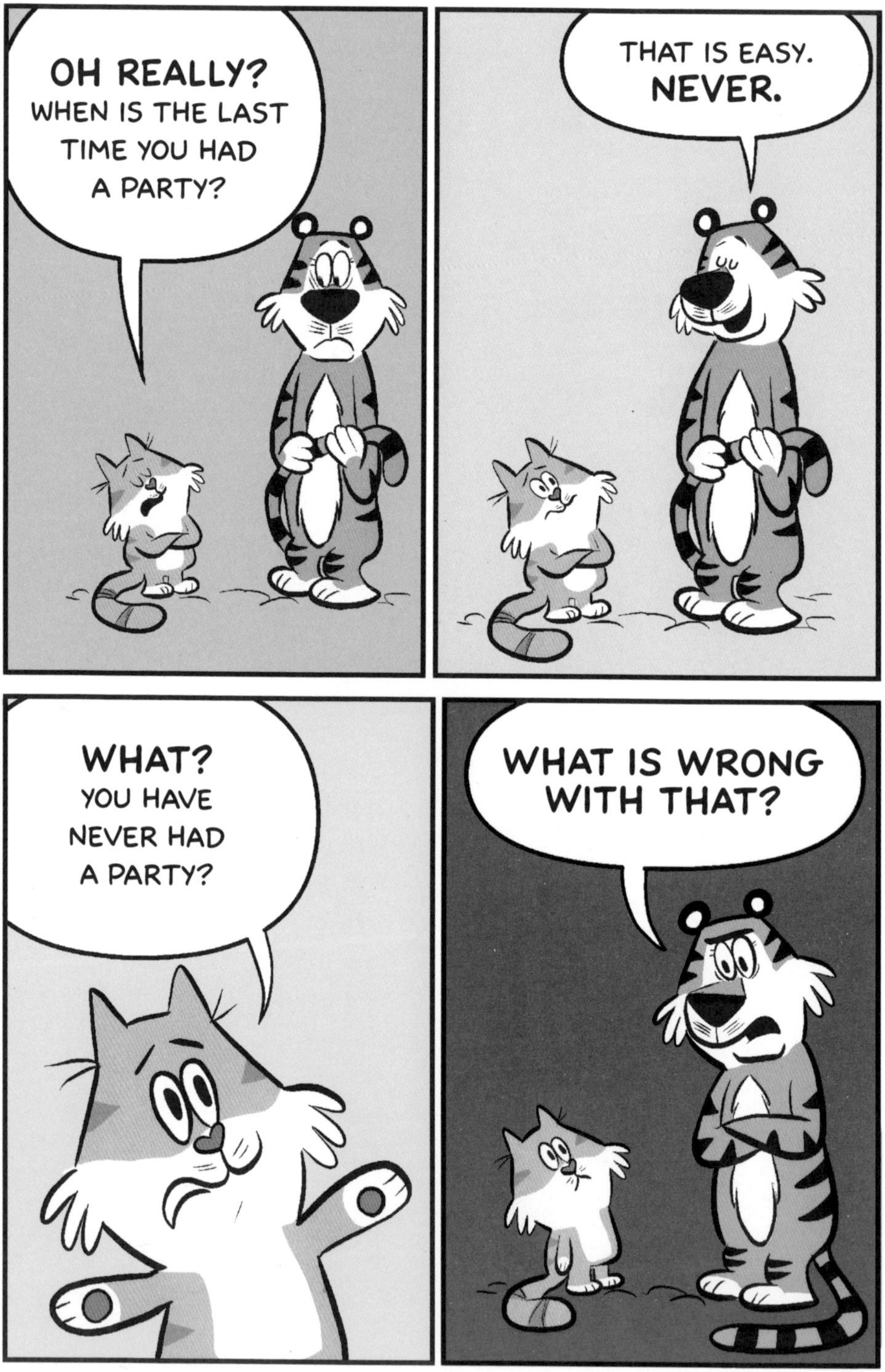
OH REALLY? WHEN IS THE LAST TIME YOU HAD A PARTY?
THAT IS EASY. NEVER.
WHAT? YOU HAVE NEVER HAD A PARTY?
WHAT IS WRONG WITH THAT?

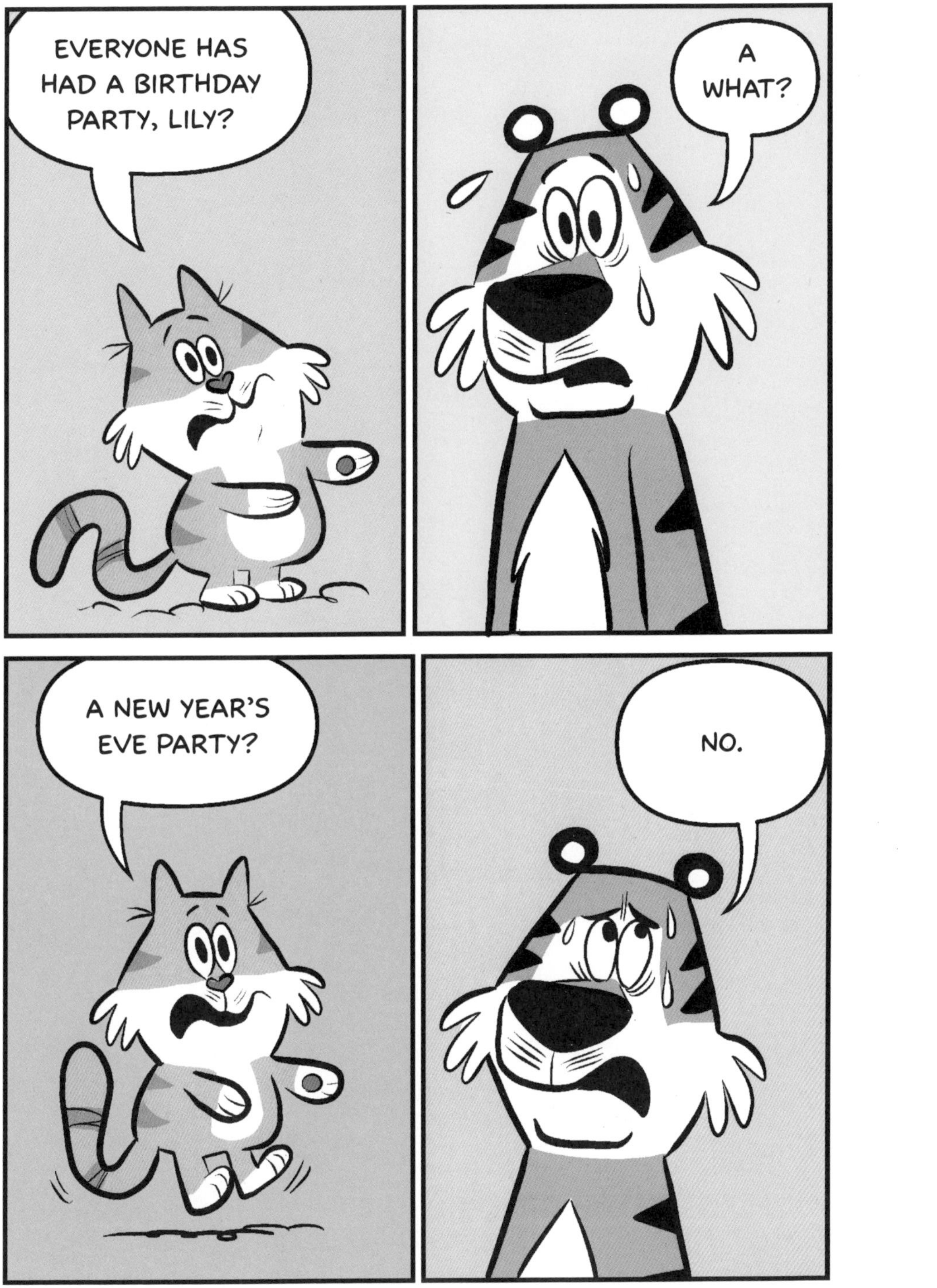
EVERYONE HAS HAD A BIRTHDAY PARTY, LILY?
A WHAT?
A NEW YEAR'S EVE PARTY?
NO.

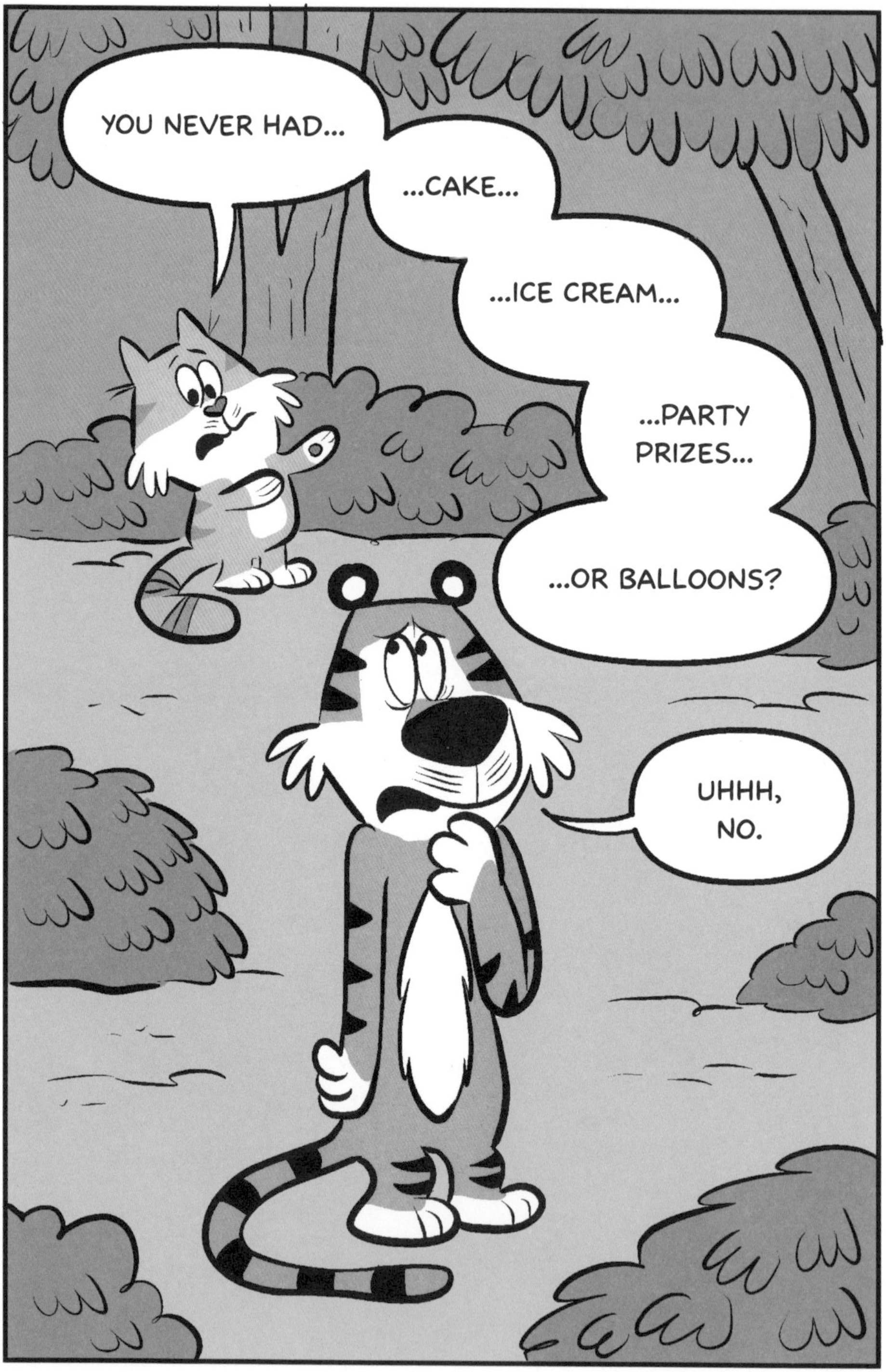
YOU NEVER HAD...
...CAKE...
...ICE CREAM...
...PARTY PRIZES...
...OR BALLOONS?
UHHH, NO.

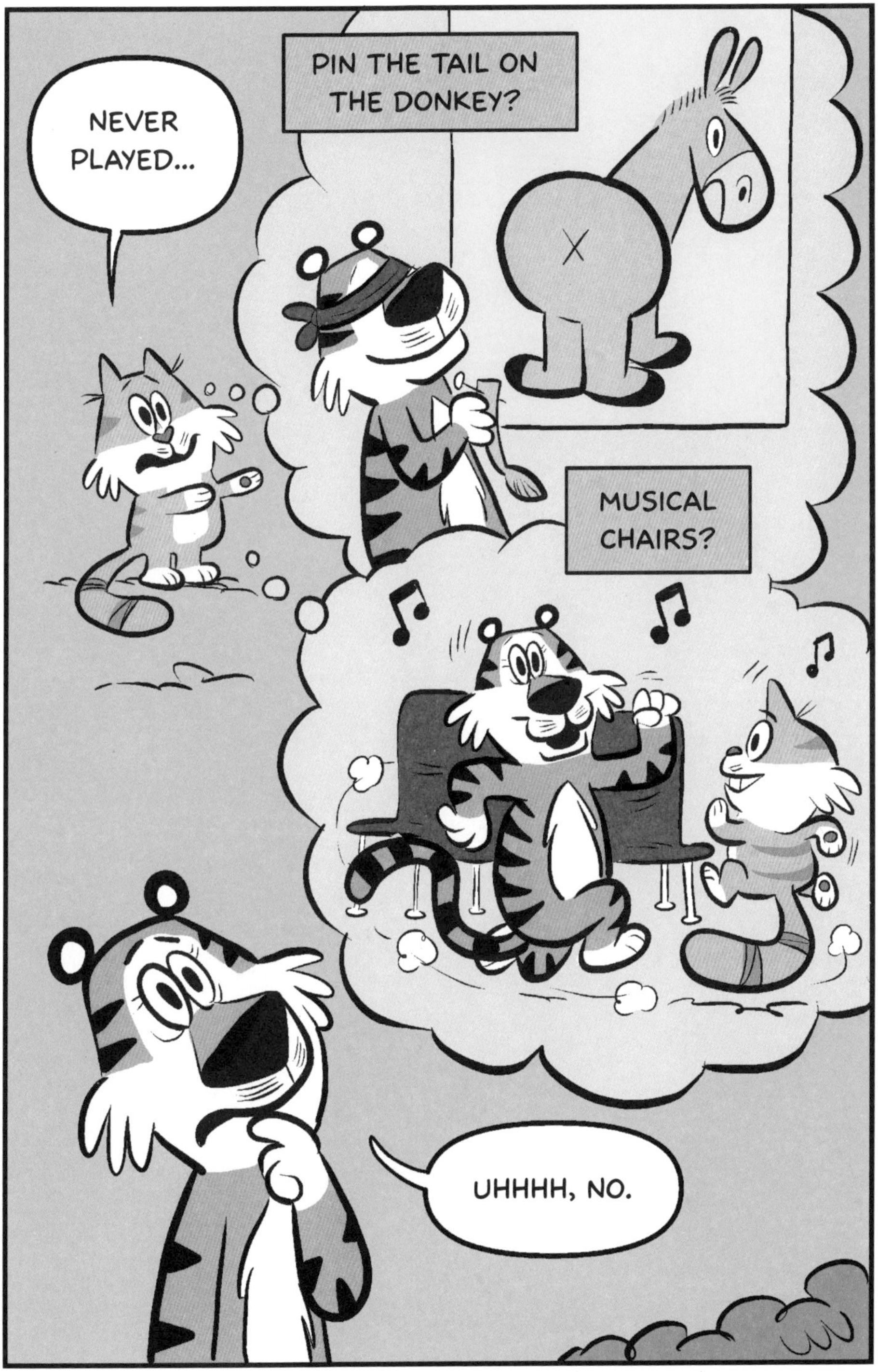
NEVER PLAYED...
PIN THE TAIL ON THE DONKEY?
MUSICAL CHAIRS?
UHHHH, NO.

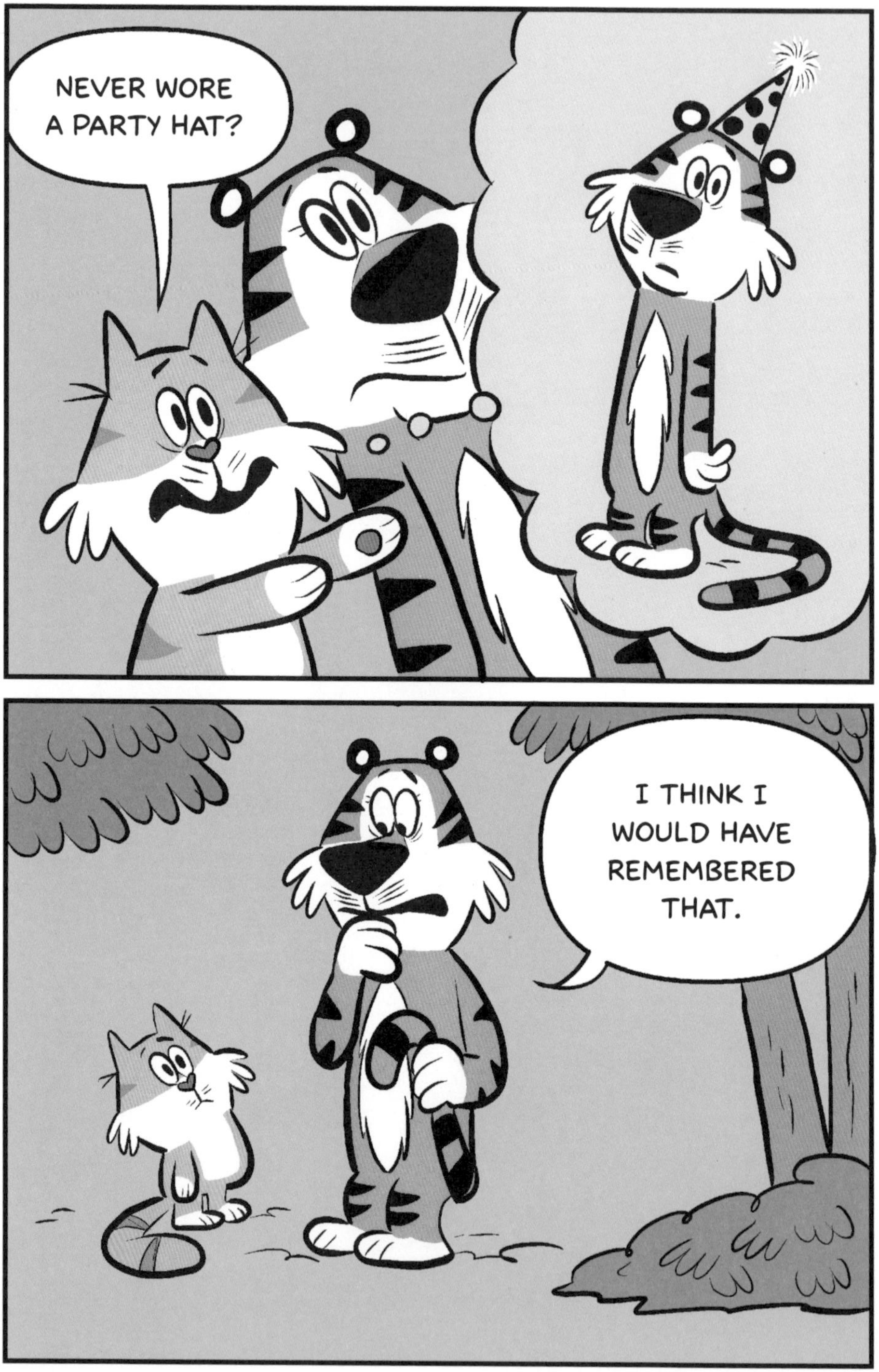
NEVER WORE A PARTY HAT?
I THINK I WOULD HAVE REMEMBERED THAT.

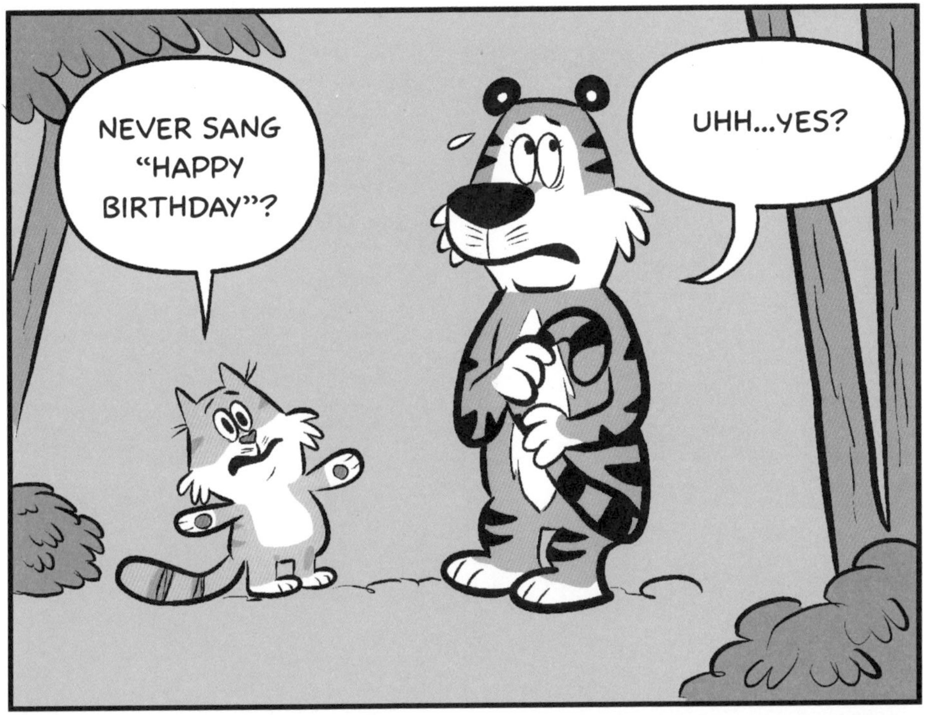
NEVER SANG "HAPPY BIRTHDAY"?
UHH...YES?

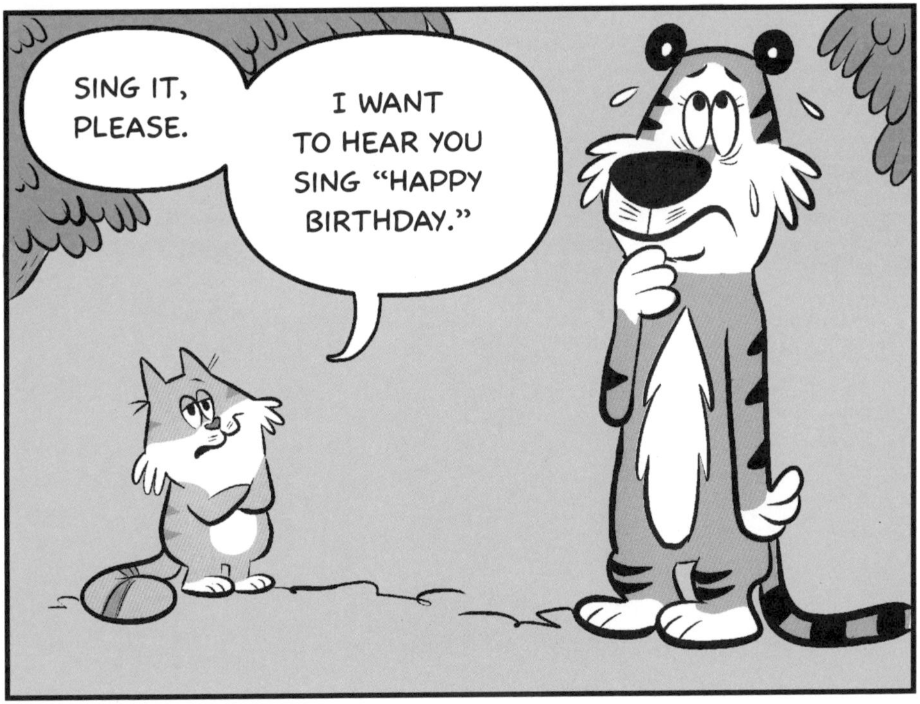
SING IT, PLEASE.
I WANT TO HEAR YOU SING "HAPPY BIRTHDAY."

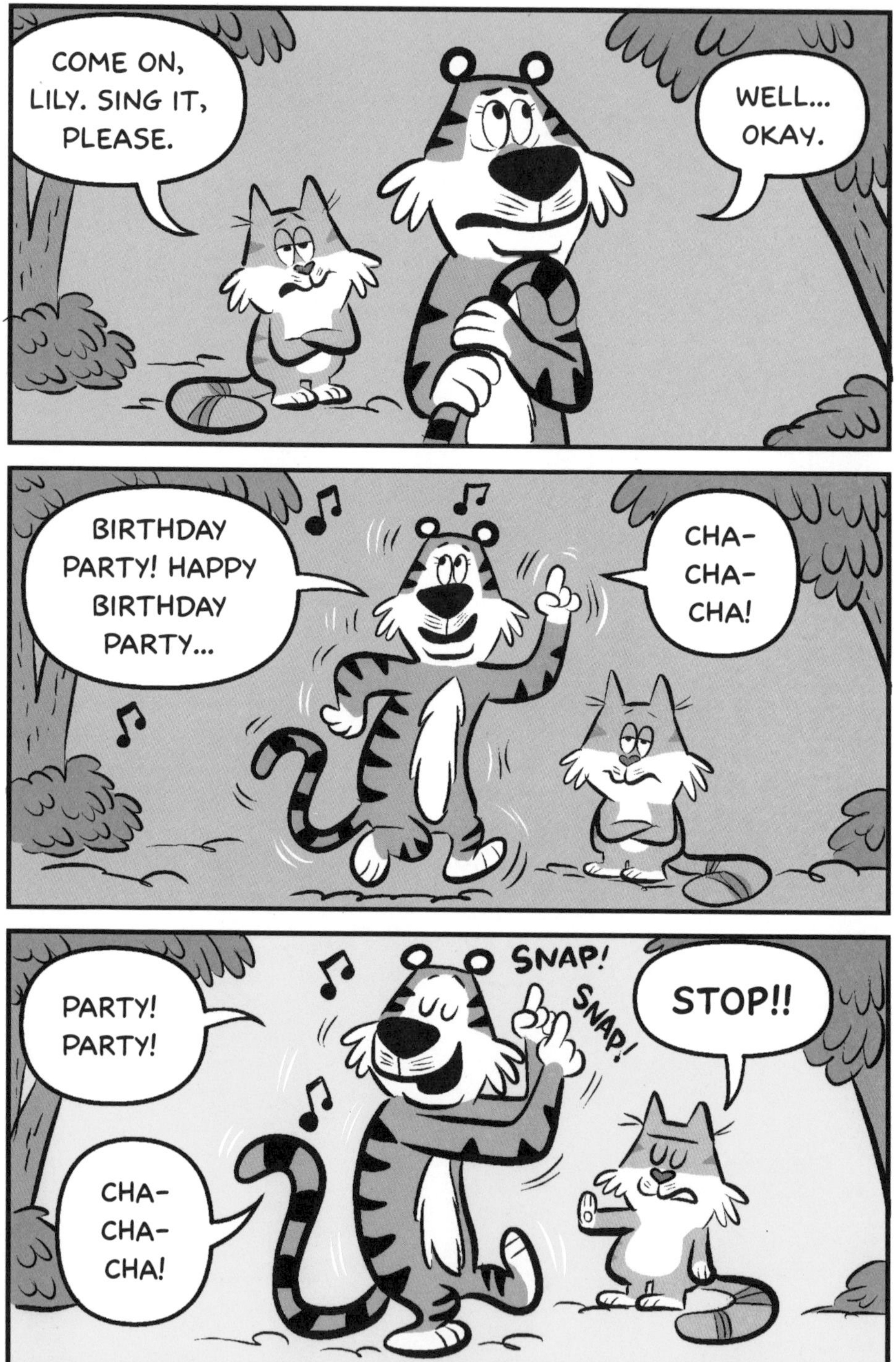
COME ON, LILY. SING IT, PLEASE.
WELL... OKAY.
BIRTHDAY PARTY! HAPPY BIRTHDAY PARTY...
CHA-CHA-CHA!
PARTY! PARTY!
SNAP!
SNAP!
CHA-CHA-CHA!
STOP!!

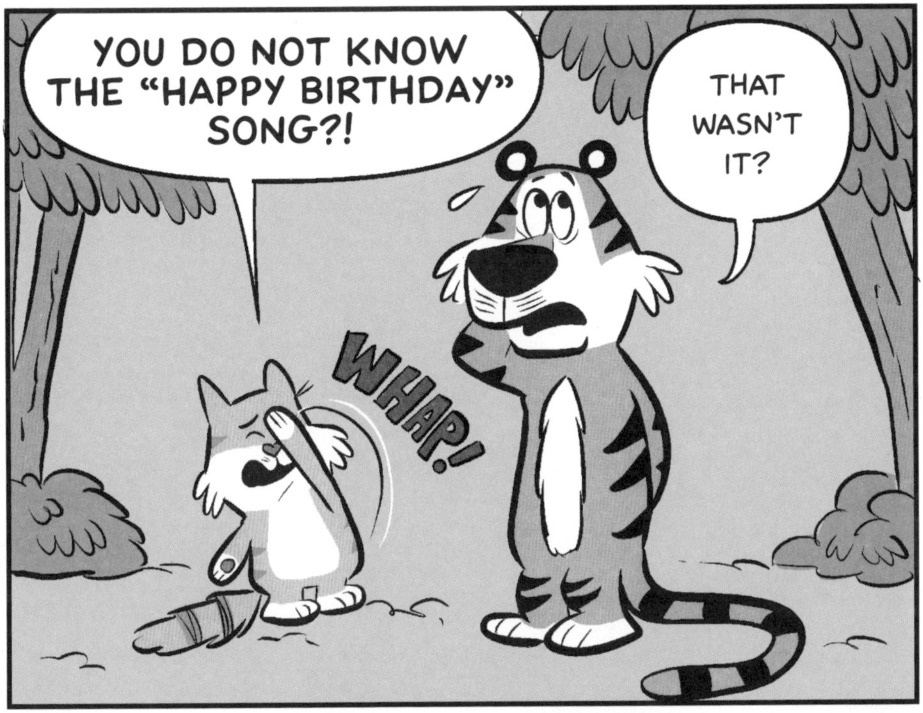
YOU DO NOT KNOW THE "HAPPY BIRTHDAY" SONG?!
THAT WASN'T IT?
WHAP!

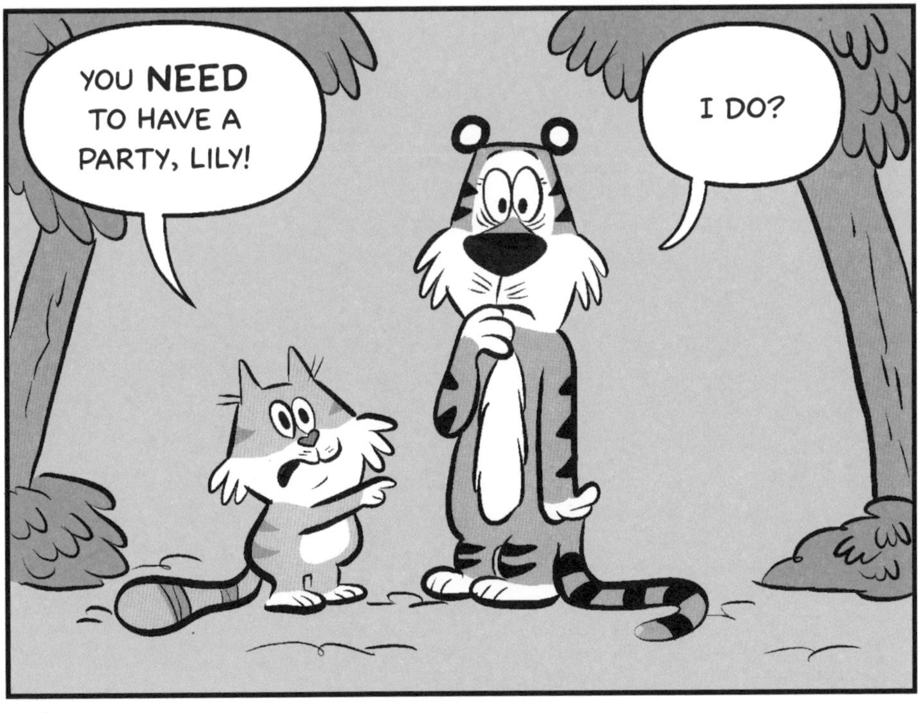
YOU **NEED** TO HAVE A PARTY, LILY!
I DO?

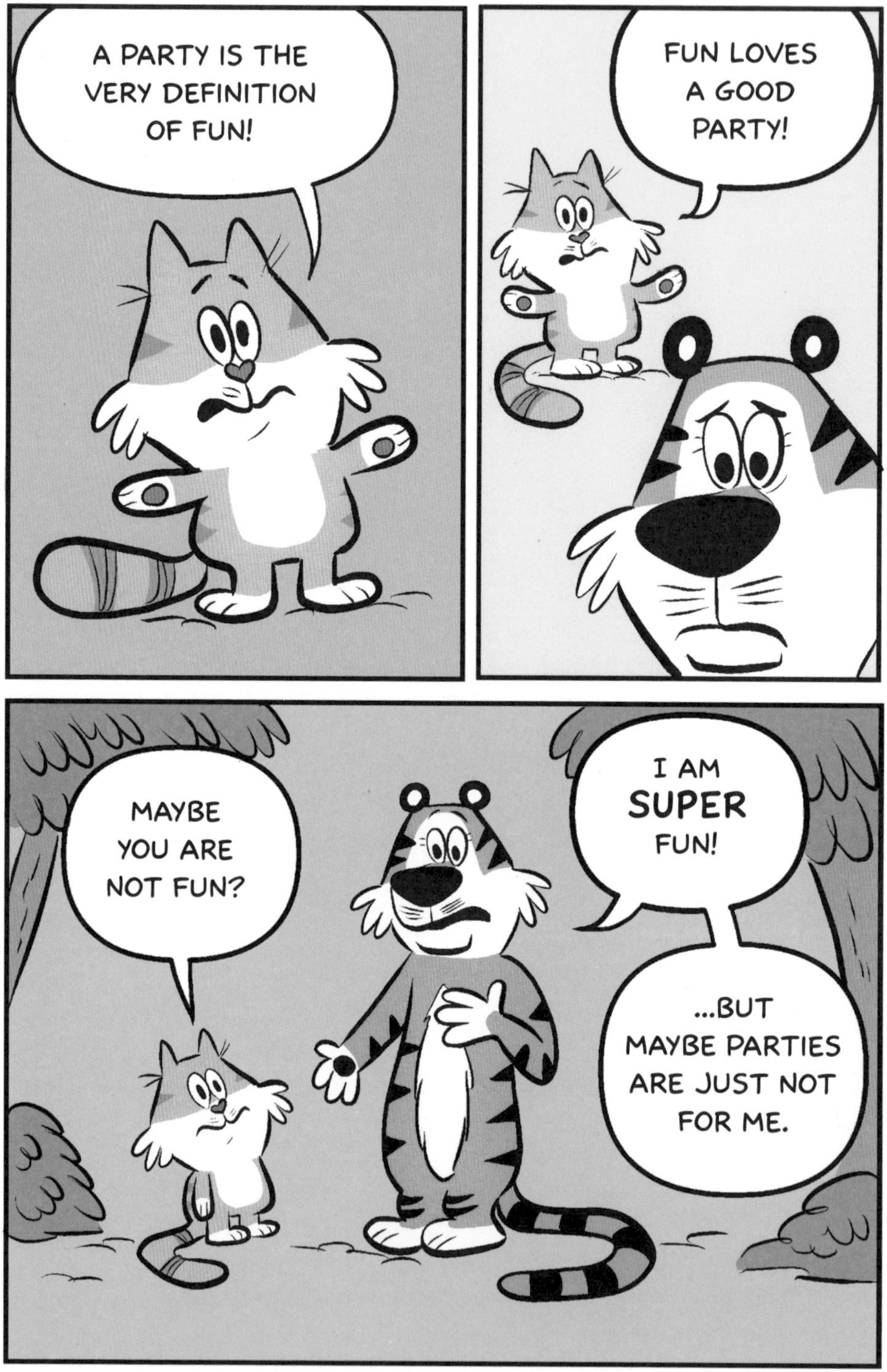
A PARTY IS THE VERY DEFINITION OF FUN!
FUN LOVES A GOOD PARTY!
MAYBE YOU ARE NOT FUN?
I AM **SUPER** FUN!
...BUT MAYBE PARTIES ARE JUST NOT FOR ME.

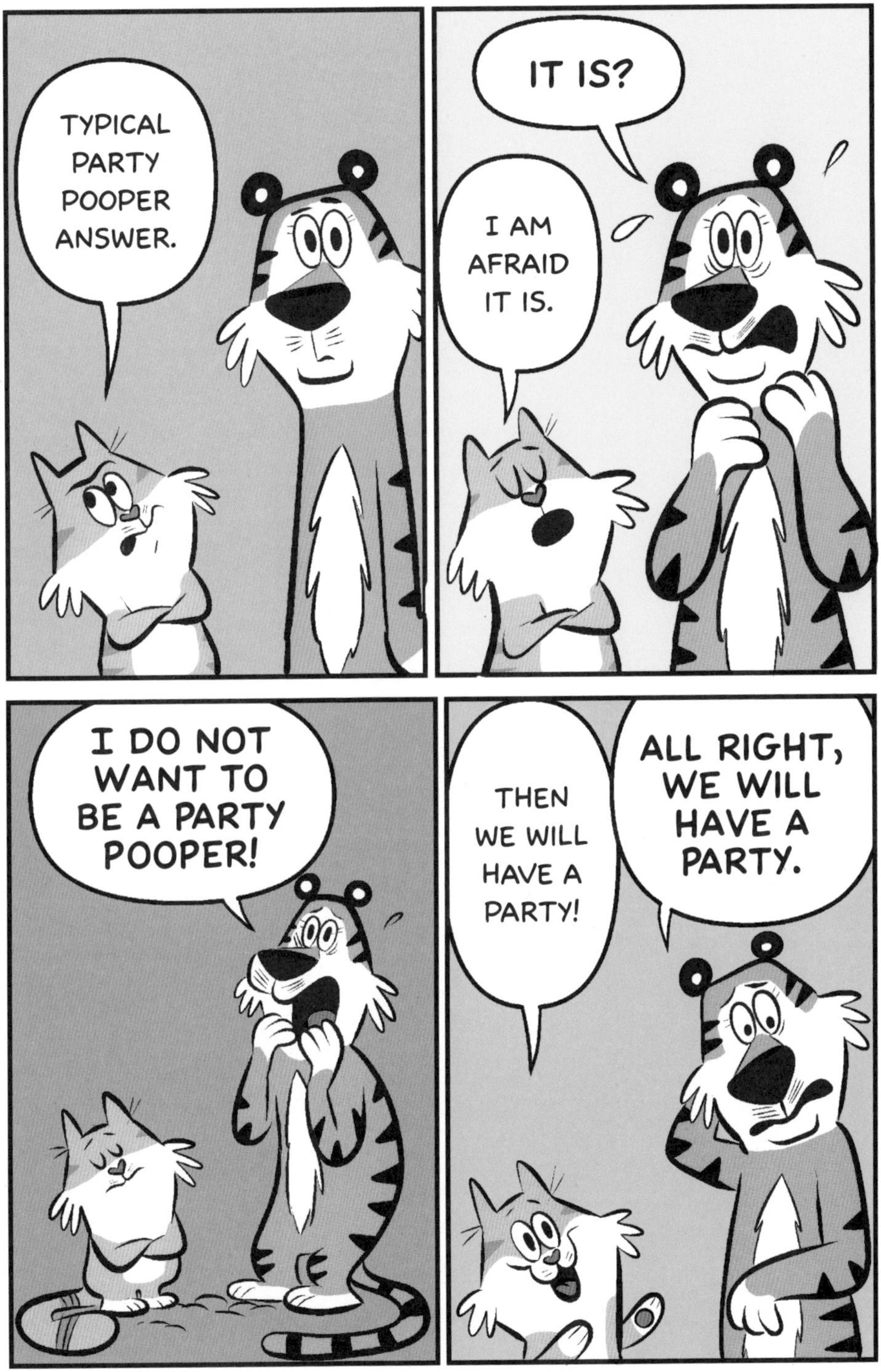
TYPICAL PARTY POOPER ANSWER.
IT IS?
I AM AFRAID IT IS.
I DO NOT WANT TO BE A PARTY POOPER!
ALL RIGHT, WE WILL HAVE A PARTY.
THEN WE WILL HAVE A PARTY!

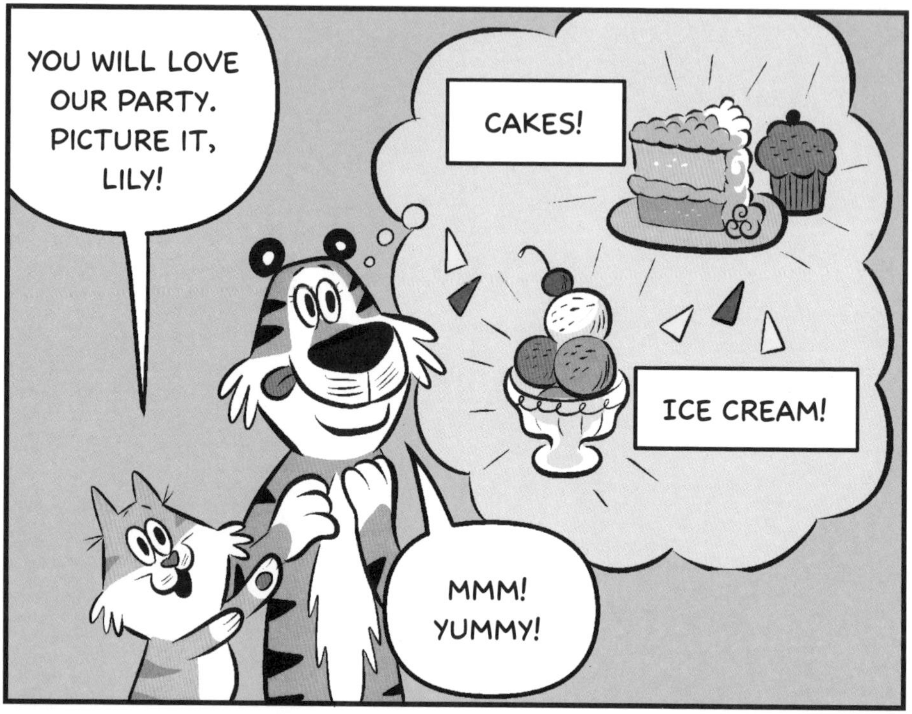
YOU WILL LOVE OUR PARTY. PICTURE IT, LILY!
CAKES!
ICE CREAM!
MMM! YUMMY!

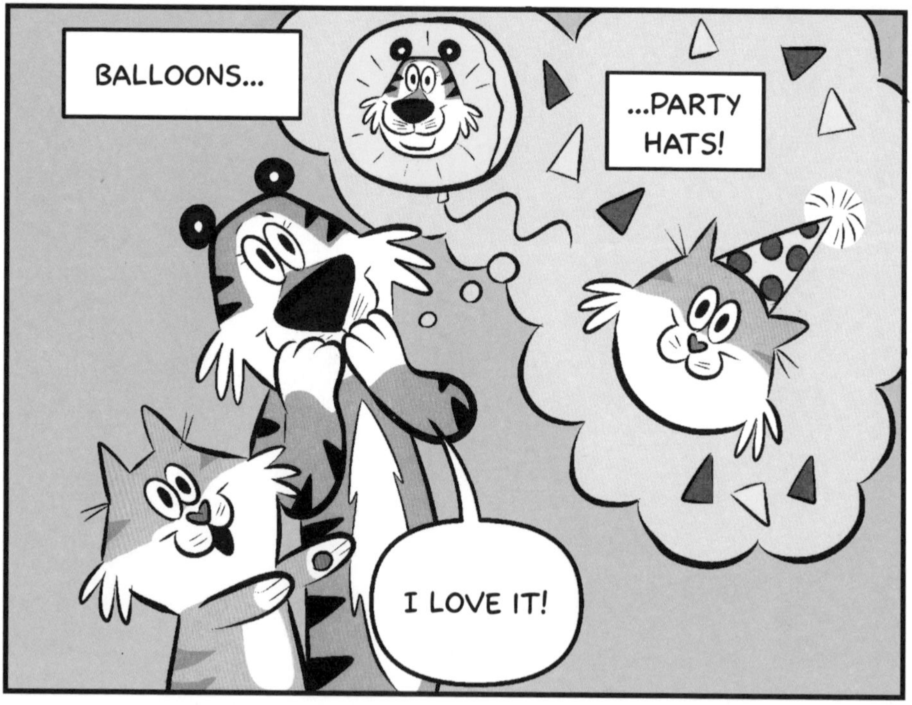
BALLOONS...
...PARTY HATS!
I LOVE IT!

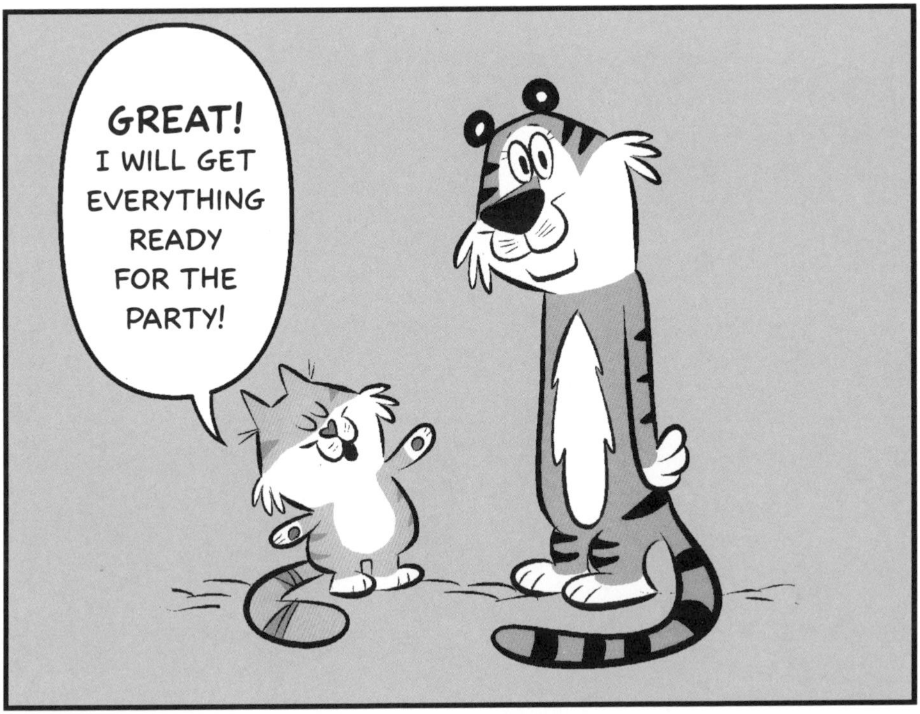
GREAT! I WILL GET EVERYTHING READY FOR THE PARTY!

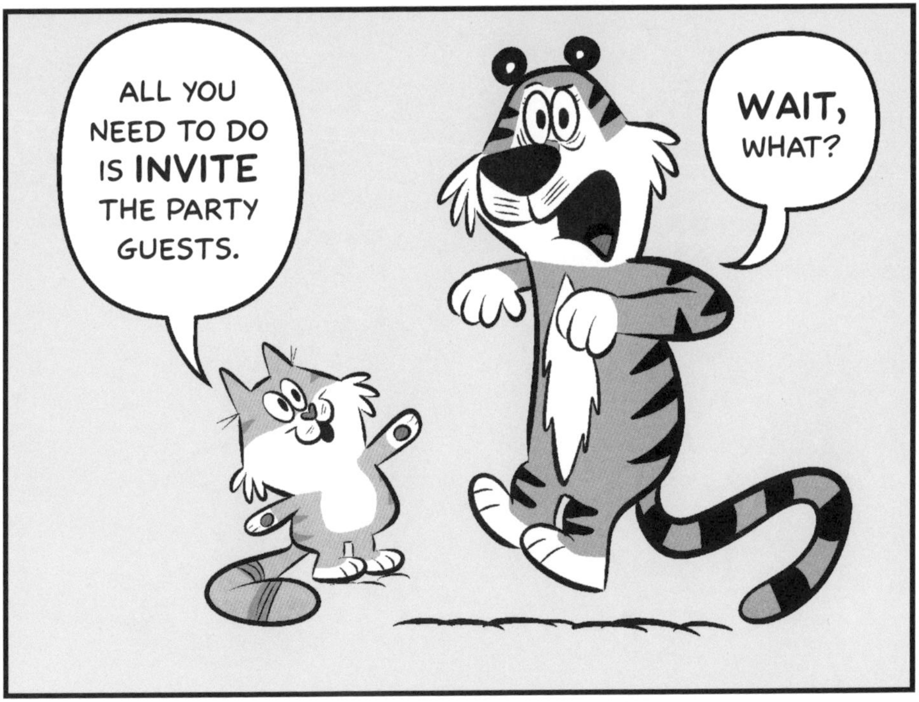
ALL YOU NEED TO DO IS INVITE THE PARTY GUESTS.
WAIT, WHAT?

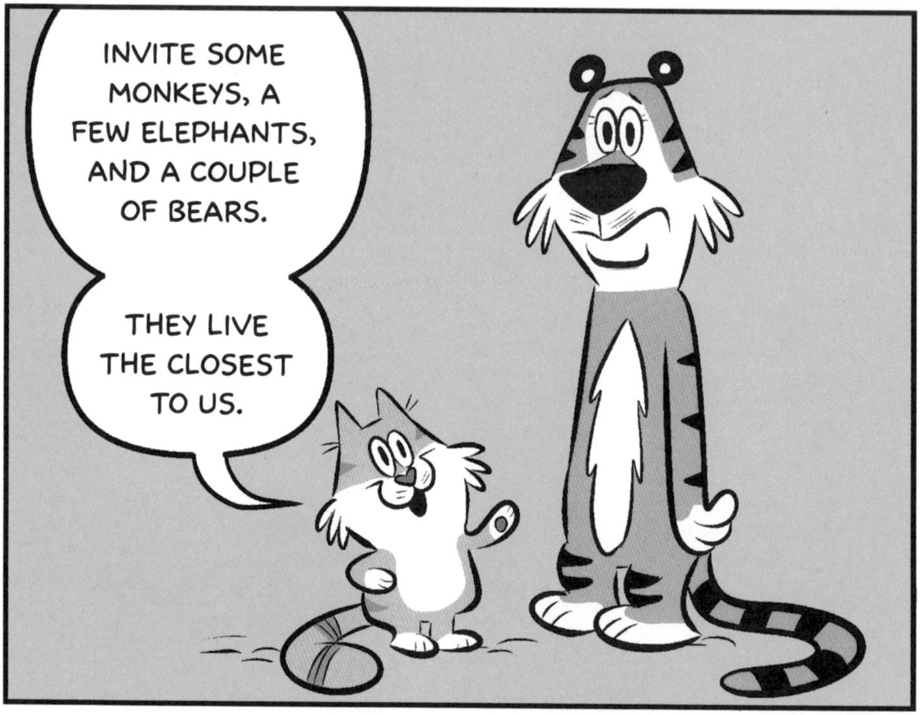
INVITE SOME MONKEYS, A FEW ELEPHANTS, AND A COUPLE OF BEARS.
THEY LIVE THE CLOSEST TO US.

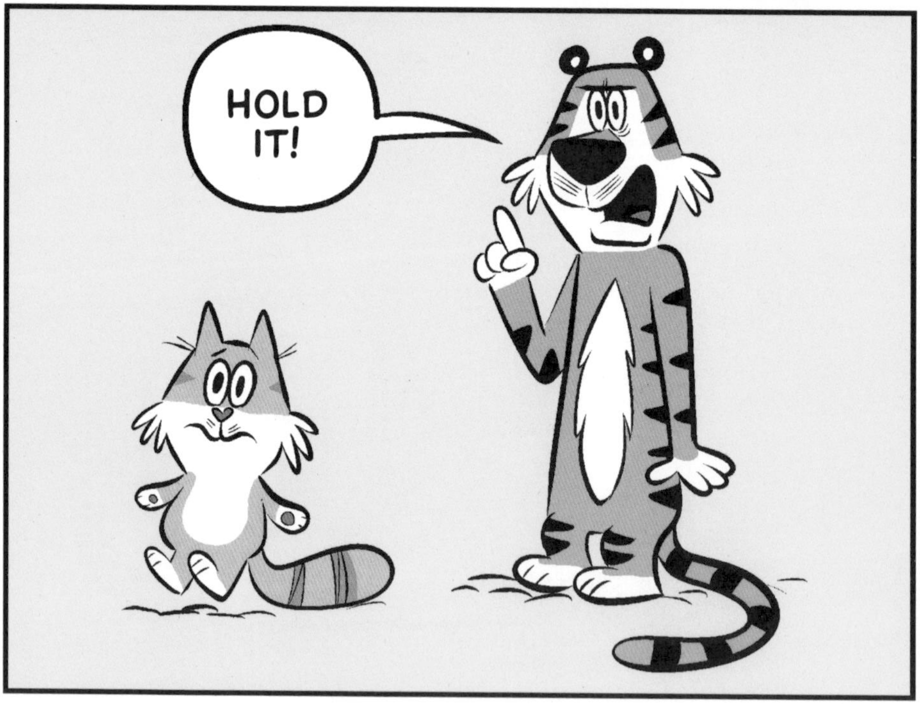
HOLD IT!

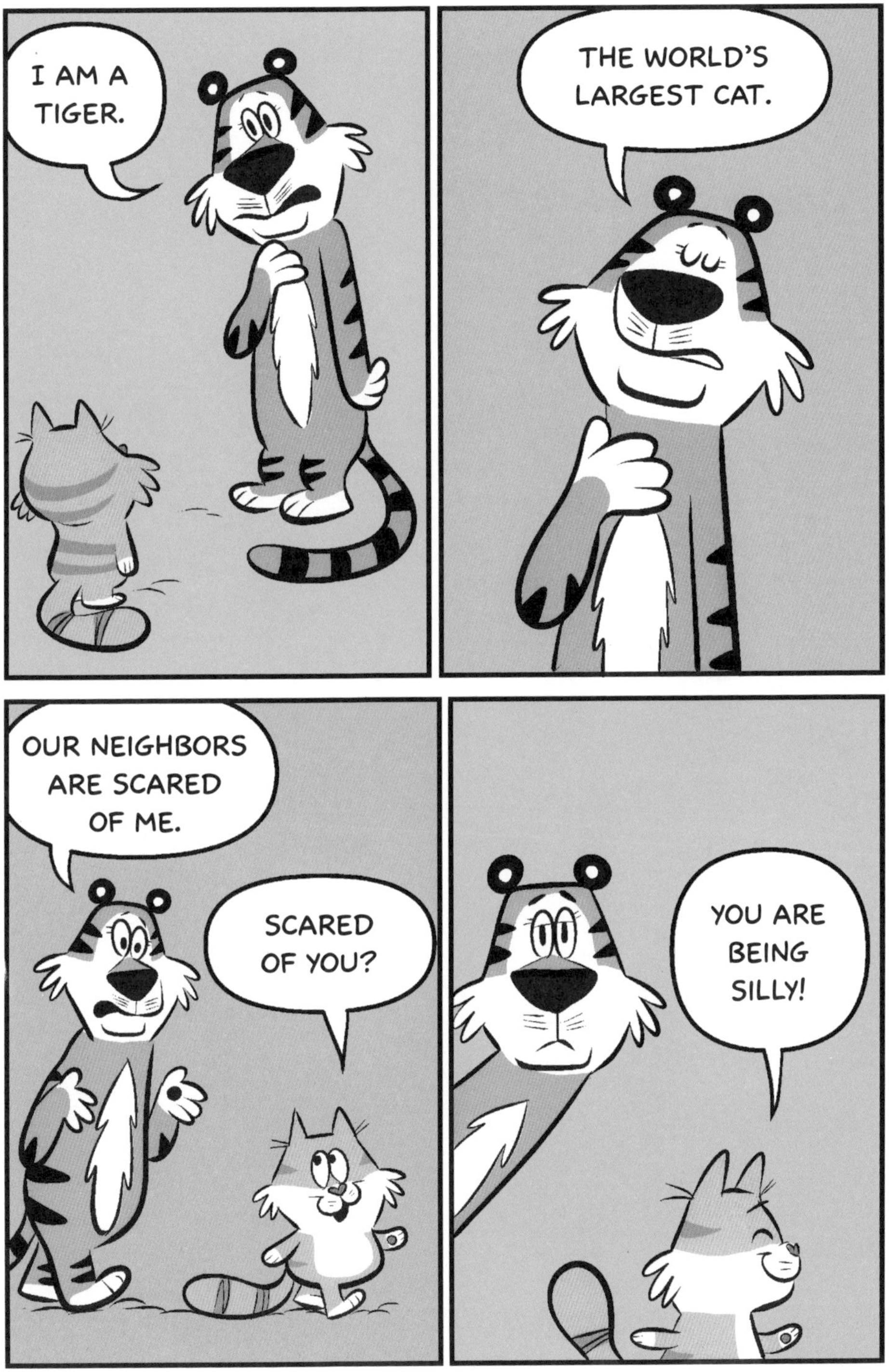
I AM A TIGER.
THE WORLD'S LARGEST CAT.
OUR NEIGHBORS ARE SCARED OF ME.
SCARED OF YOU?
YOU ARE BEING SILLY!

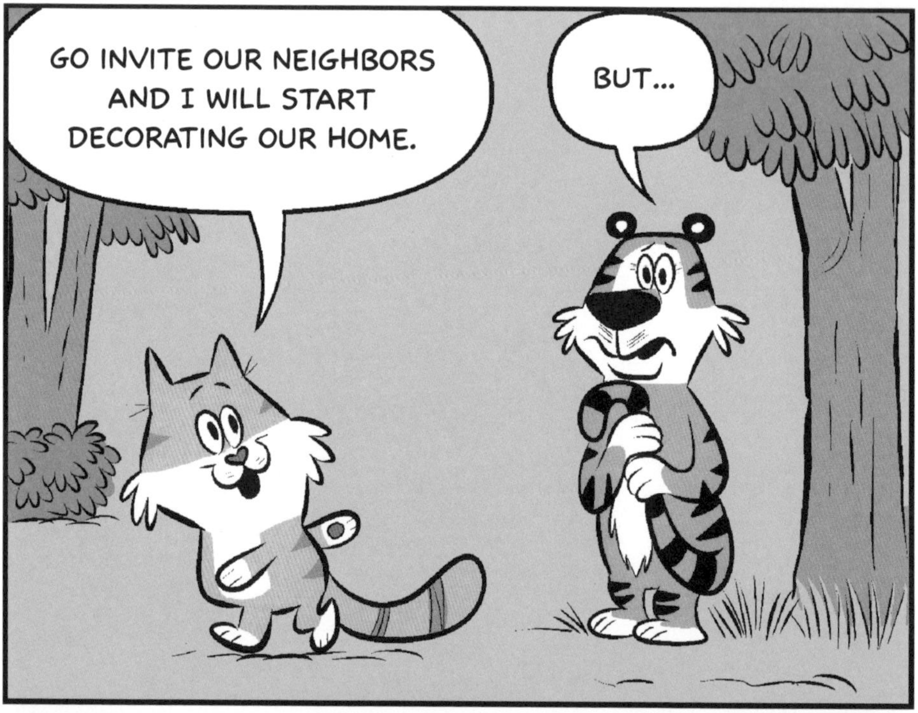
GO INVITE OUR NEIGHBORS AND I WILL START DECORATING OUR HOME.
BUT...

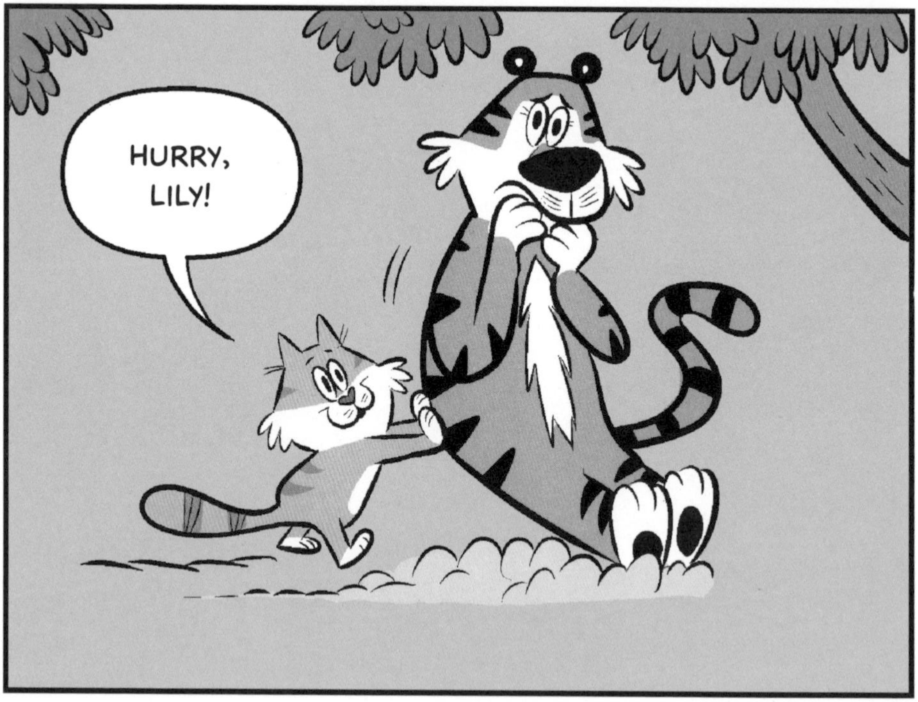
HURRY, LILY!

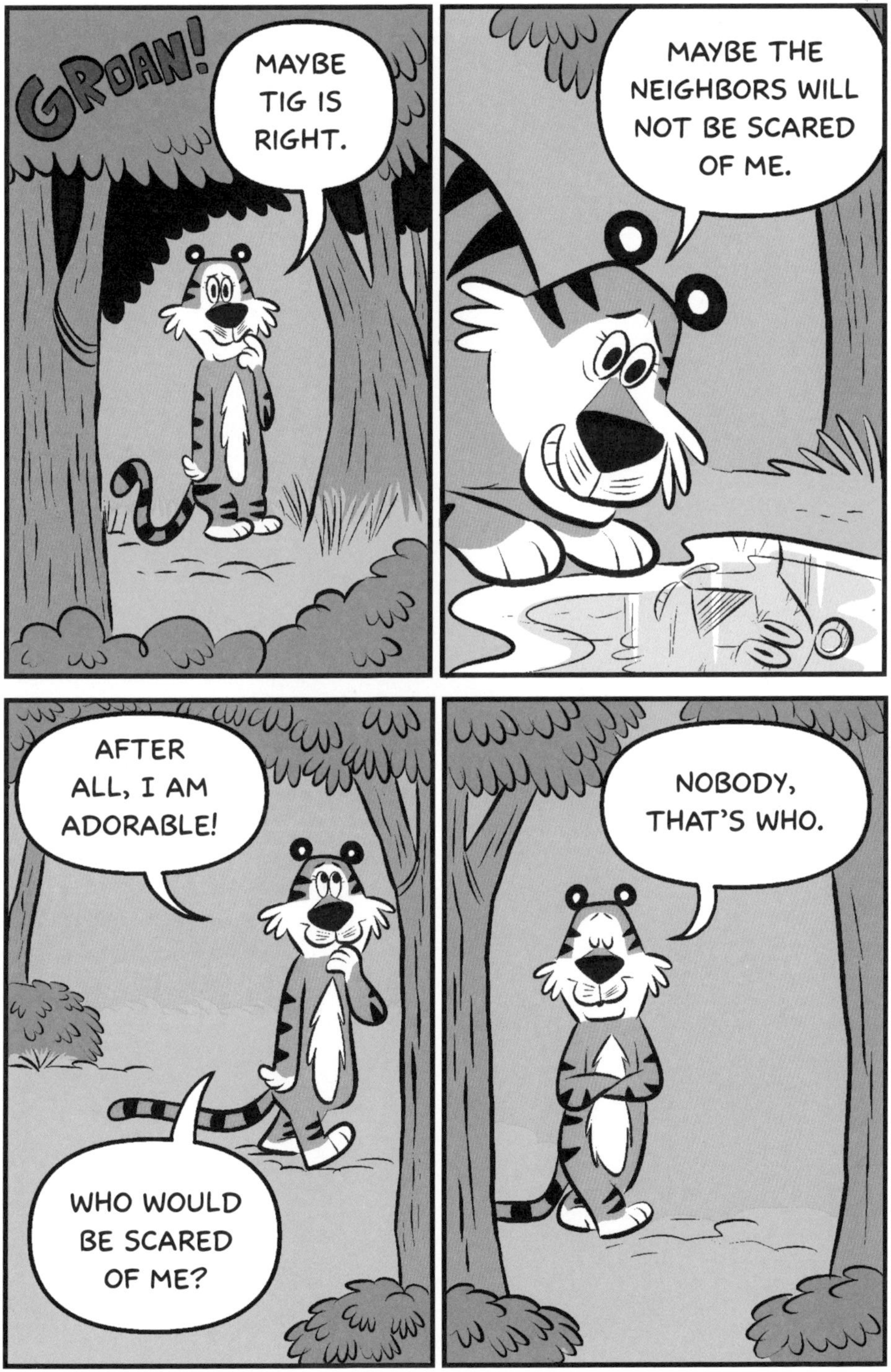
GROAN!
MAYBE TIG IS RIGHT.
MAYBE THE NEIGHBORS WILL NOT BE SCARED OF ME.
AFTER ALL, I AM ADORABLE!
WHO WOULD BE SCARED OF ME?
NOBODY, THAT'S WHO.

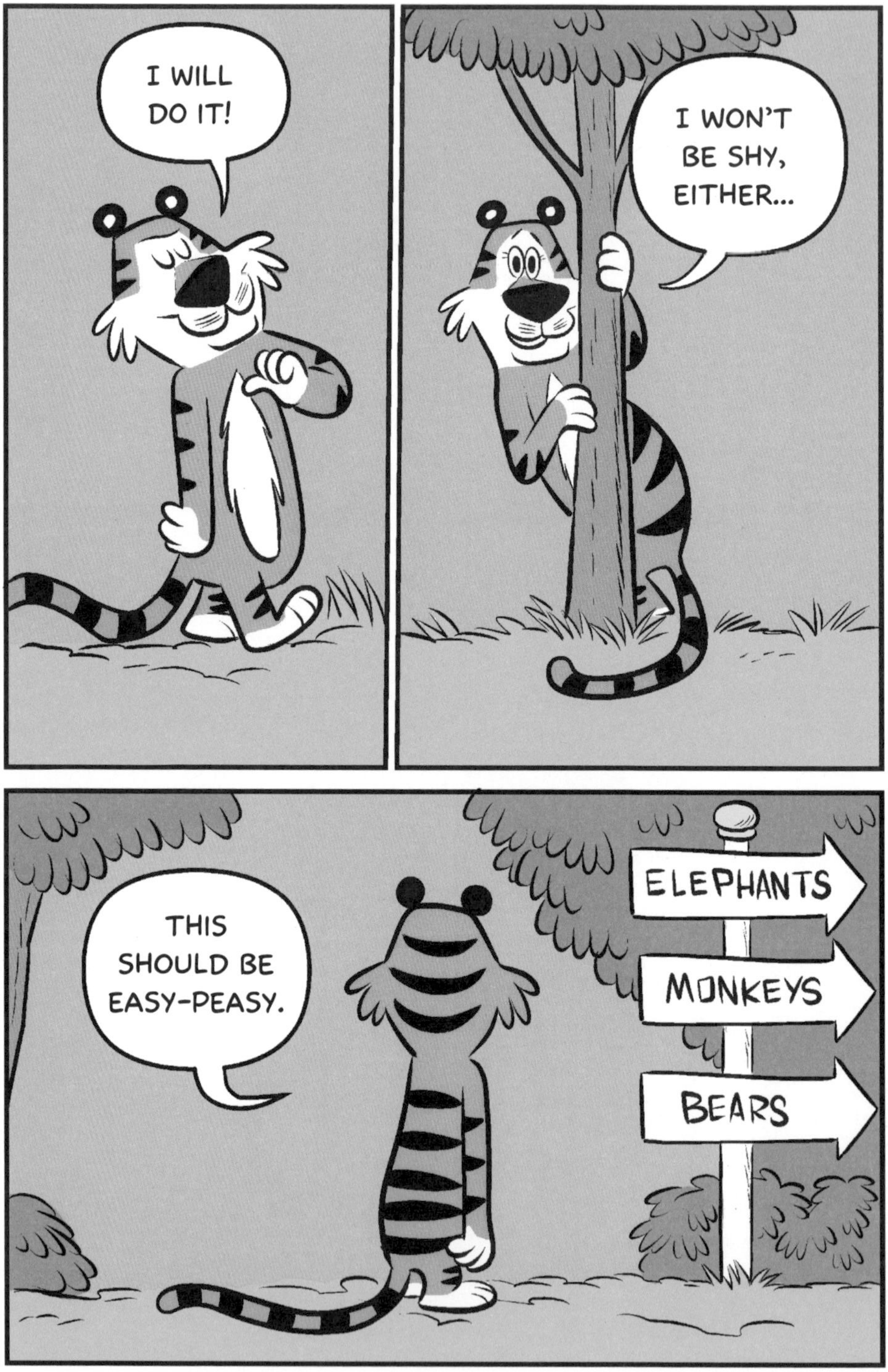
I WILL DO IT!
I WON'T BE SHY, EITHER...
THIS SHOULD BE EASY-PEASY.
ELEPHANTS
MONKEYS
BEARS

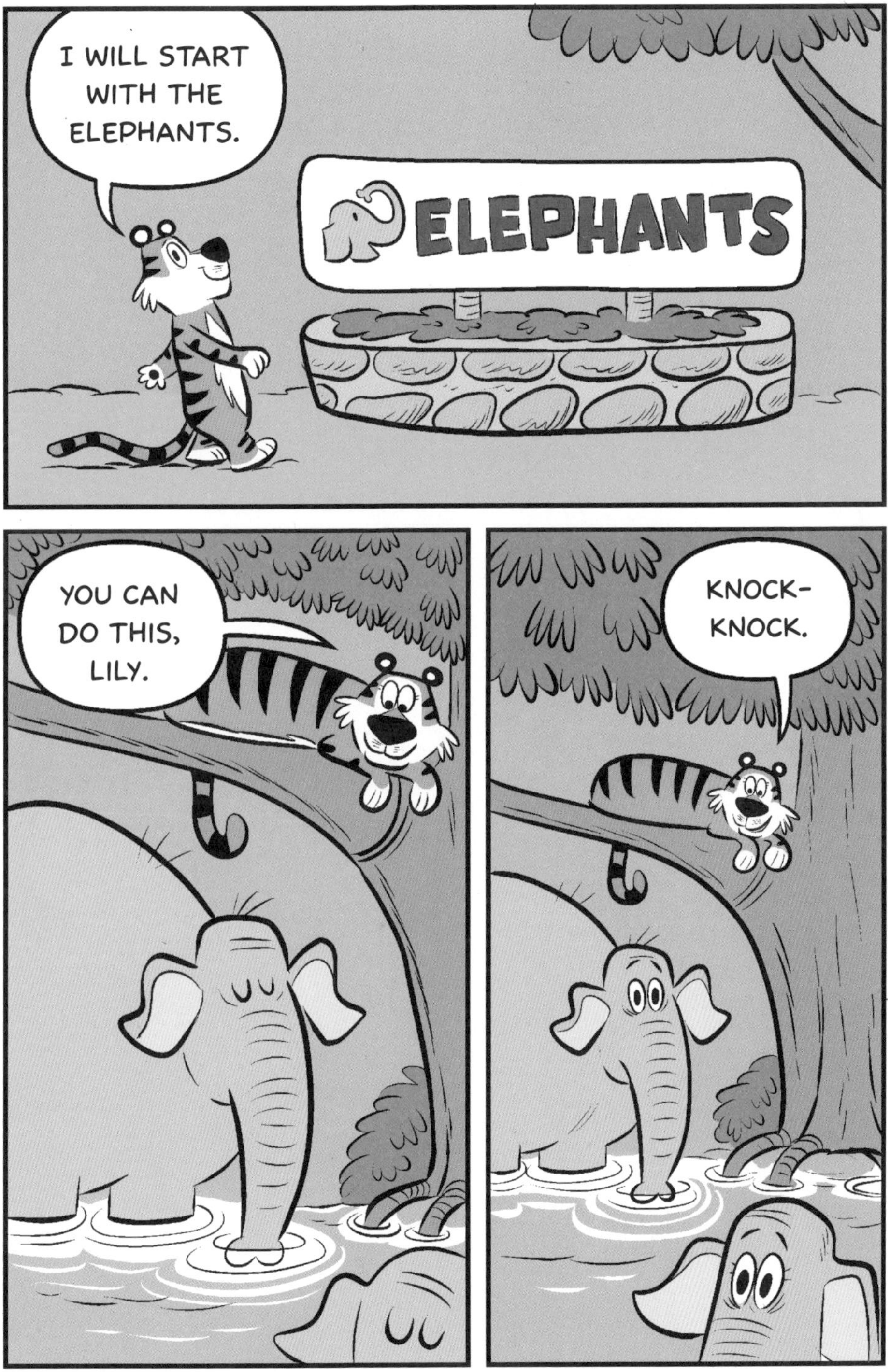
I WILL START WITH THE ELEPHANTS.
ELEPHANTS
YOU CAN DO THIS, LILY.
KNOCK-KNOCK.

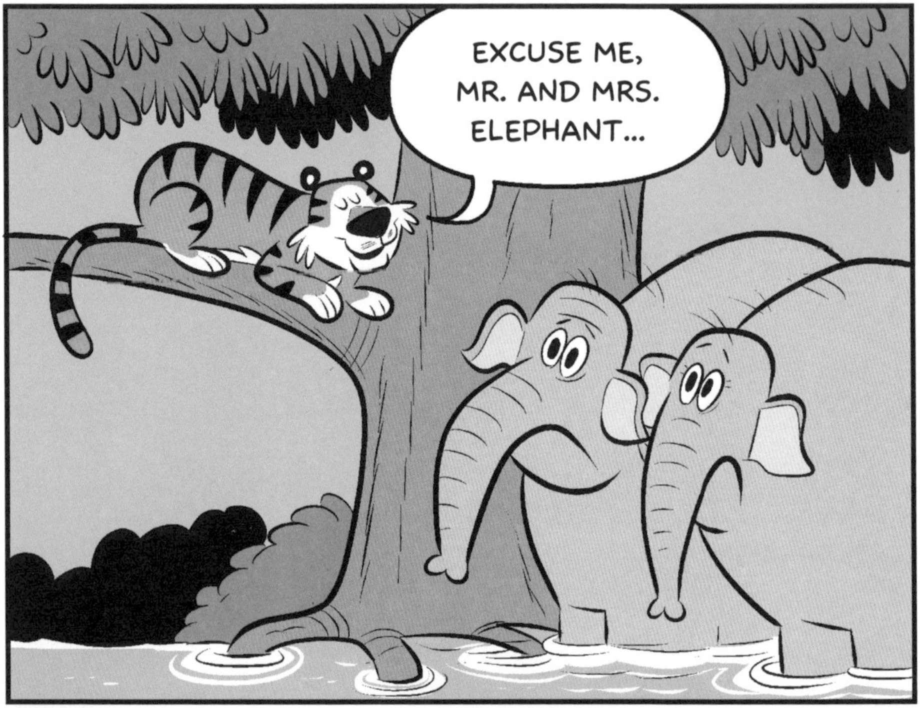
EXCUSE ME, MR. AND MRS. ELEPHANT...

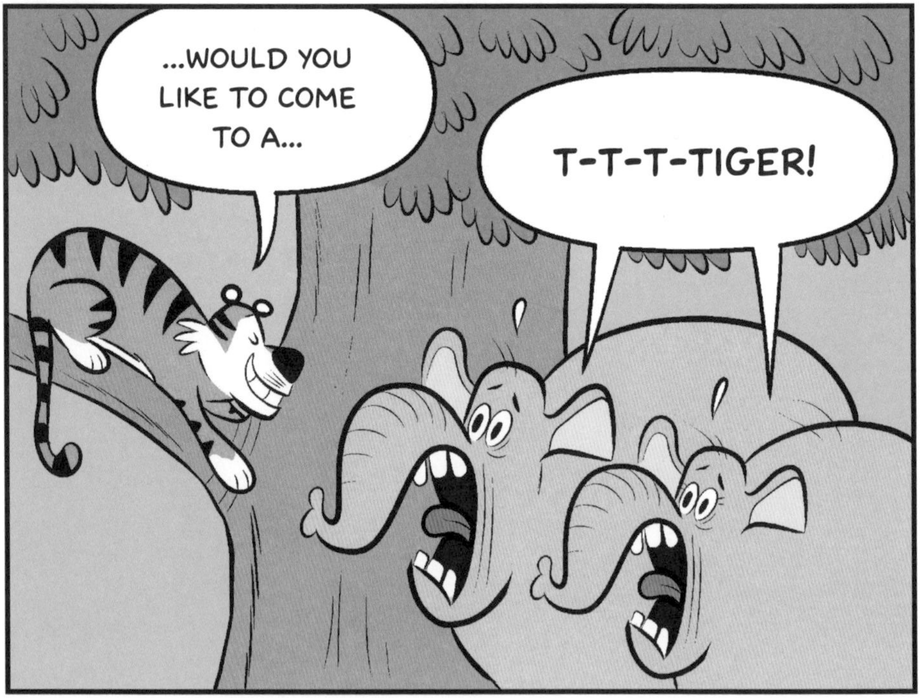
...WOULD YOU LIKE TO COME TO A...
T-T-T-TIGER!

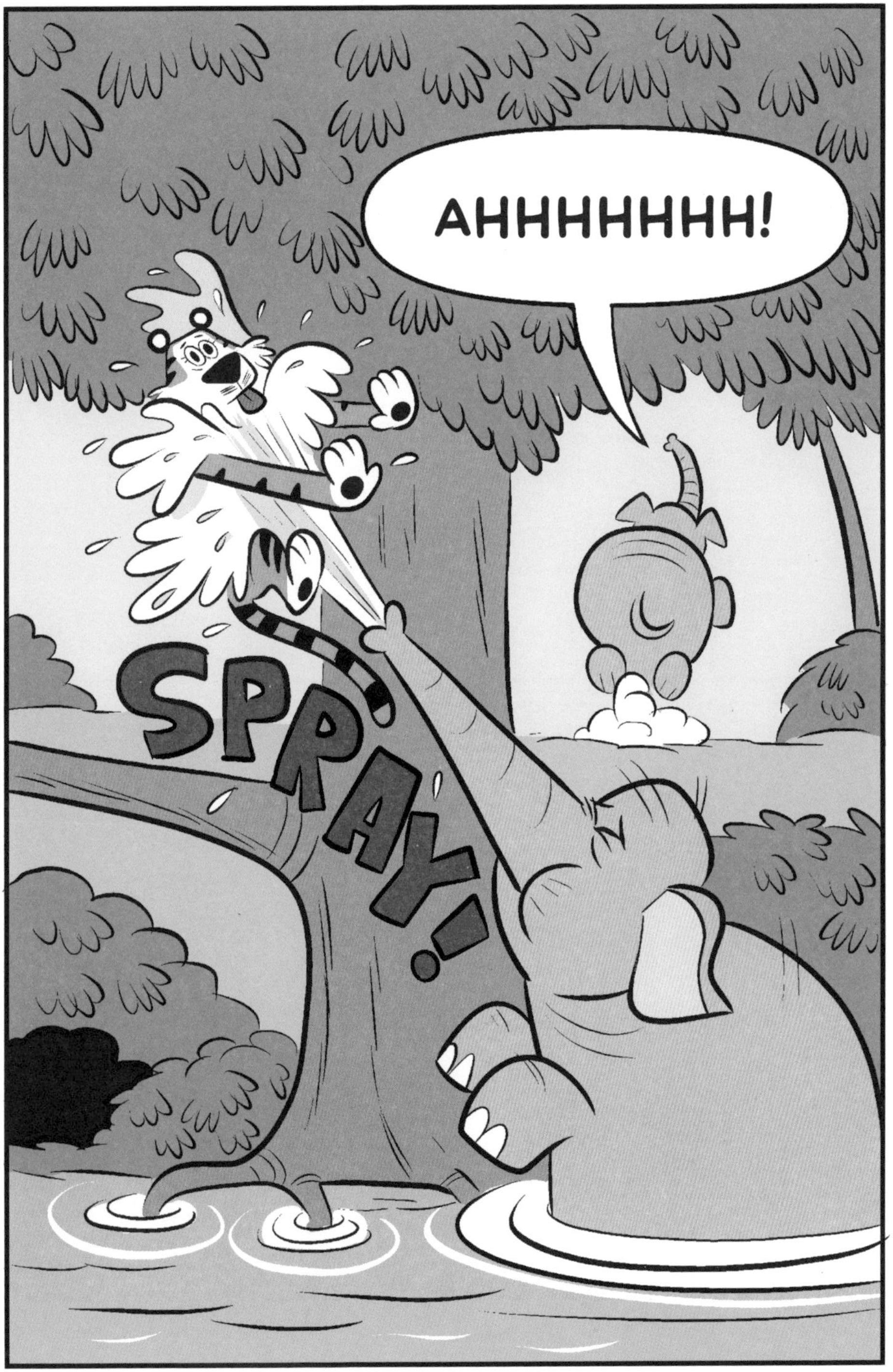
AHHHHHHH!
SPRAY!

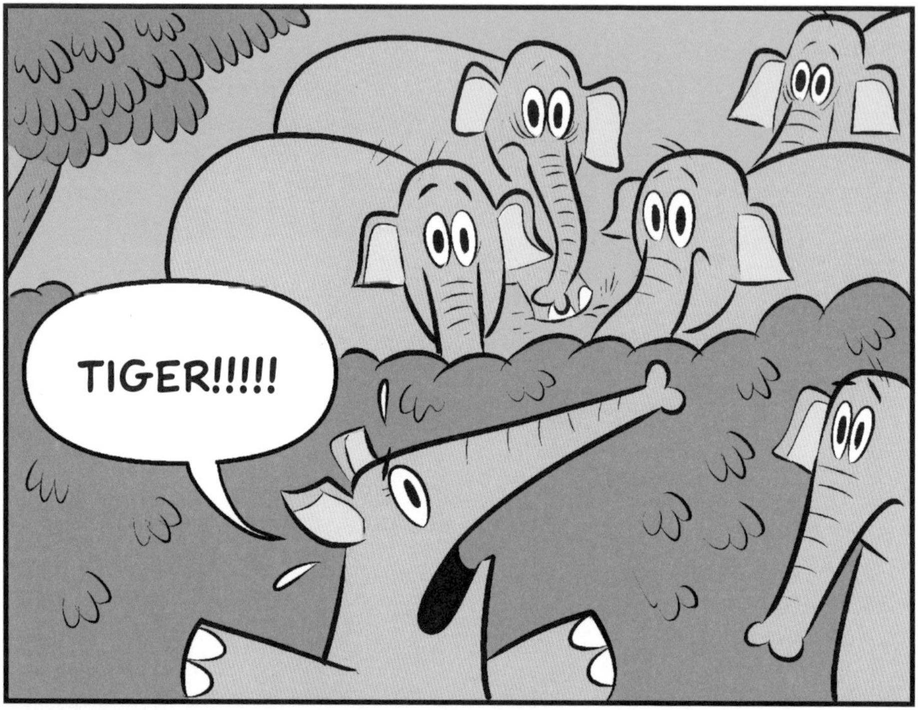
TIGER!!!!!

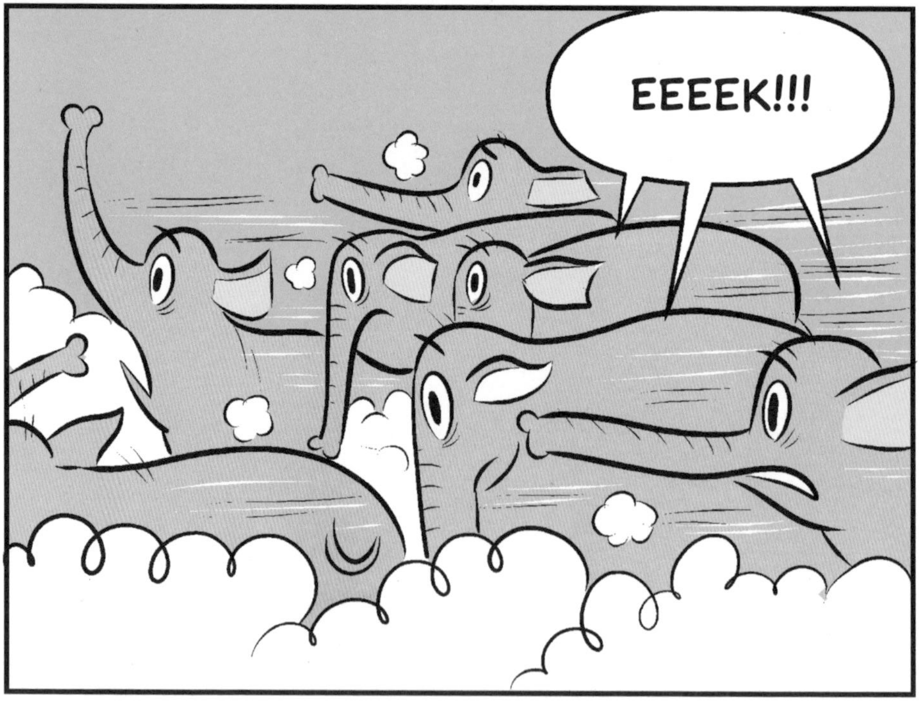
EEEEK!!!

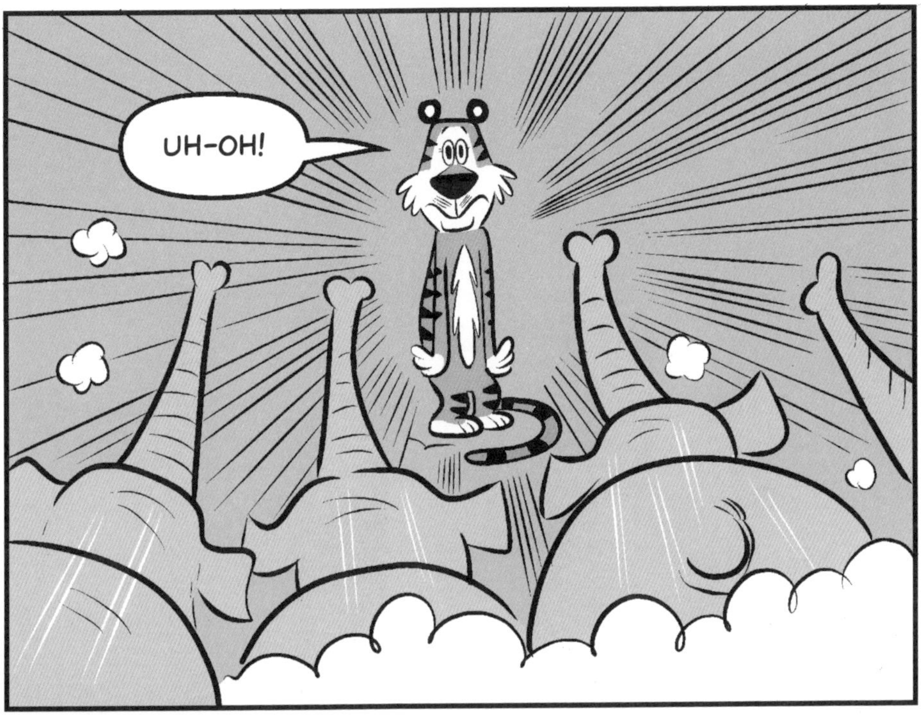
UH-OH!

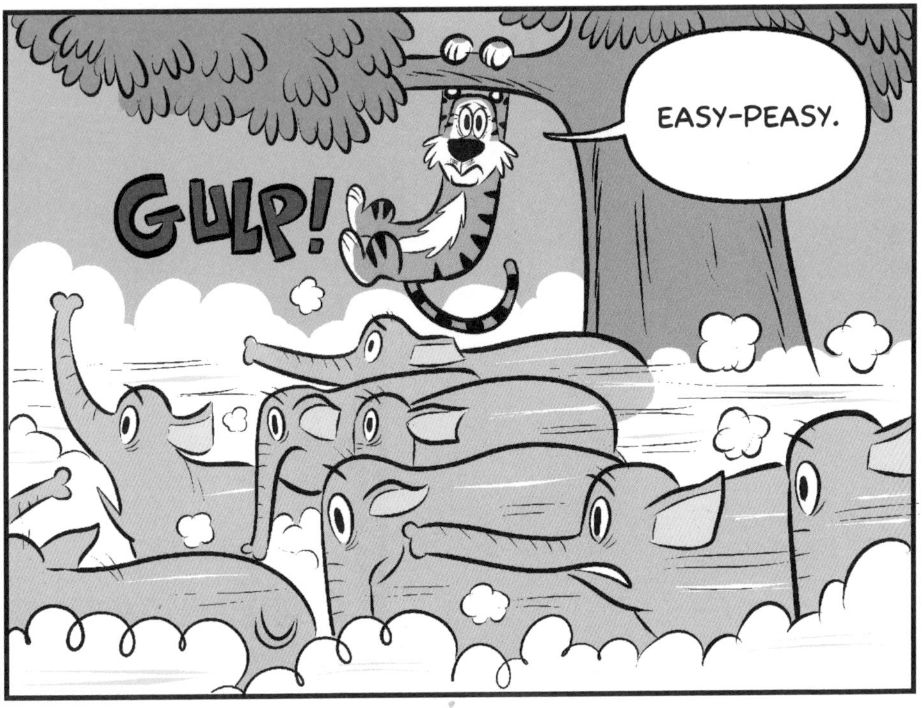
EASY-PEASY.
GULP!

Chapter TWO

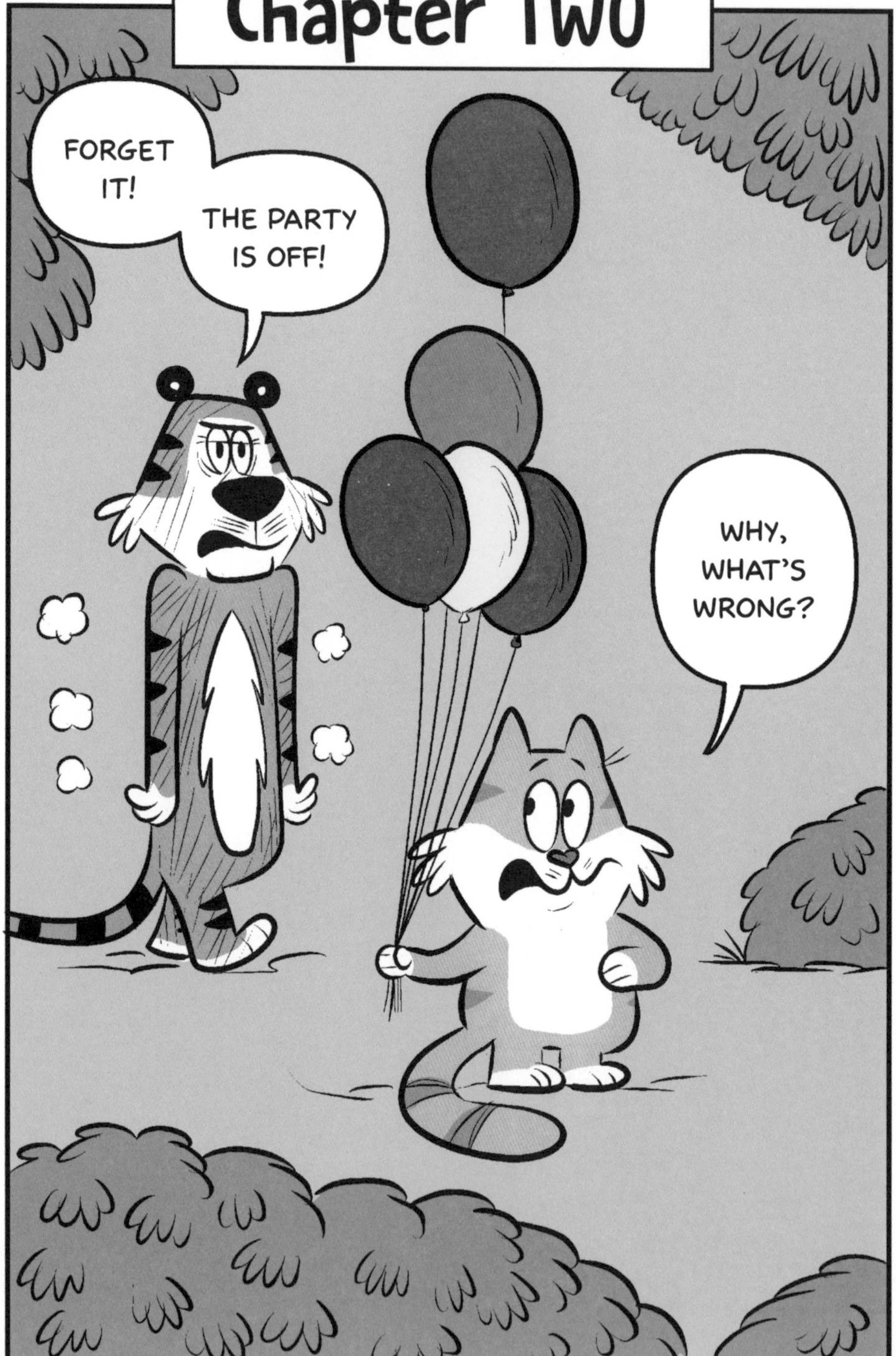
FORGET IT!
THE PARTY IS OFF!
WHY, WHAT'S WRONG?

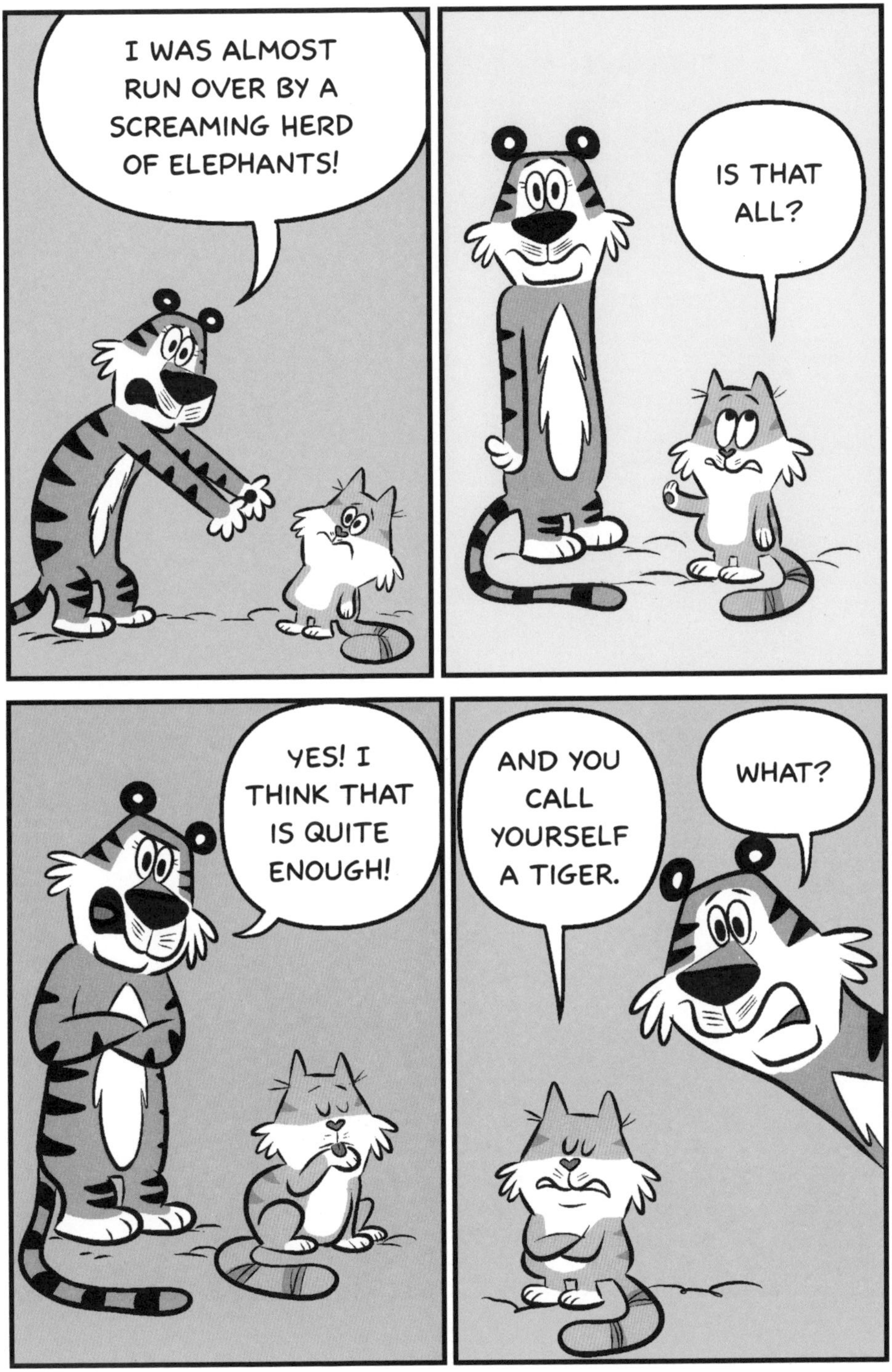
I WAS ALMOST RUN OVER BY A SCREAMING HERD OF ELEPHANTS!
IS THAT ALL?
YES! I THINK THAT IS QUITE ENOUGH!
AND YOU CALL YOURSELF A TIGER.
WHAT?

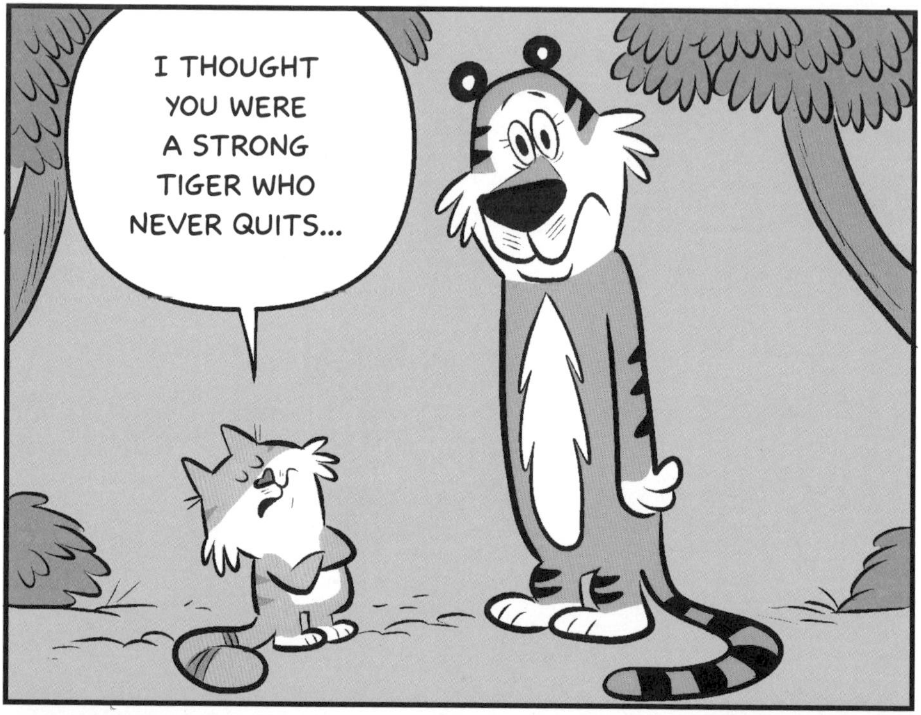
I THOUGHT YOU WERE A STRONG TIGER WHO NEVER QUITS...

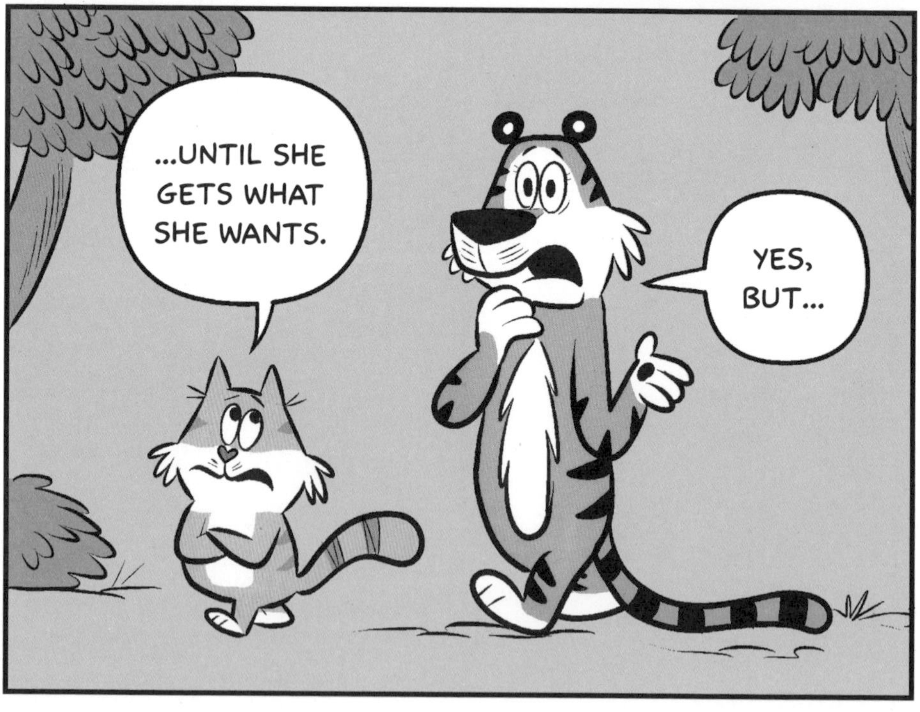
...UNTIL SHE GETS WHAT SHE WANTS.
YES, BUT...

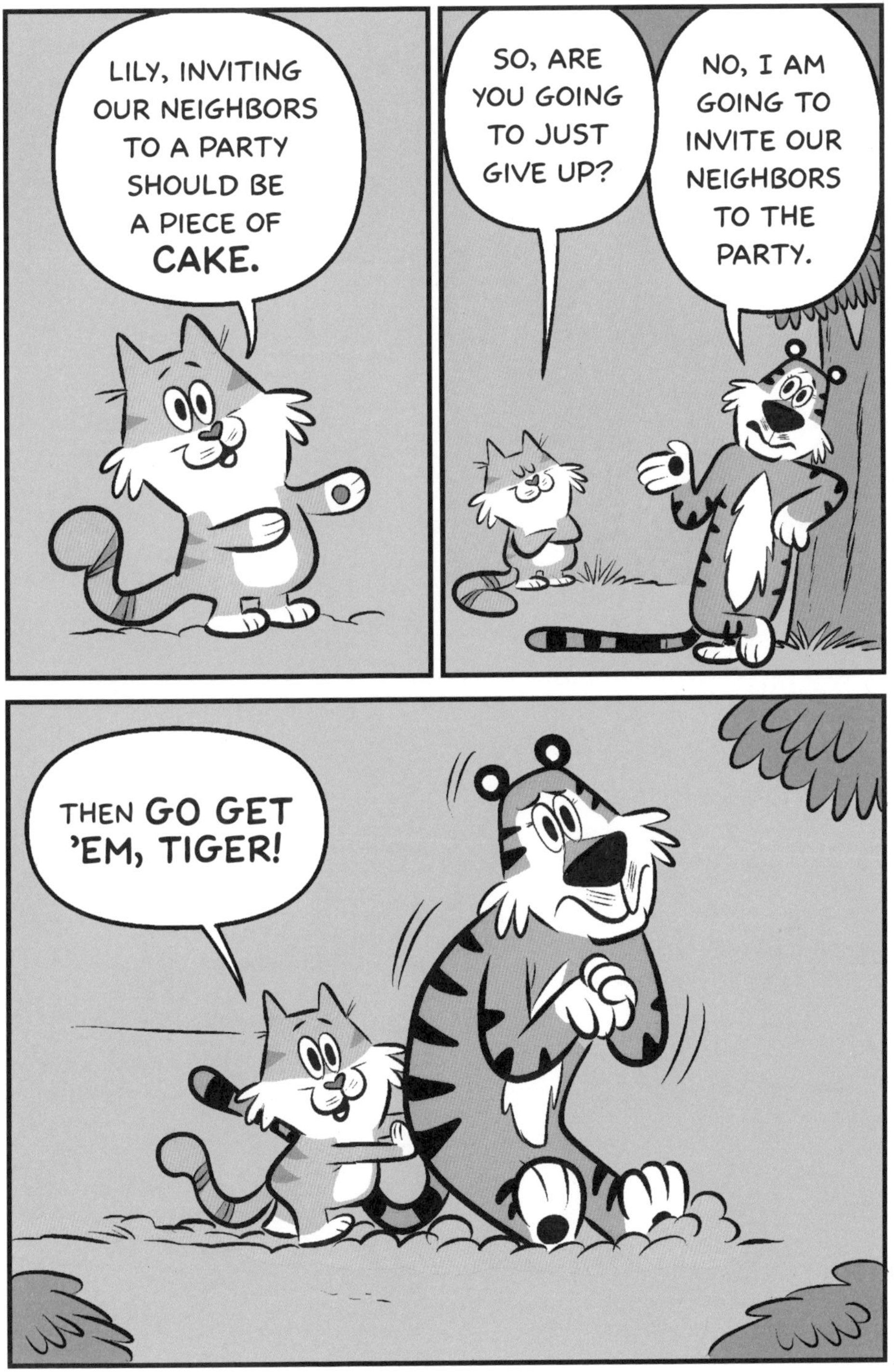
LILY, INVITING OUR NEIGHBORS TO A PARTY SHOULD BE A PIECE OF CAKE.
SO, ARE YOU GOING TO JUST GIVE UP?
NO, I AM GOING TO INVITE OUR NEIGHBORS TO THE PARTY.
THEN GO GET 'EM, TIGER!

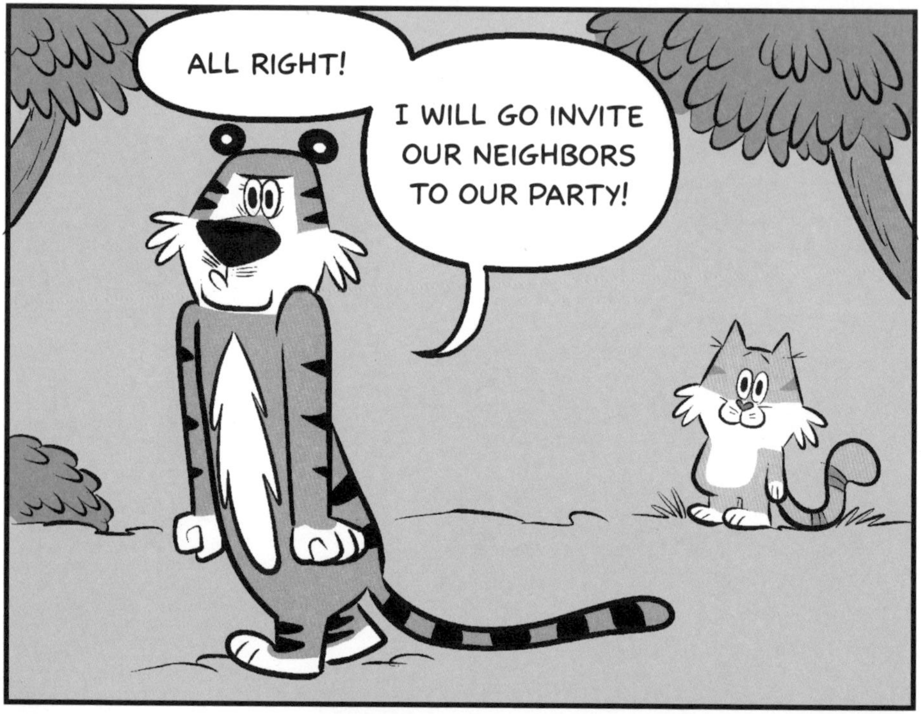
ALL RIGHT!
I WILL GO INVITE OUR NEIGHBORS TO OUR PARTY!

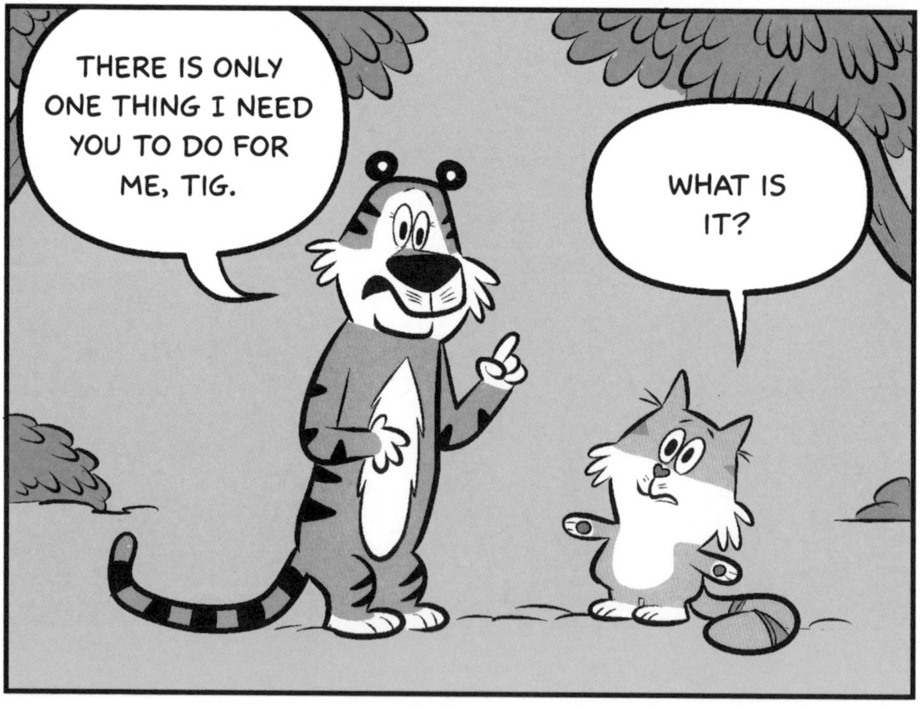
THERE IS ONLY ONE THING I NEED YOU TO DO FOR ME, TIG.
WHAT IS IT?

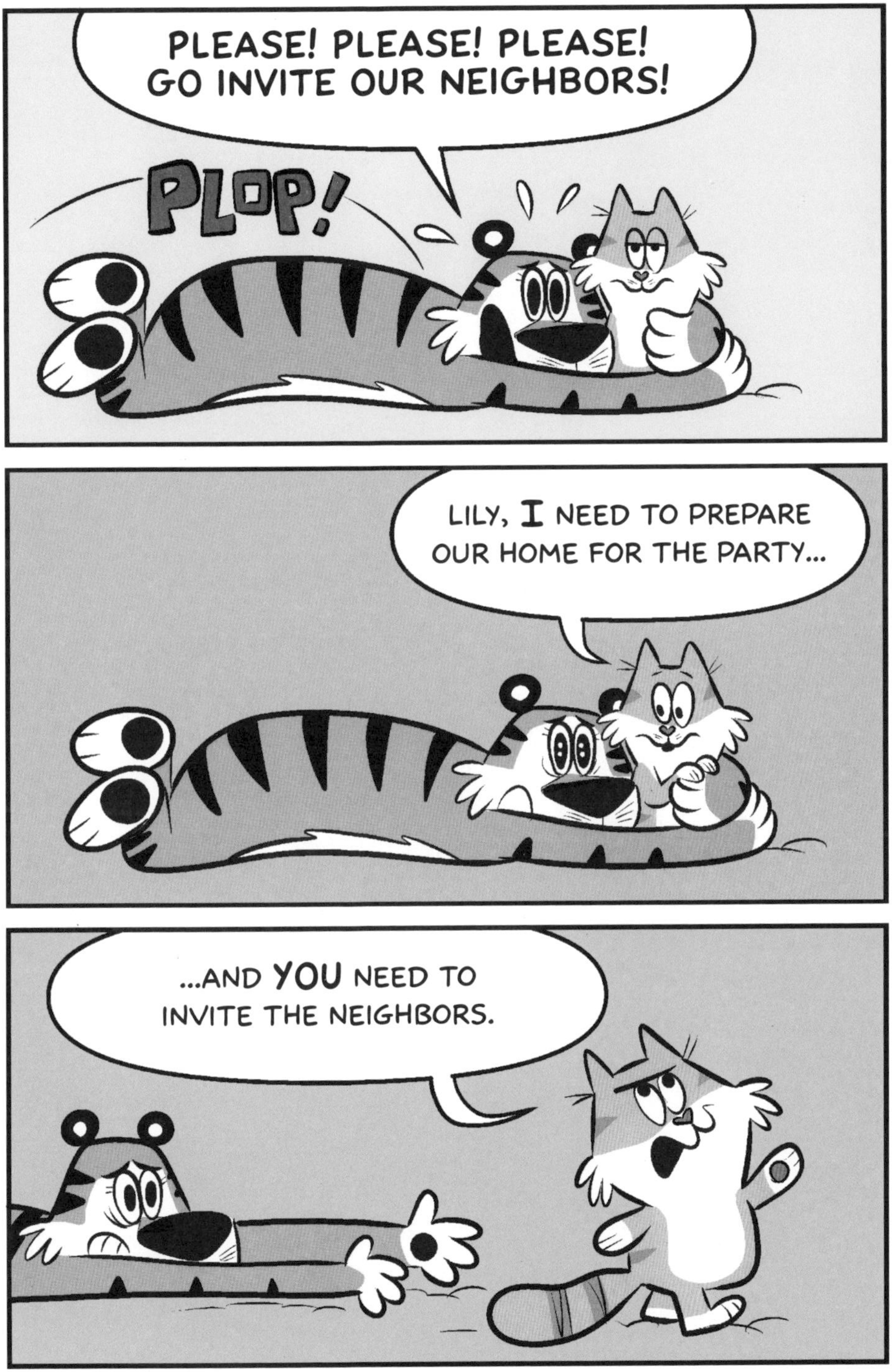
PLEASE! PLEASE! PLEASE! GO INVITE OUR NEIGHBORS!
PLOP!
LILY, I NEED TO PREPARE OUR HOME FOR THE PARTY...
...AND YOU NEED TO INVITE THE NEIGHBORS.

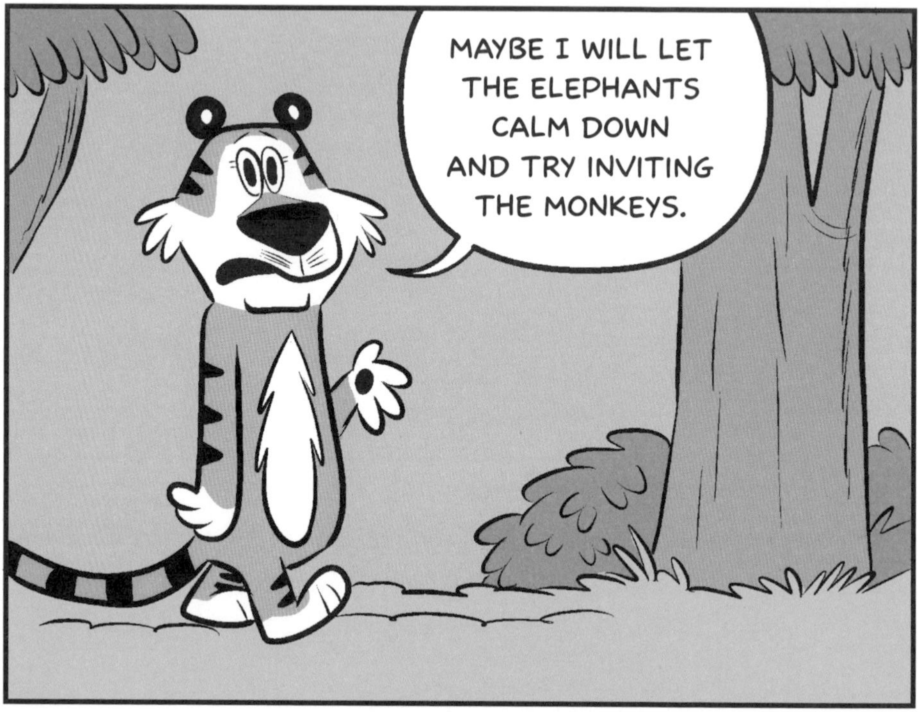
MAYBE I WILL LET THE ELEPHANTS CALM DOWN AND TRY INVITING THE MONKEYS.

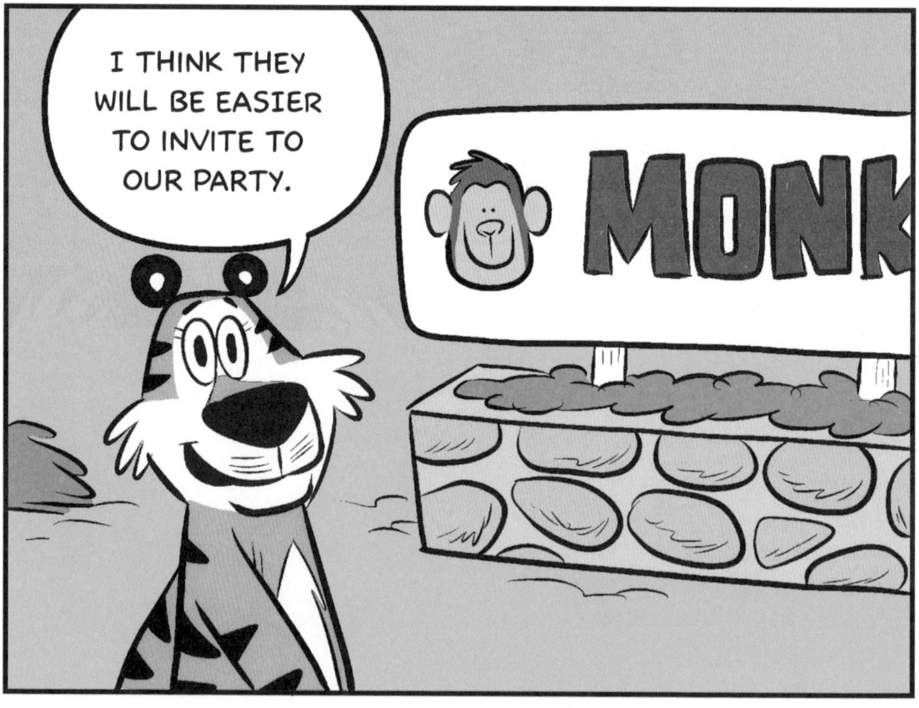
I THINK THEY WILL BE EASIER TO INVITE TO OUR PARTY.
MONK

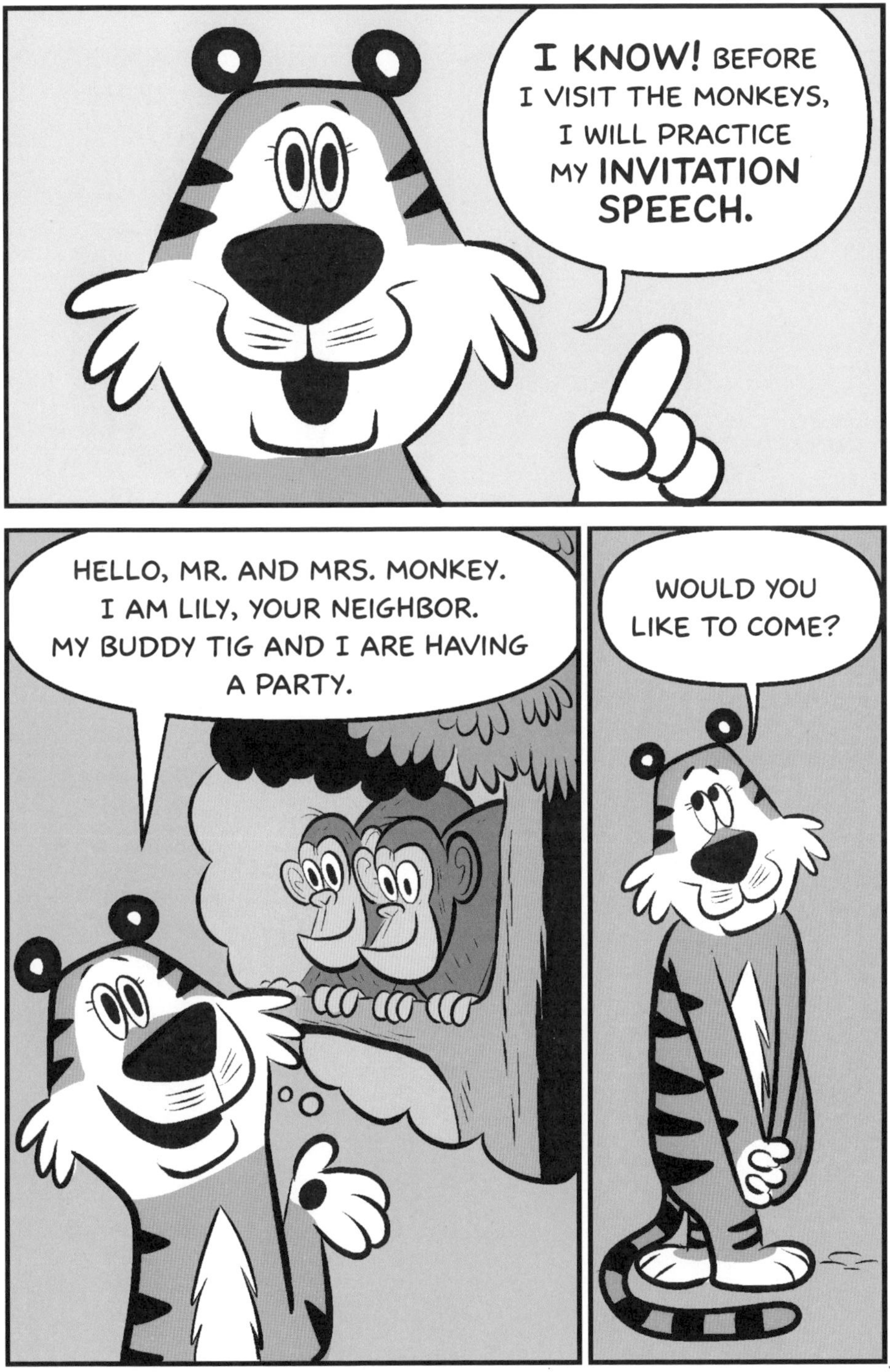
I KNOW! BEFORE I VISIT THE MONKEYS, I WILL PRACTICE MY INVITATION SPEECH.
HELLO, MR. AND MRS. MONKEY. I AM LILY, YOUR NEIGHBOR. MY BUDDY TIG AND I ARE HAVING A PARTY.
WOULD YOU LIKE TO COME?

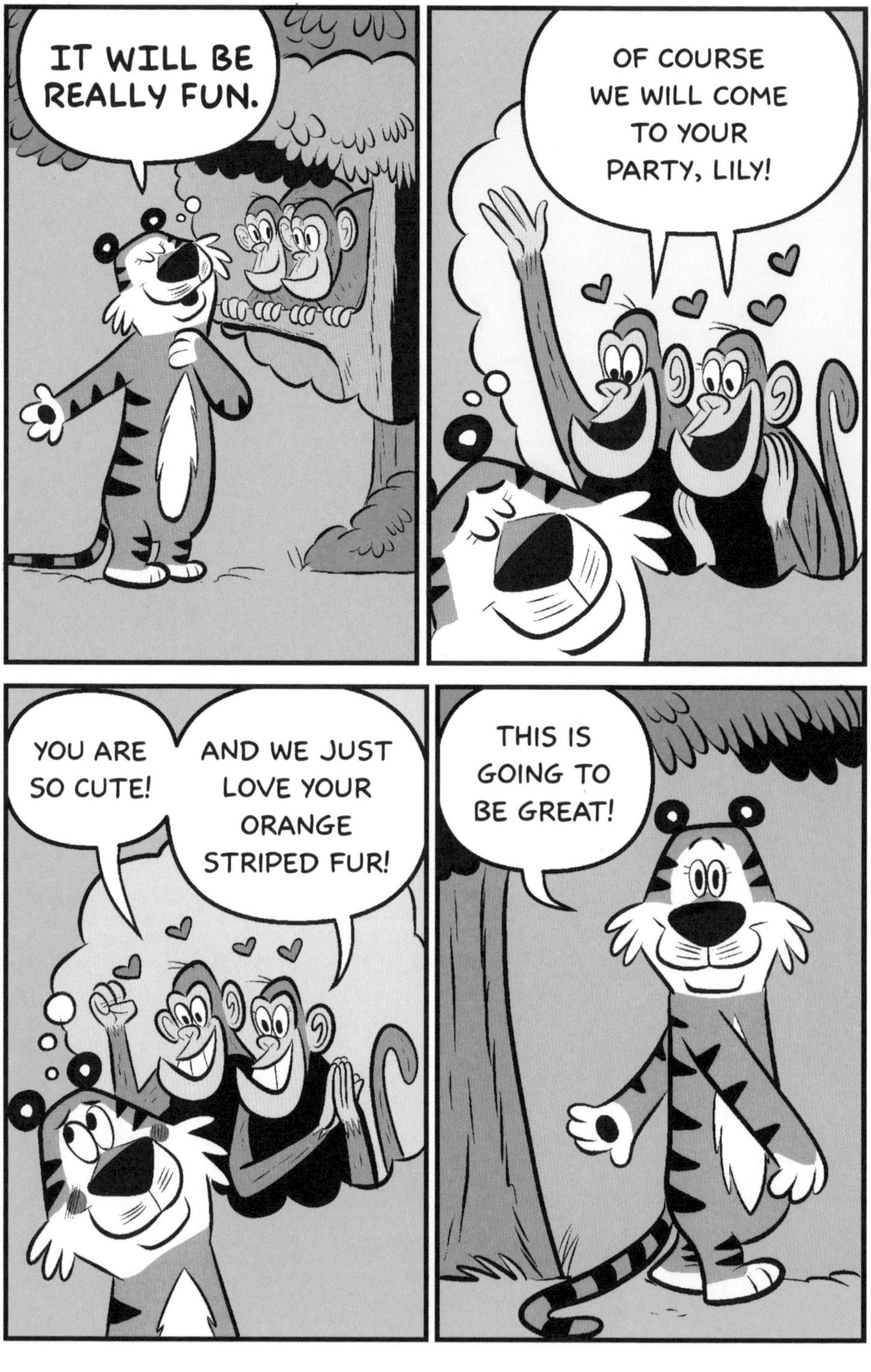
IT WILL BE REALLY FUN.
OF COURSE WE WILL COME TO YOUR PARTY, LILY!
YOU ARE SO CUTE!
AND WE JUST LOVE YOUR ORANGE STRIPED FUR!
THIS IS GOING TO BE GREAT!

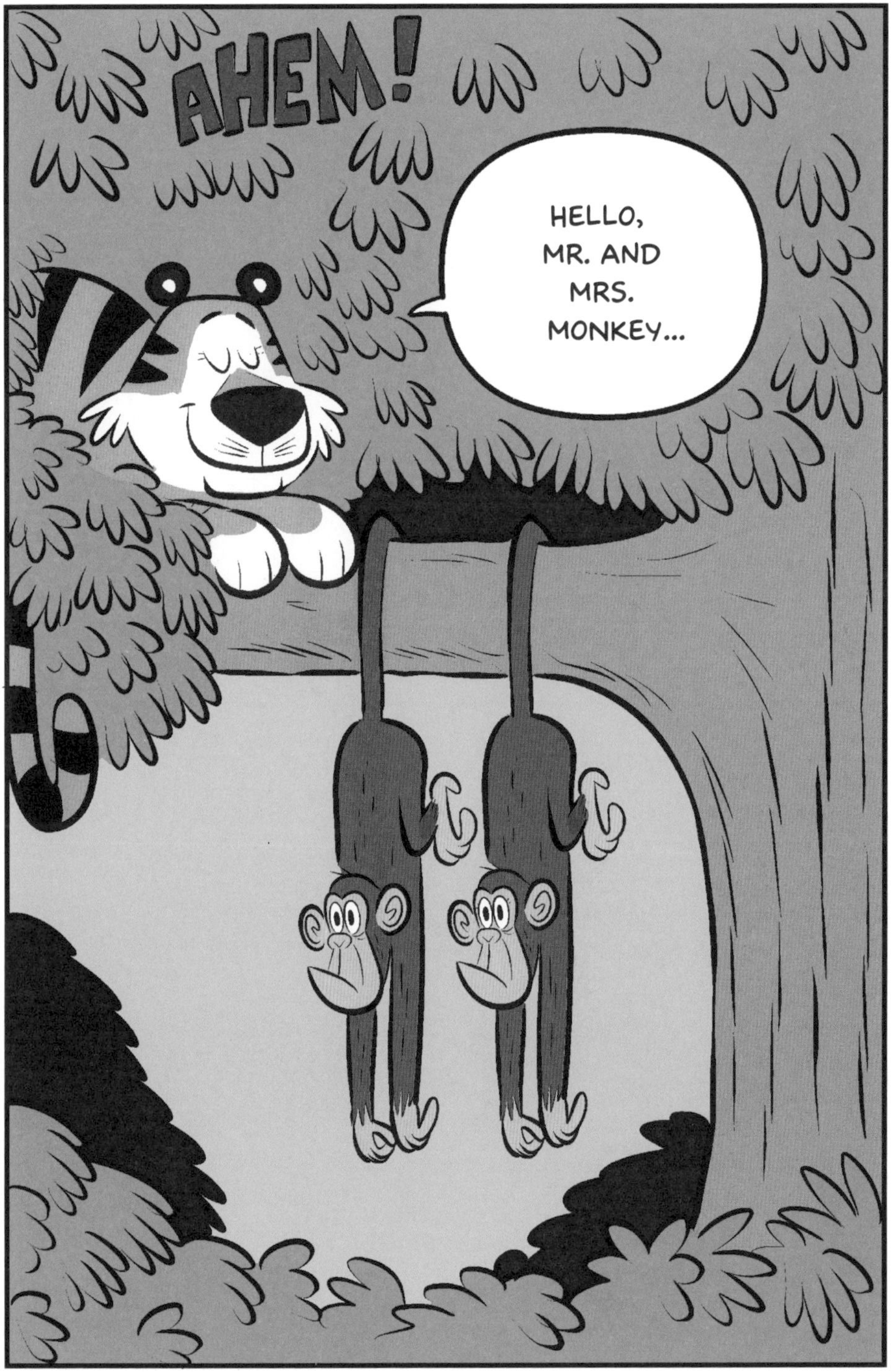
AHEM!
HELLO, MR. AND MRS. MONKEY...

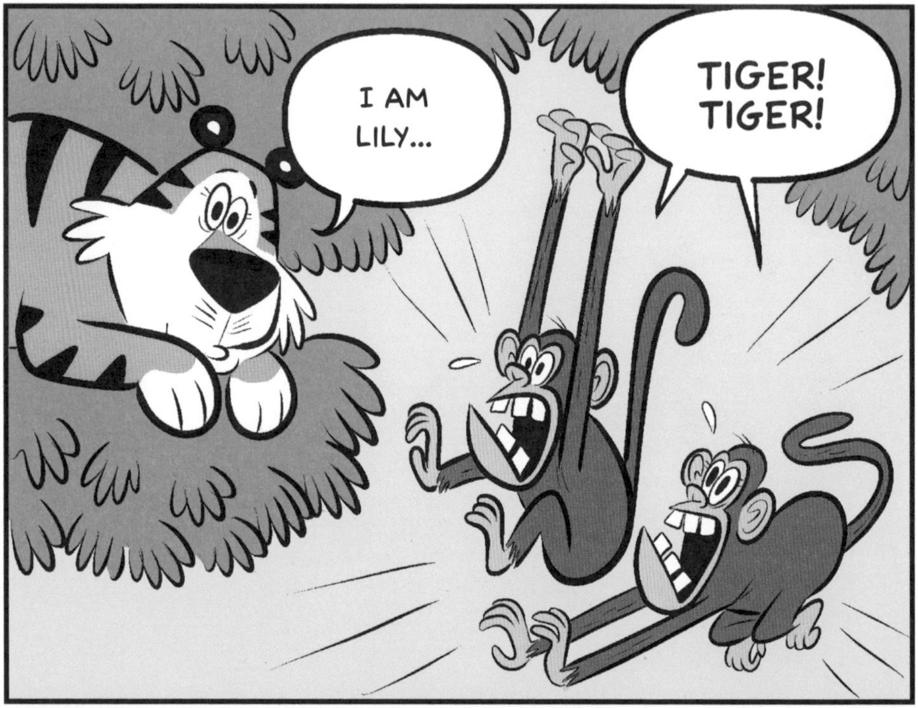
I AM LILY...
TIGER! TIGER!

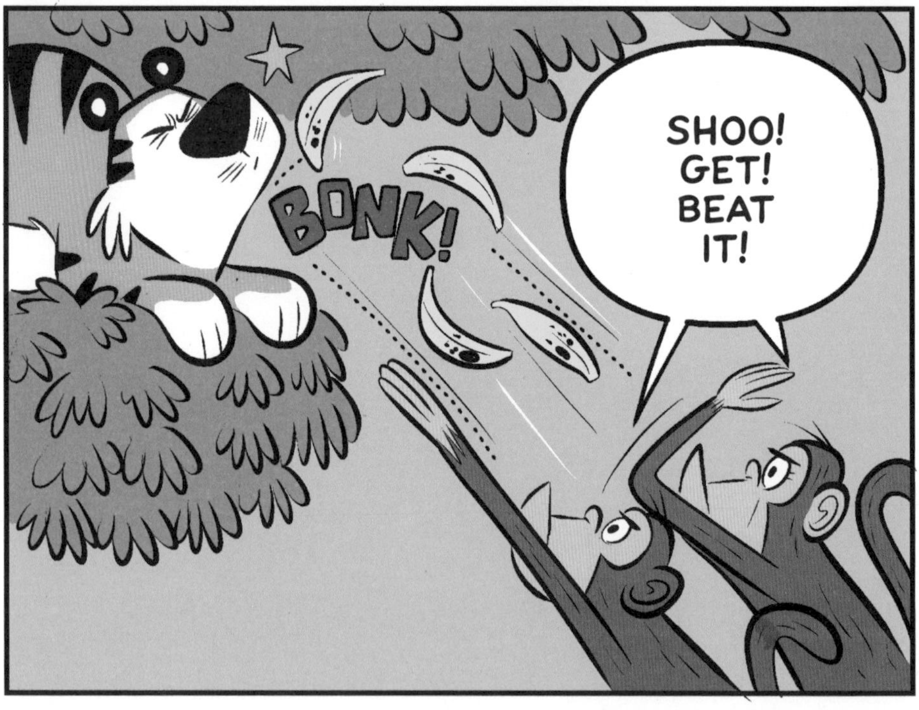
BONK!
SHOO! GET! BEAT IT!

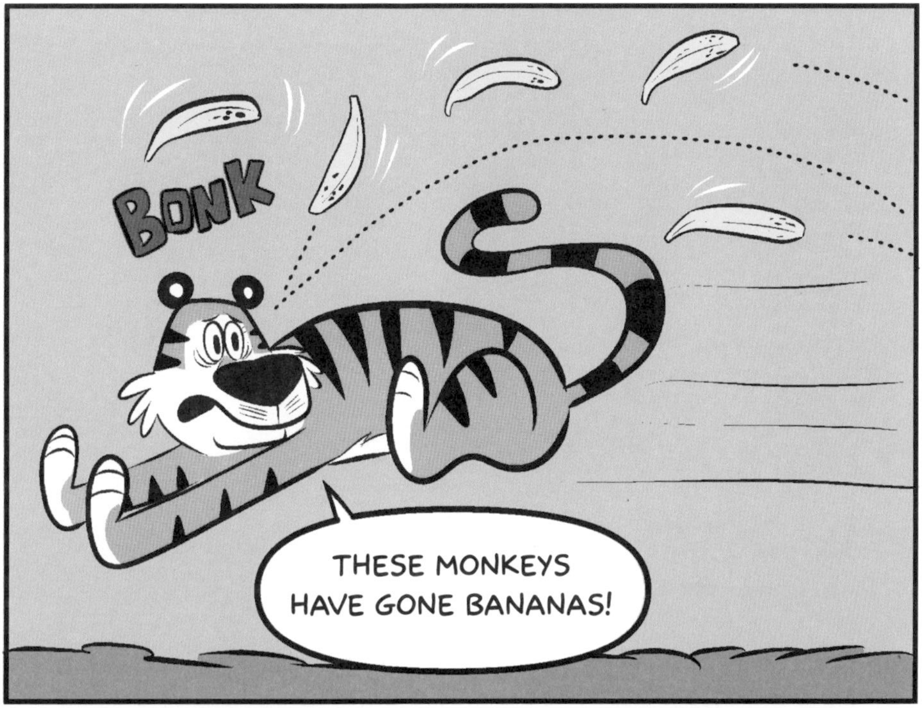
BONK
THESE MONKEYS HAVE GONE BANANAS!

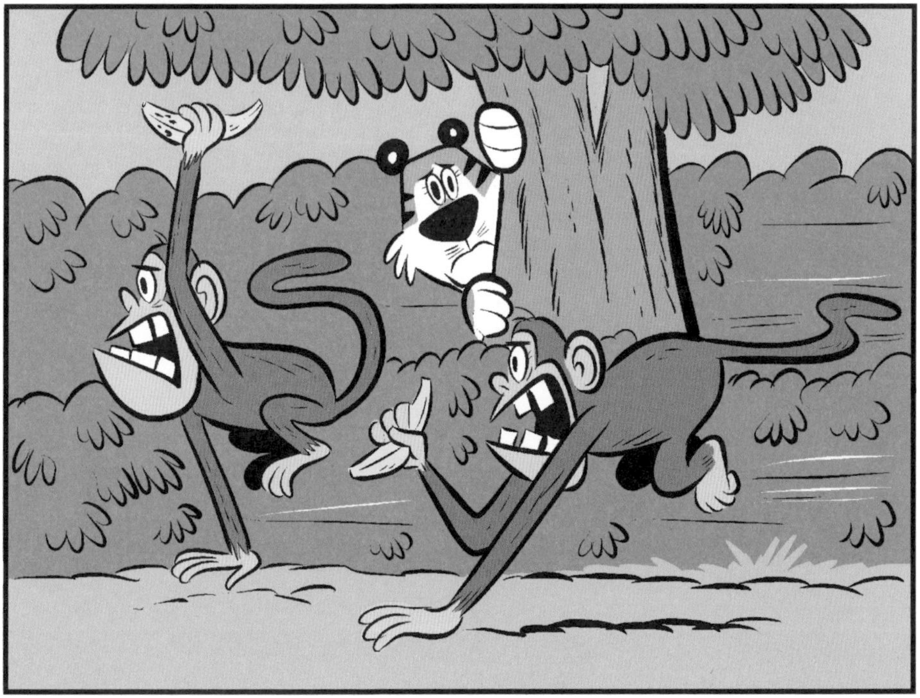

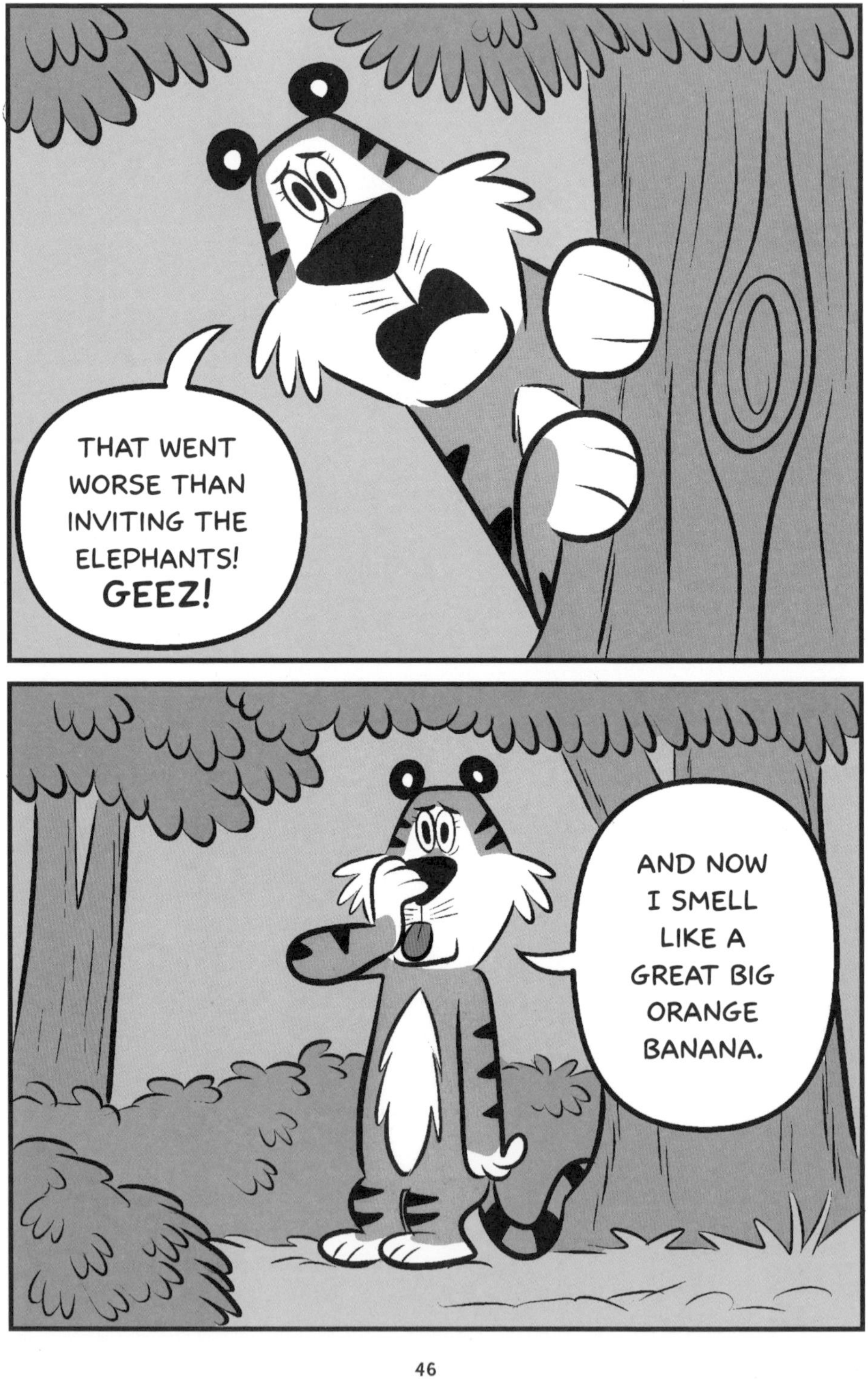
THAT WENT WORSE THAN INVITING THE ELEPHANTS! GEEZ!
AND NOW I SMELL LIKE A GREAT BIG ORANGE BANANA.

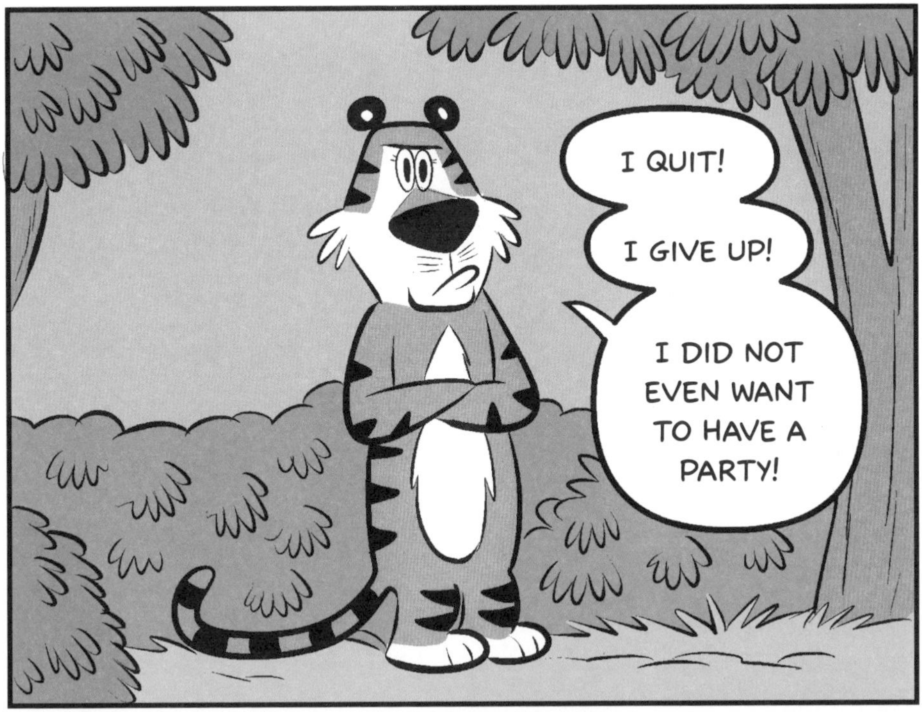
I QUIT!
I GIVE UP!
I DID NOT EVEN WANT TO HAVE A PARTY!

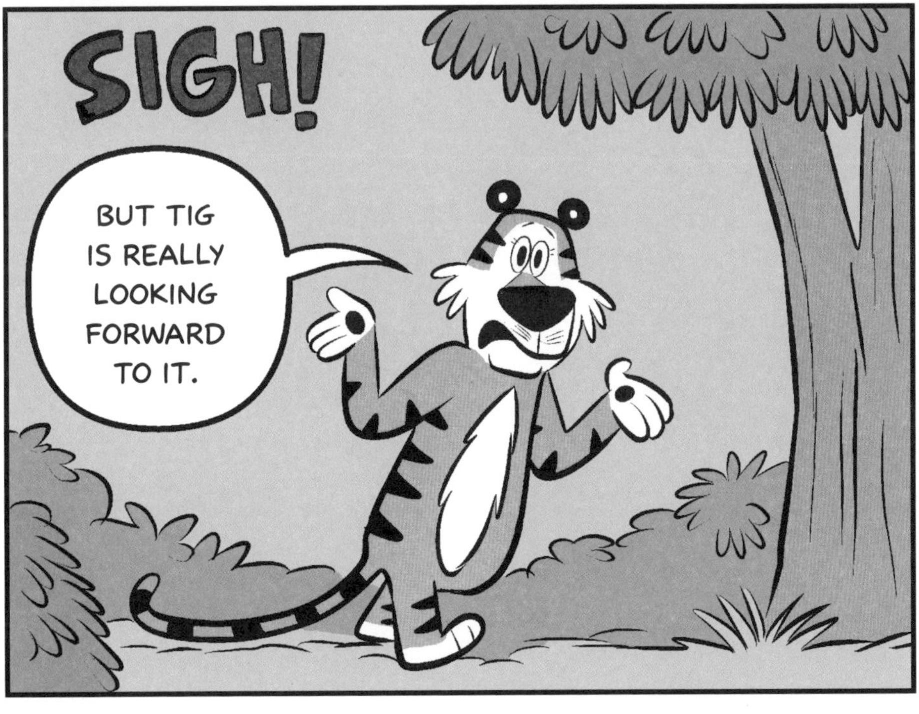
SIGH!
BUT TIG IS REALLY LOOKING FORWARD TO IT.

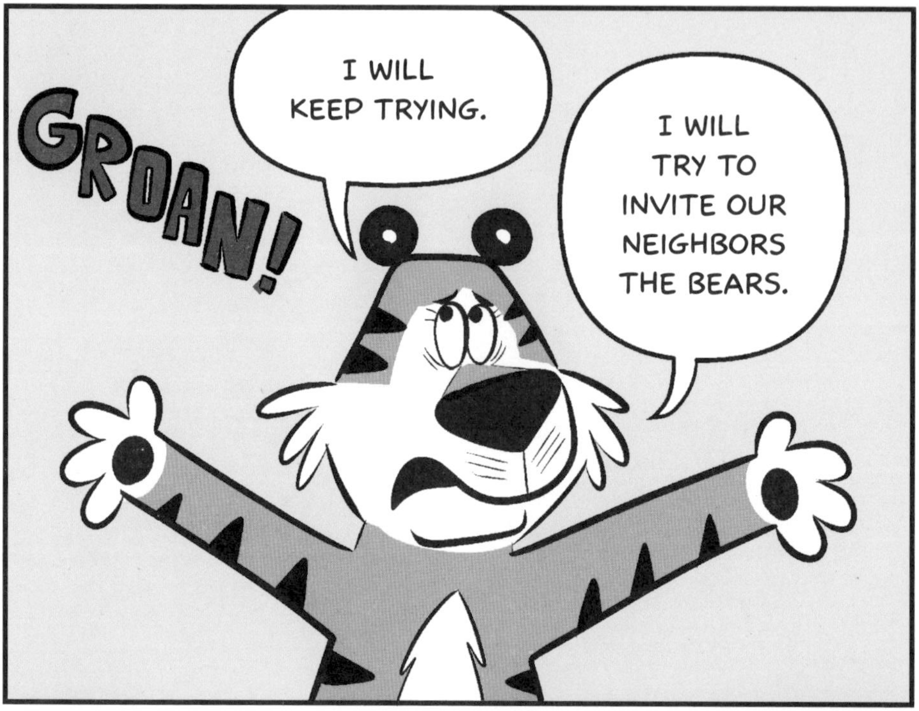
GROAN!
I WILL KEEP TRYING.
I WILL TRY TO INVITE OUR NEIGHBORS THE BEARS.

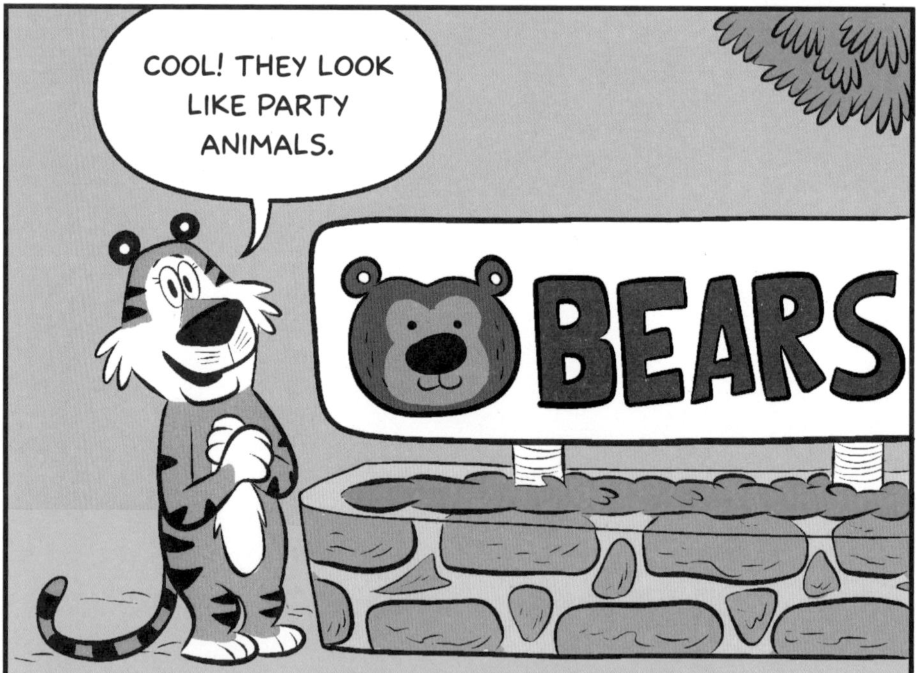
COOL! THEY LOOK LIKE PARTY ANIMALS.
BEARS

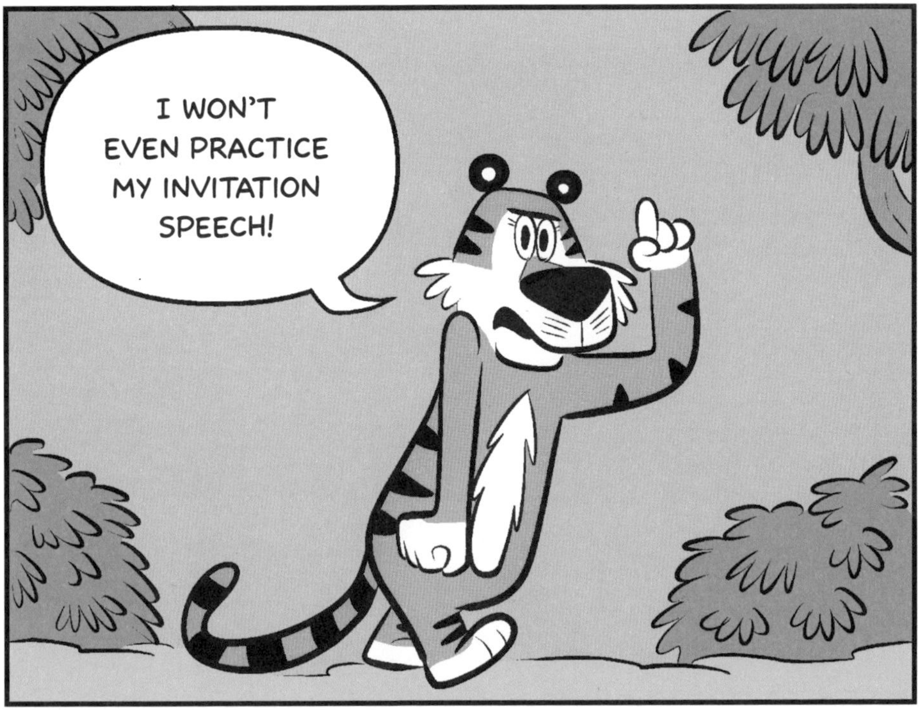
I WON'T EVEN PRACTICE MY INVITATION SPEECH!

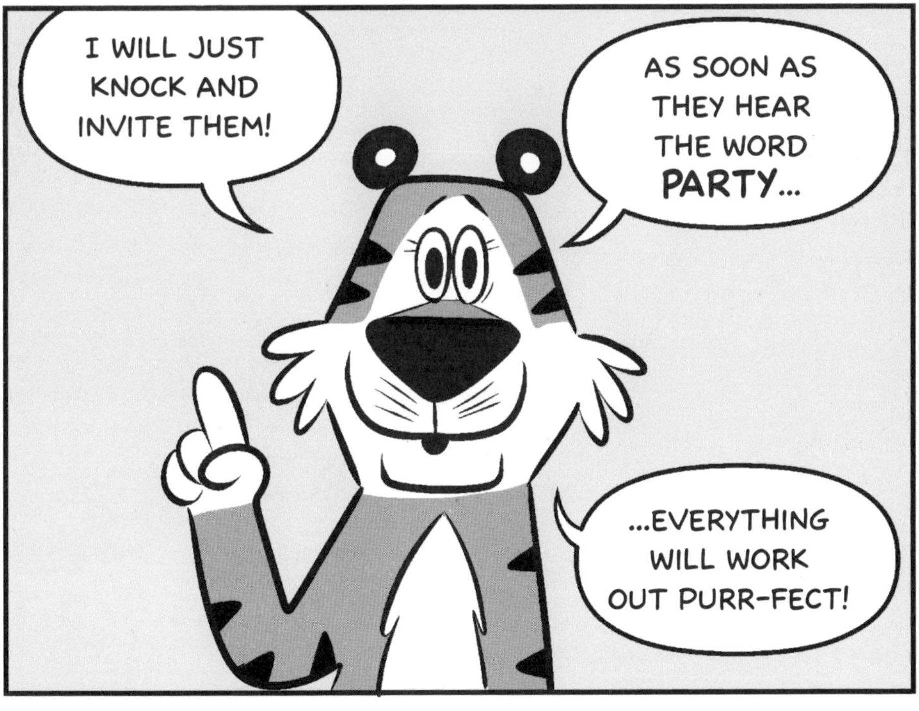
I WILL JUST KNOCK AND INVITE THEM!
AS SOON AS THEY HEAR THE WORD **PARTY**...
...EVERYTHING WILL WORK OUT PURR-FECT!

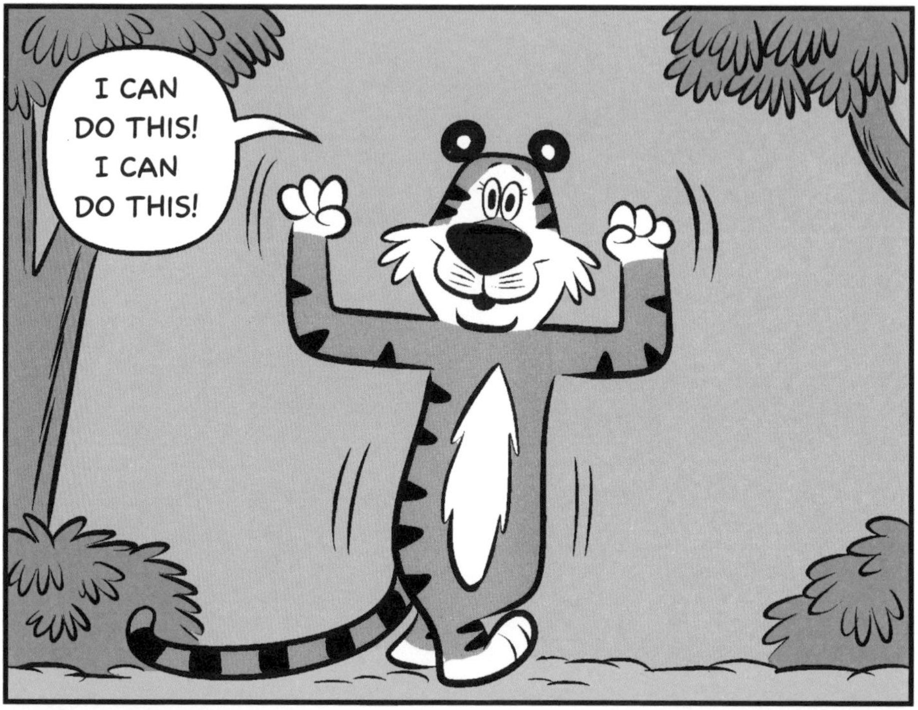
I CAN DO THIS! I CAN DO THIS!

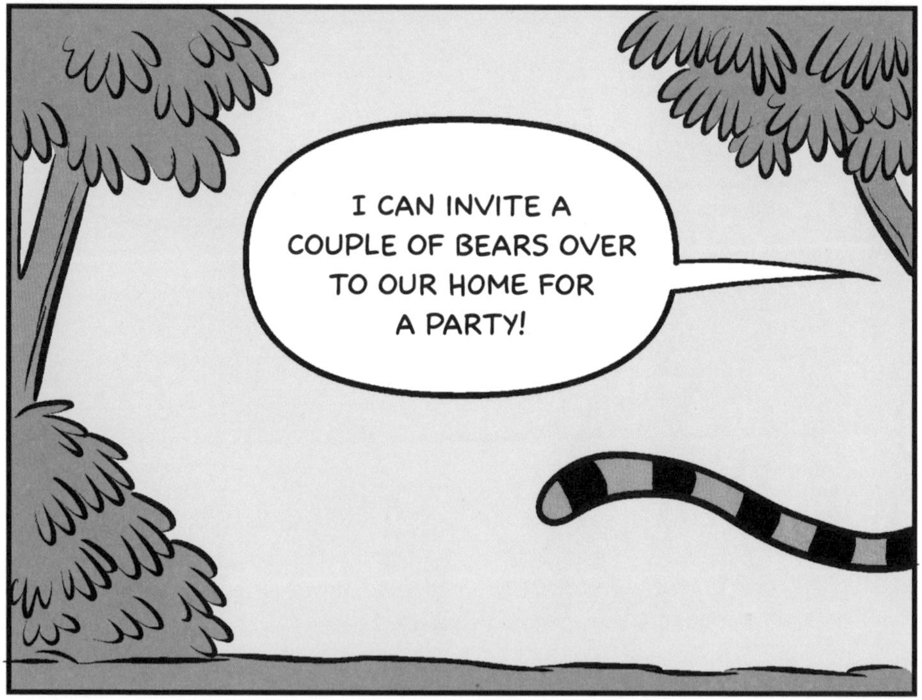
I CAN INVITE A COUPLE OF BEARS OVER TO OUR HOME FOR A PARTY!

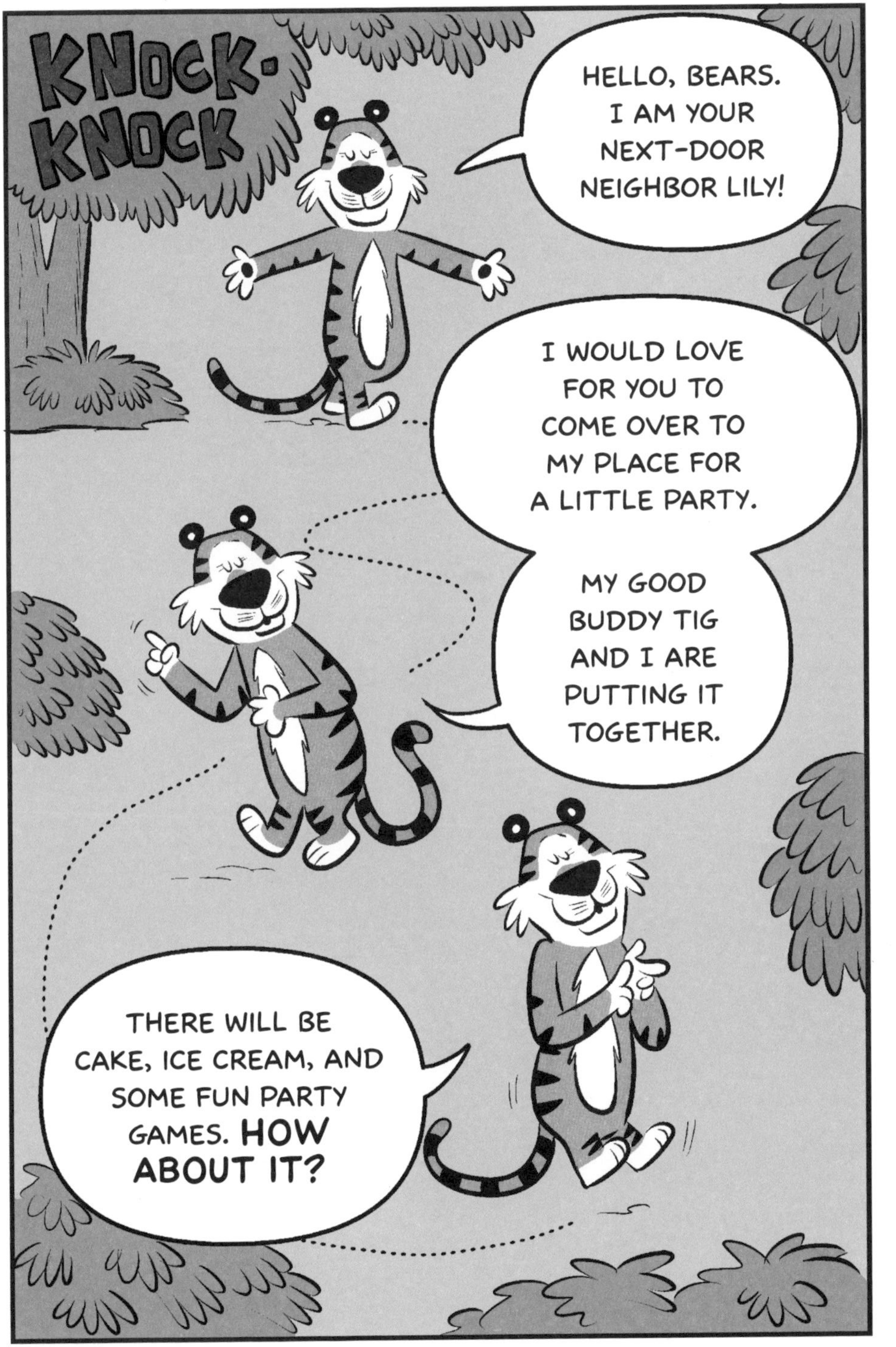
KNOCK-KNOCK
HELLO, BEARS. I AM YOUR NEXT-DOOR NEIGHBOR LILY!
I WOULD LOVE FOR YOU TO COME OVER TO MY PLACE FOR A LITTLE PARTY.
MY GOOD BUDDY TIG AND I ARE PUTTING IT TOGETHER.
THERE WILL BE CAKE, ICE CREAM, AND SOME FUN PARTY GAMES. **HOW ABOUT IT?**

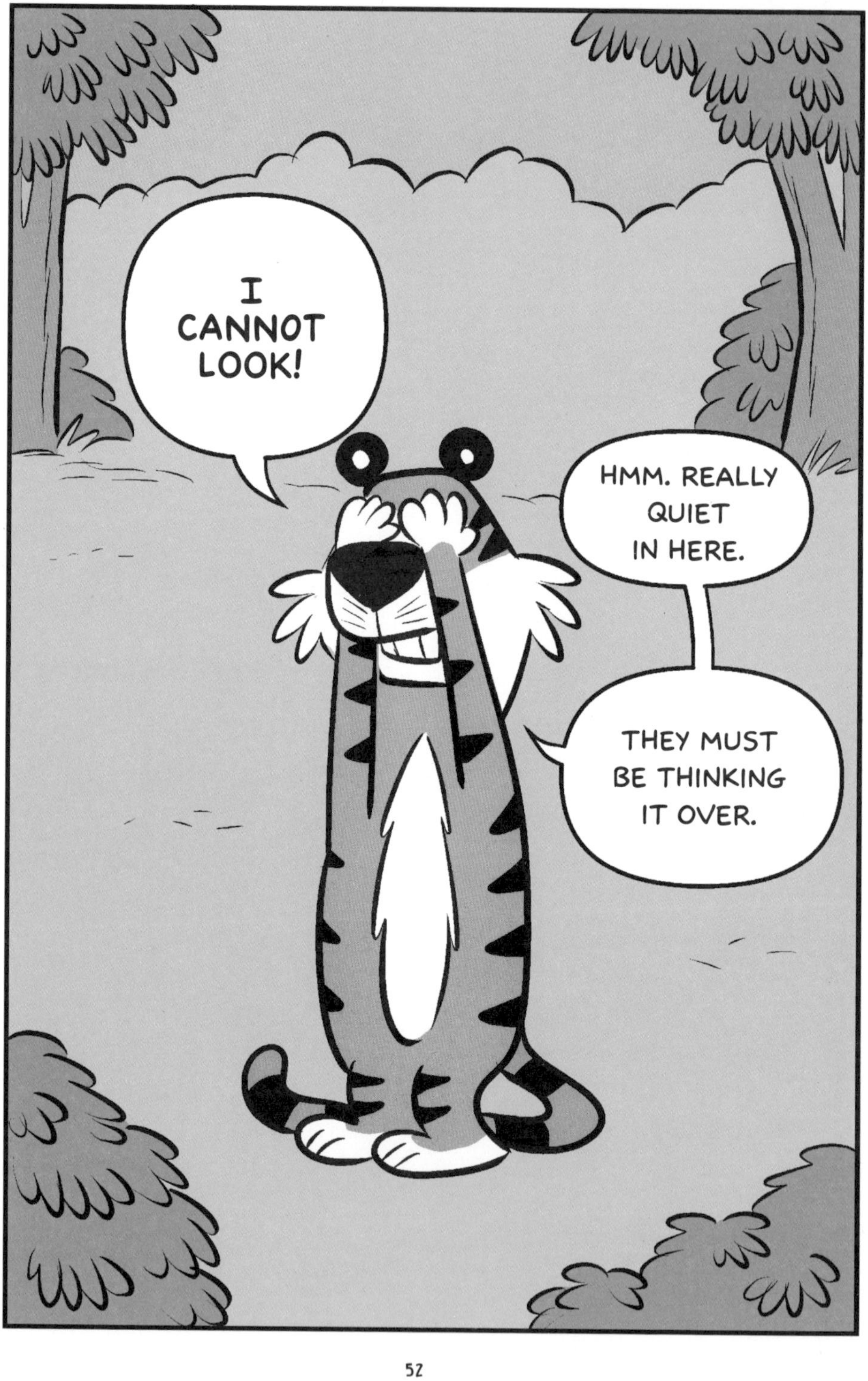
I CANNOT LOOK!
HMM. REALLY QUIET IN HERE.
THEY MUST BE THINKING IT OVER.

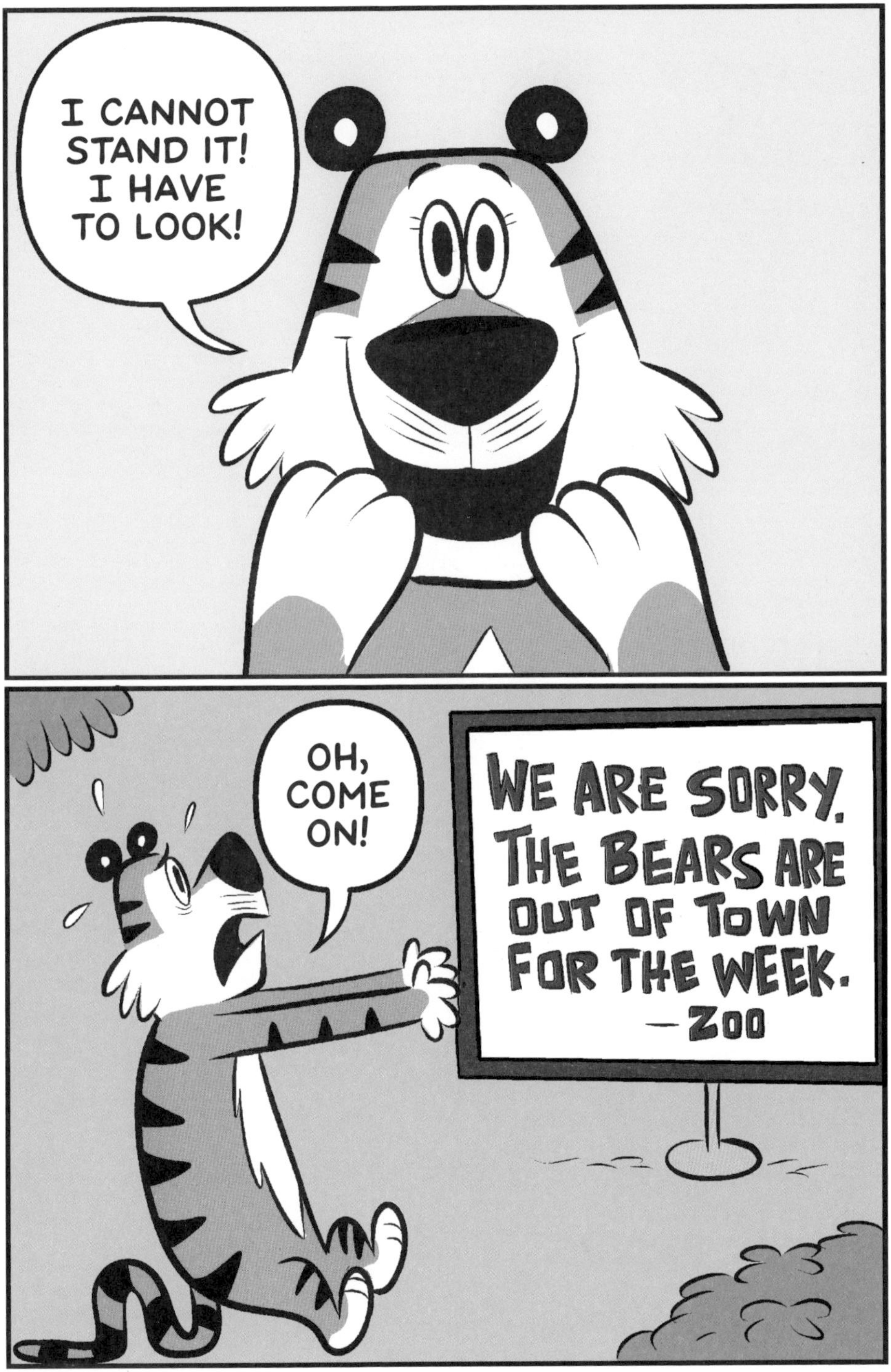
I CANNOT STAND IT! I HAVE TO LOOK!
OH, COME ON!
WE ARE SORRY. THE BEARS ARE OUT OF TOWN FOR THE WEEK.
—ZOO

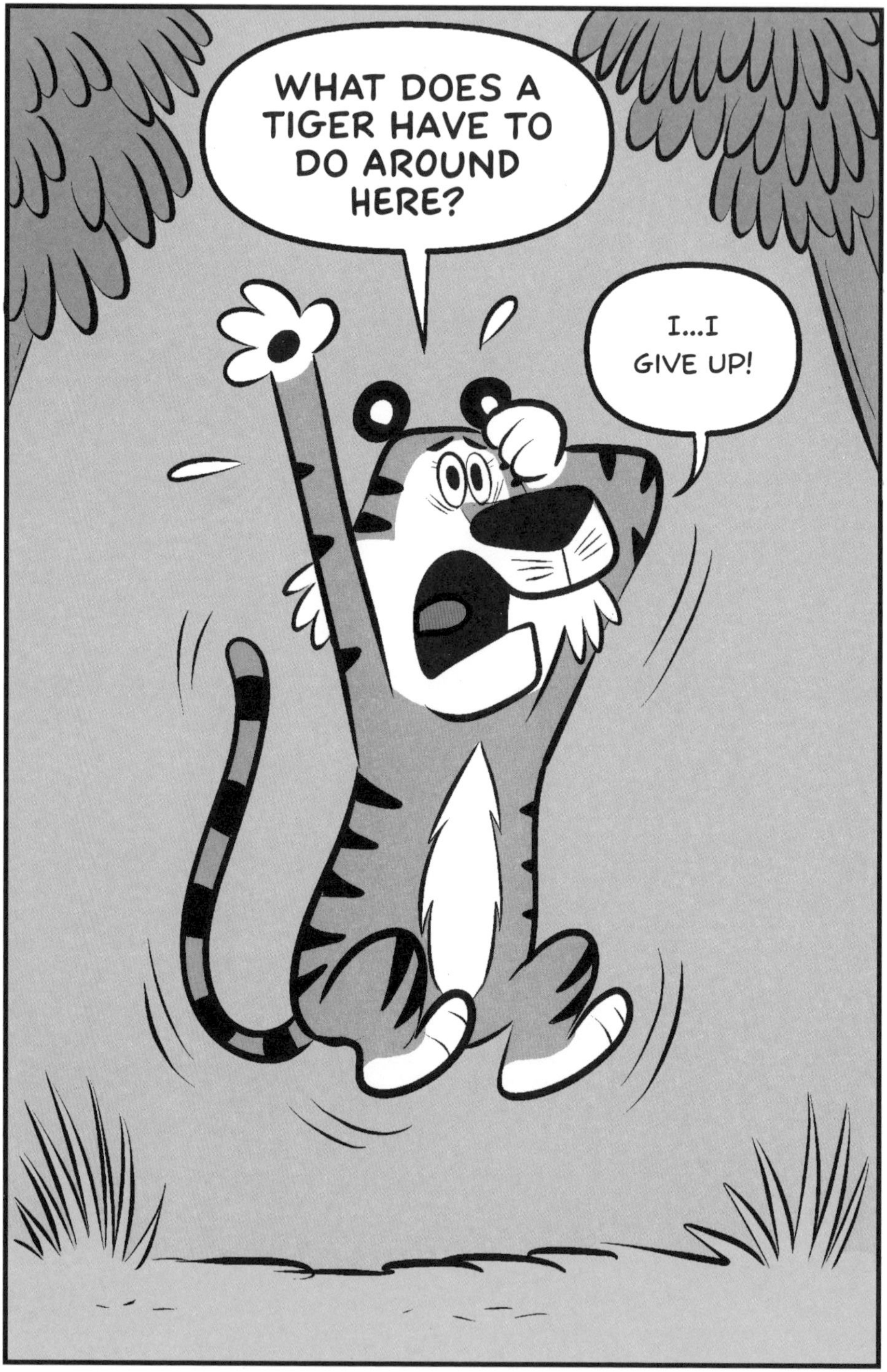
WHAT DOES A TIGER HAVE TO DO AROUND HERE?
I...I GIVE UP!

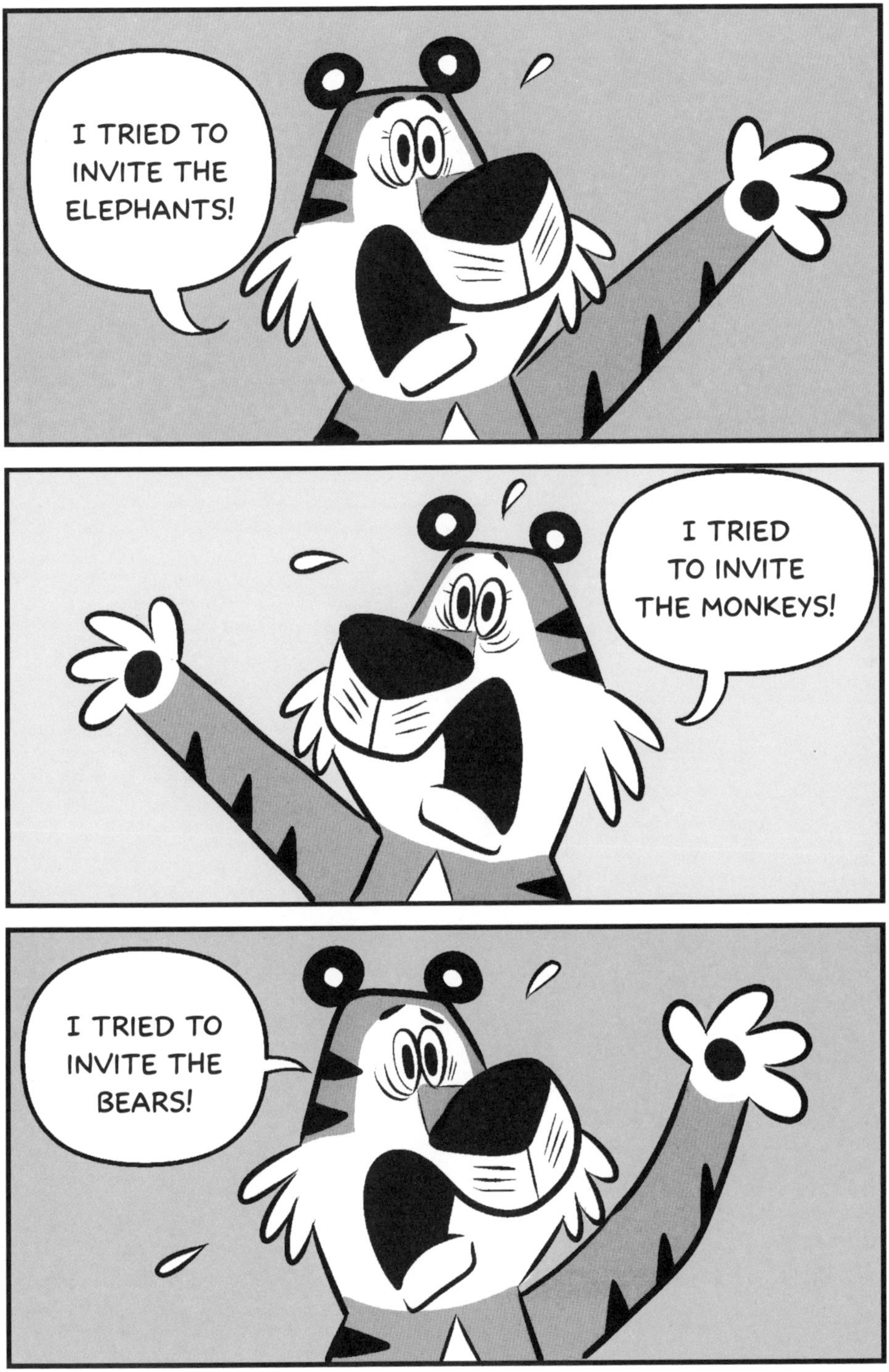
I TRIED TO INVITE THE ELEPHANTS!
I TRIED TO INVITE THE MONKEYS!
I TRIED TO INVITE THE BEARS!

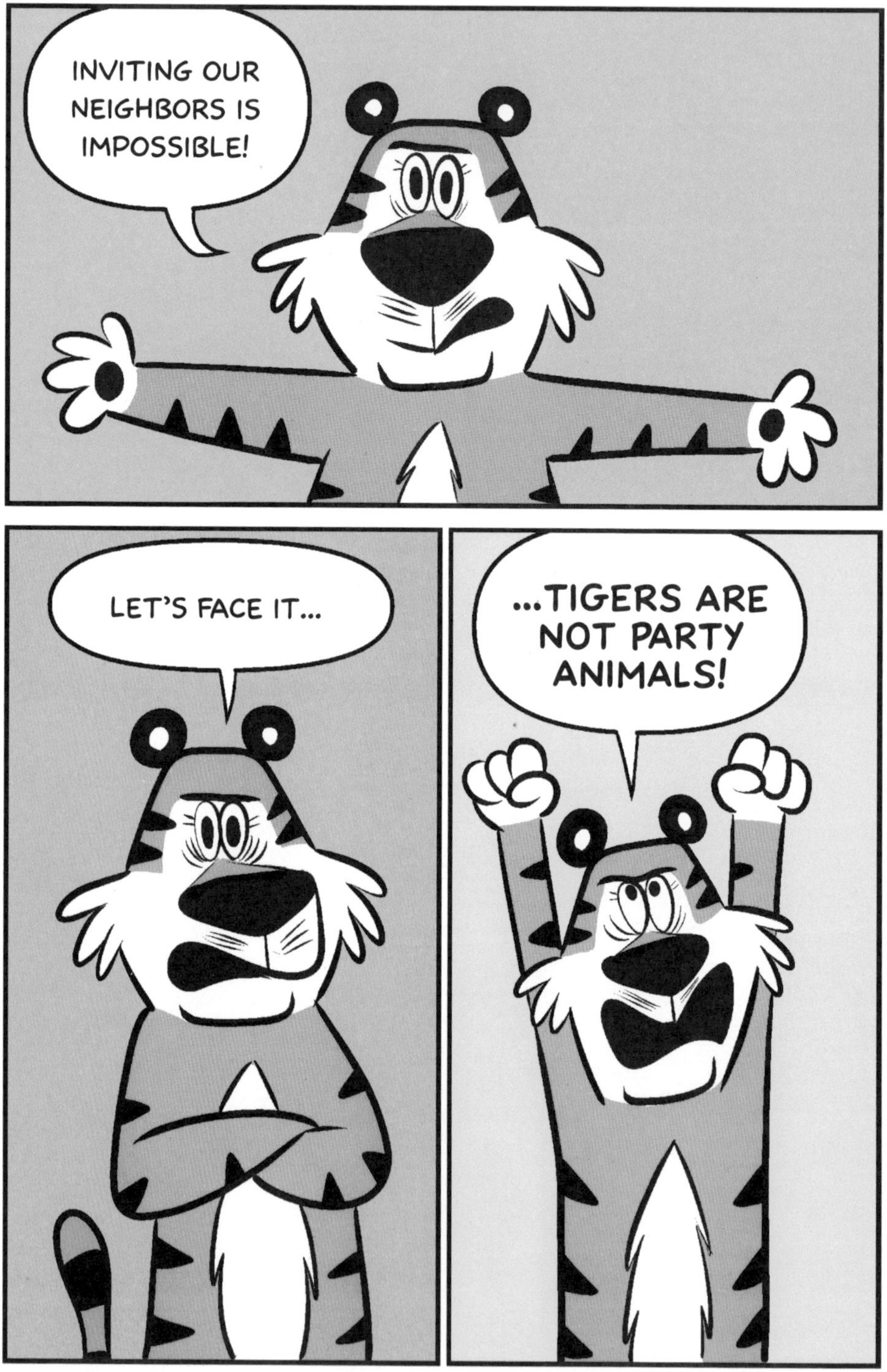
INVITING OUR NEIGHBORS IS IMPOSSIBLE!
LET'S FACE IT...
...TIGERS ARE NOT PARTY ANIMALS!

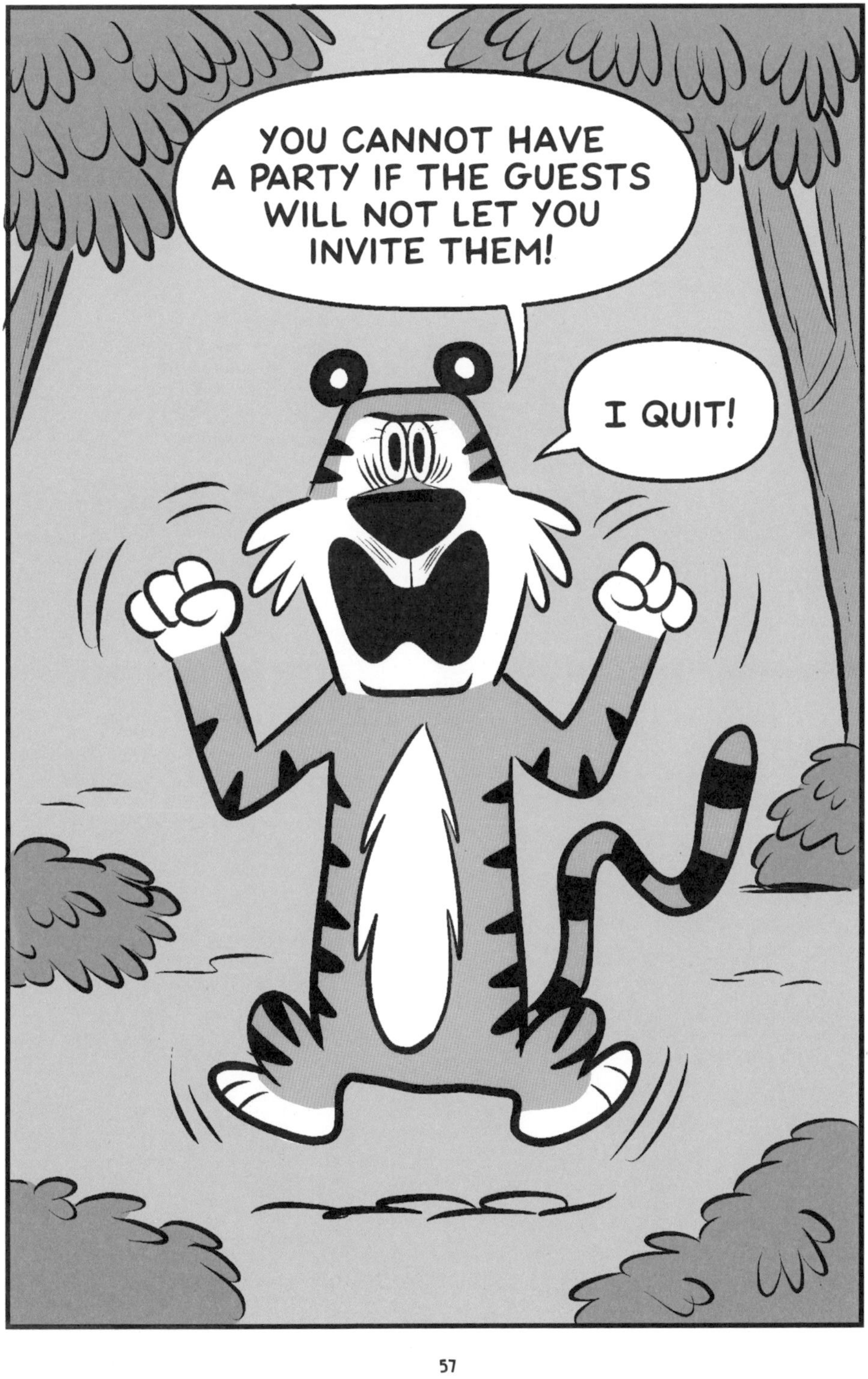
YOU CANNOT HAVE A PARTY IF THE GUESTS WILL NOT LET YOU INVITE THEM!
I QUIT!

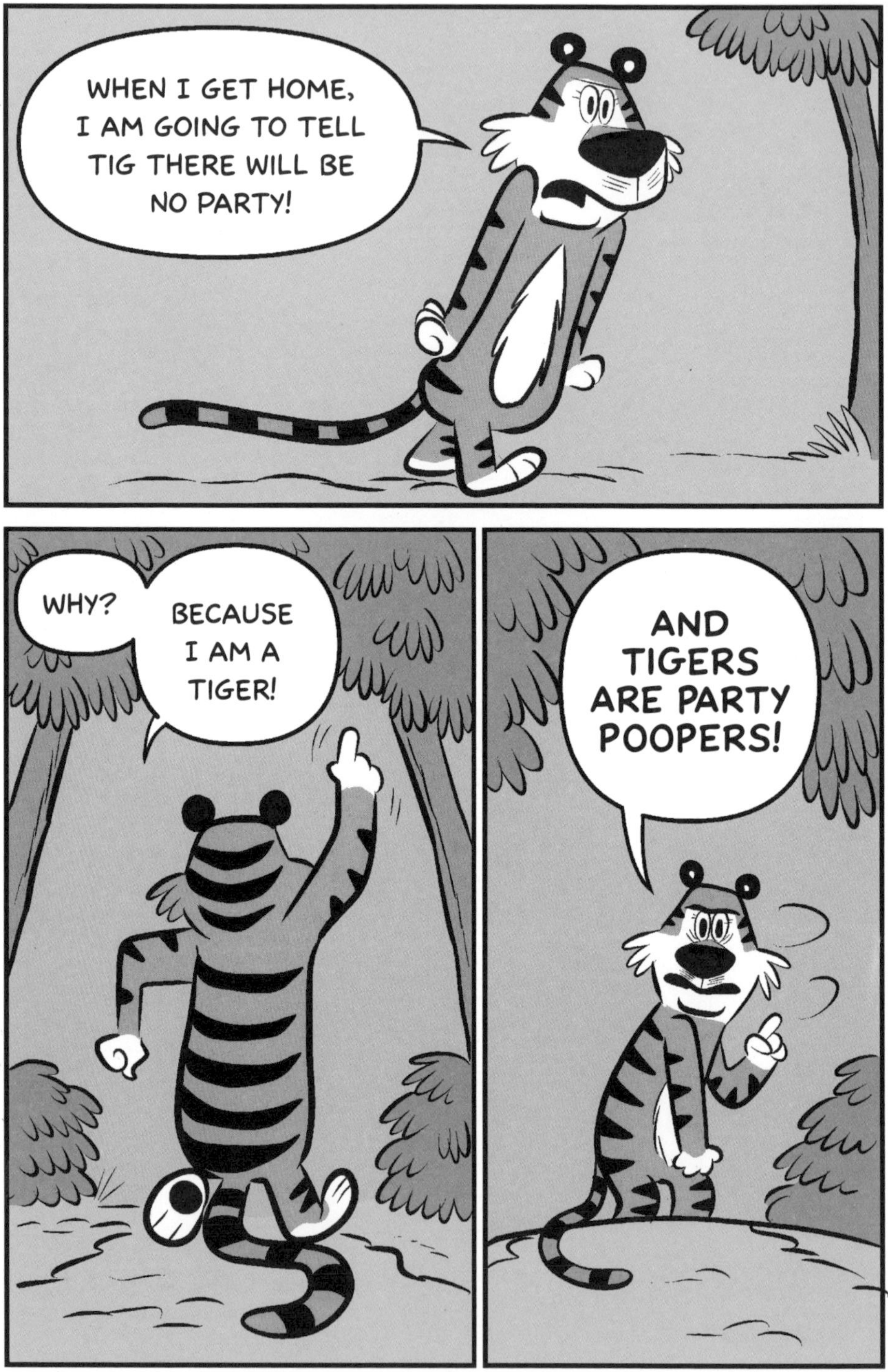
WHEN I GET HOME, I AM GOING TO TELL TIG THERE WILL BE NO PARTY!
WHY?
BECAUSE I AM A TIGER!
AND TIGERS ARE PARTY POOPERS!

Chapter THREE

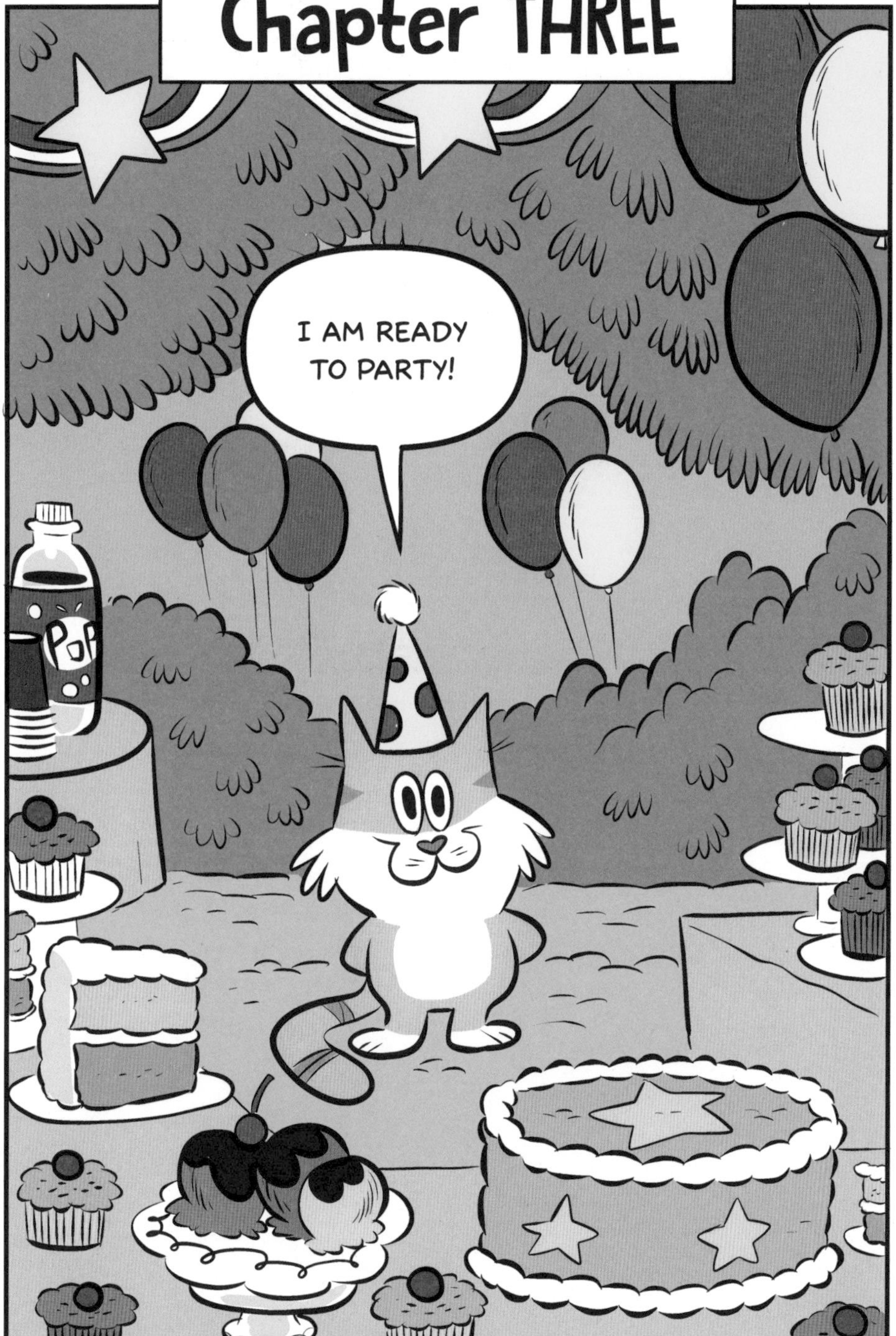
I AM READY TO PARTY!
POP

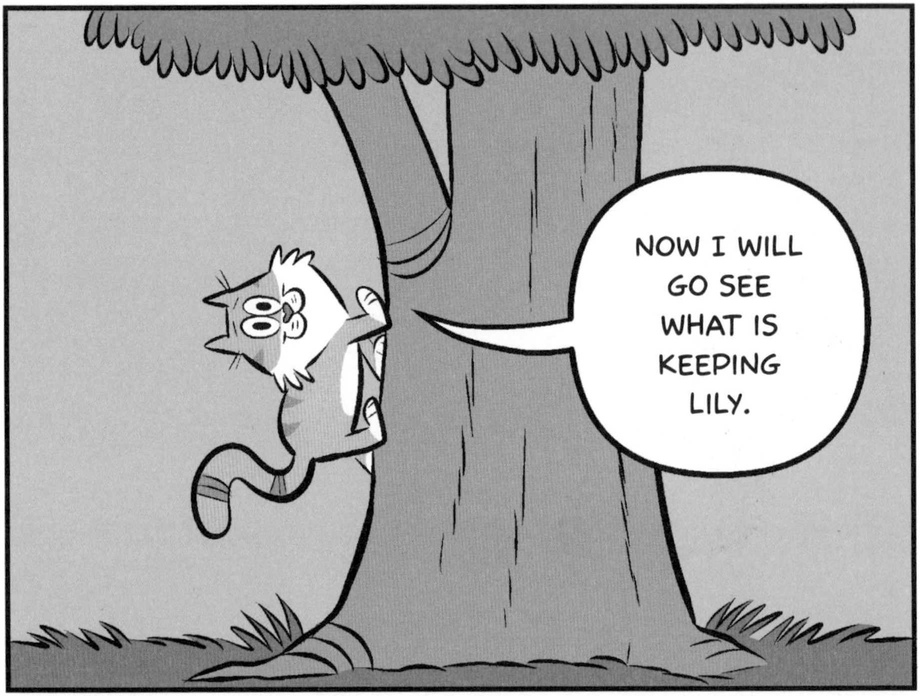
NOW I WILL GO SEE WHAT IS KEEPING LILY.

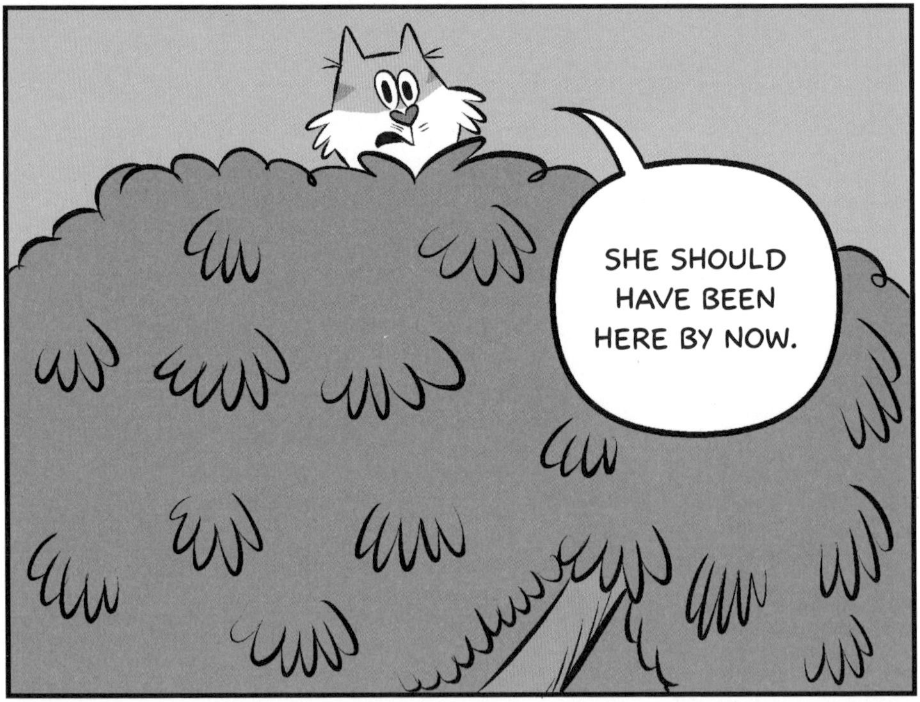
SHE SHOULD HAVE BEEN HERE BY NOW.

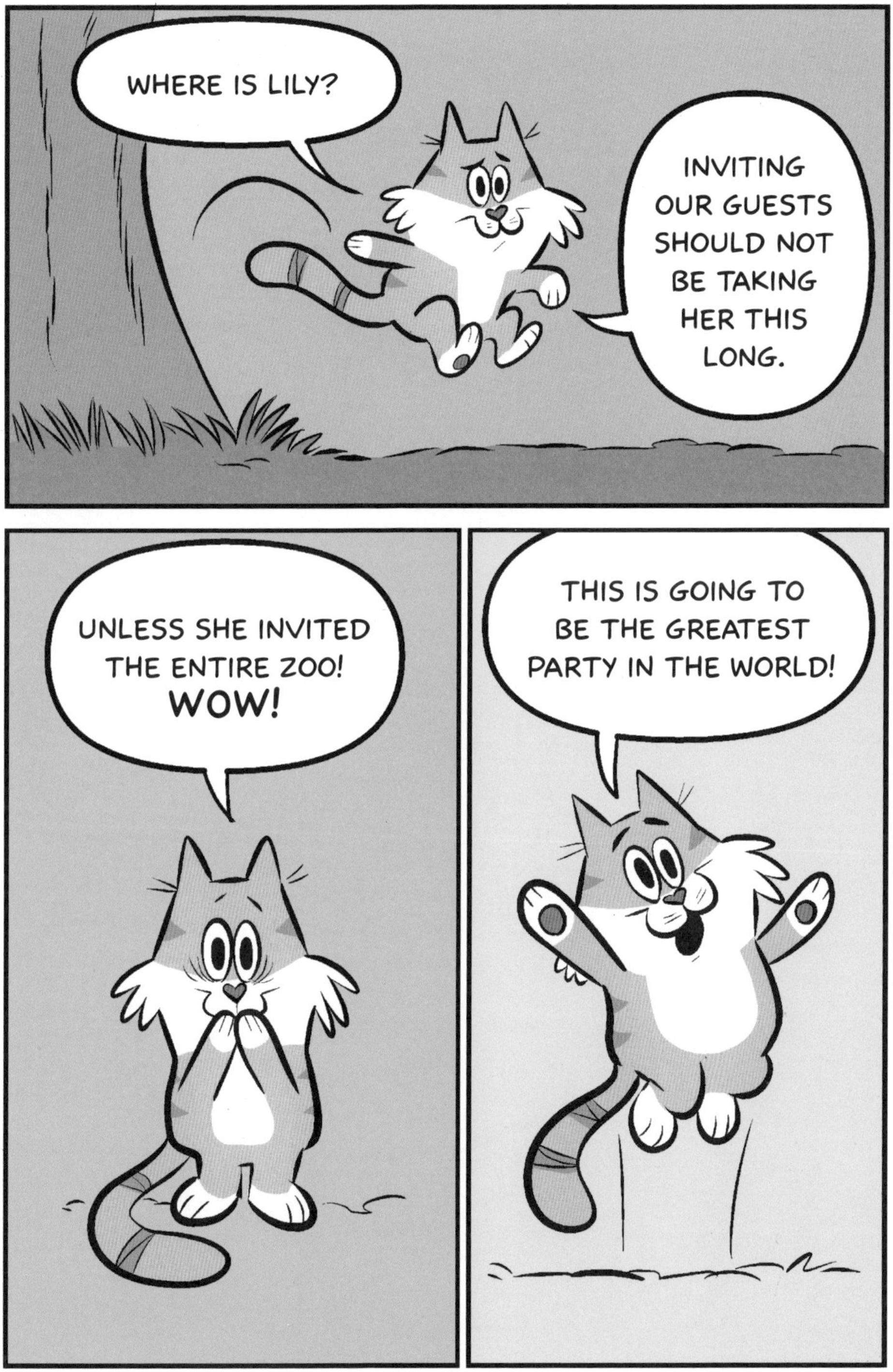
WHERE IS LILY?
INVITING OUR GUESTS SHOULD NOT BE TAKING HER THIS LONG.
UNLESS SHE INVITED THE ENTIRE ZOO! WOW!
THIS IS GOING TO BE THE GREATEST PARTY IN THE WORLD!

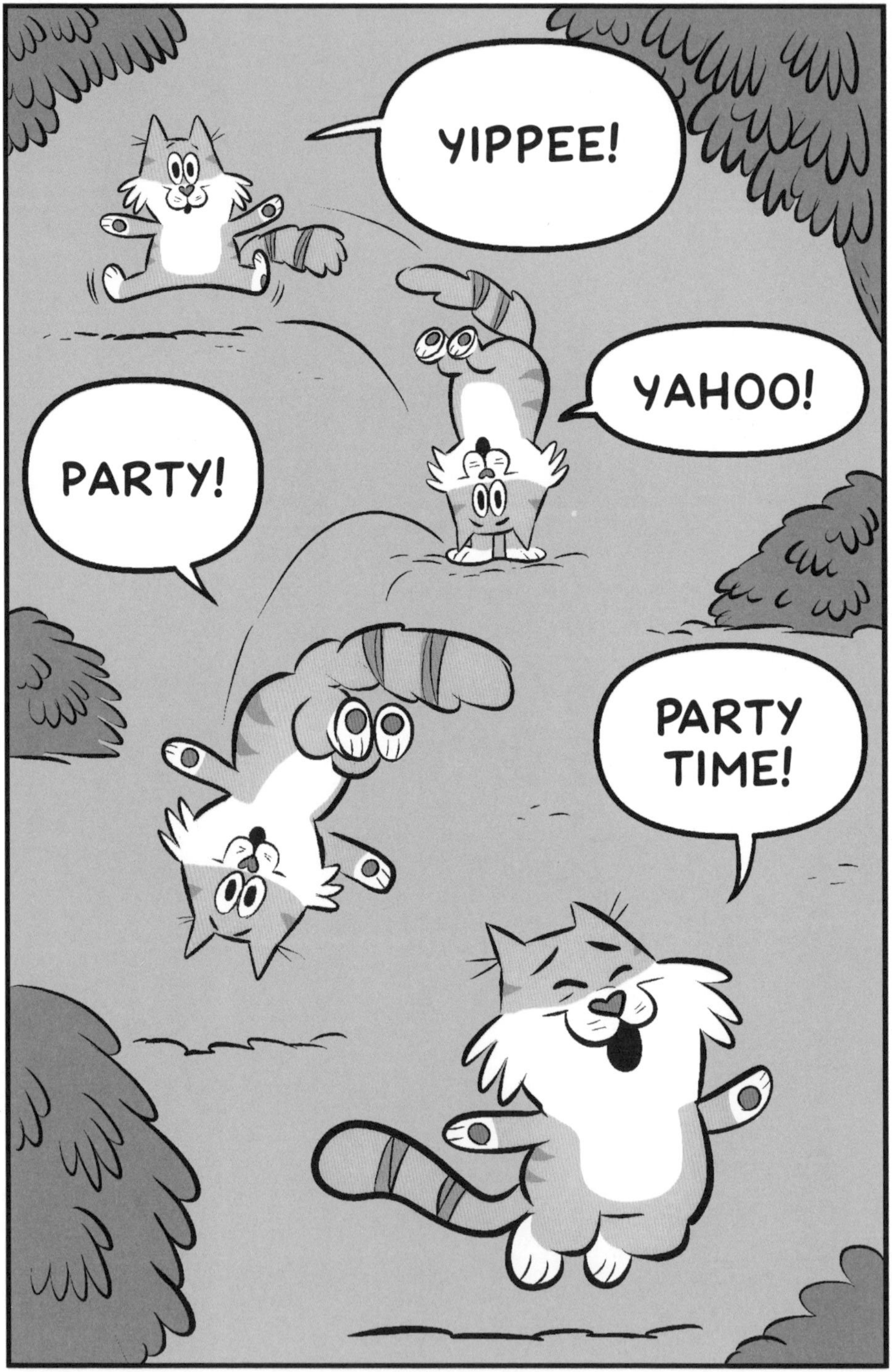
YIPPEE!
YAHOO!
PARTY!
PARTY TIME!

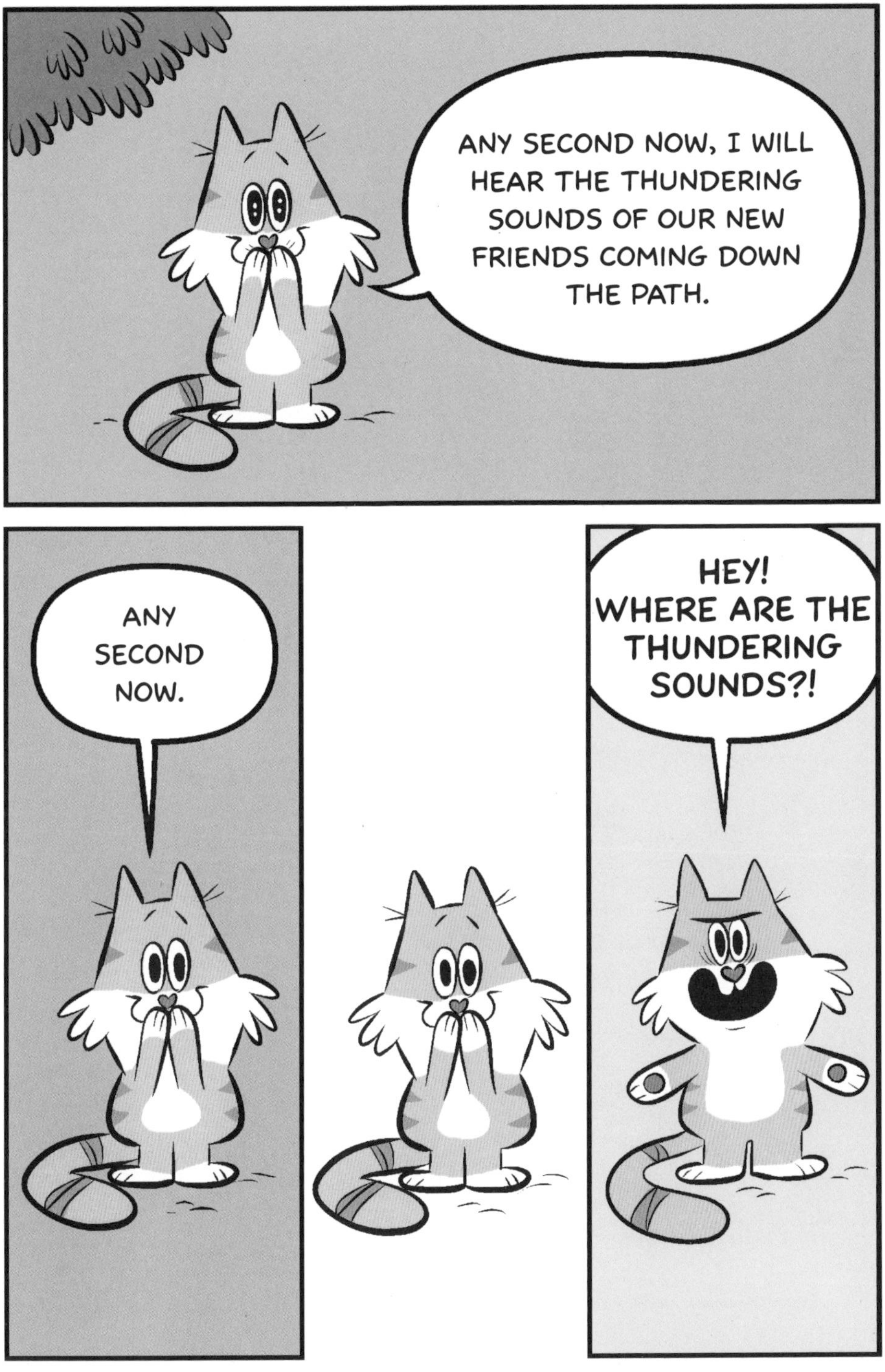
ANY SECOND NOW, I WILL HEAR THE THUNDERING SOUNDS OF OUR NEW FRIENDS COMING DOWN THE PATH.
ANY SECOND NOW.
HEY! WHERE ARE THE THUNDERING SOUNDS?!

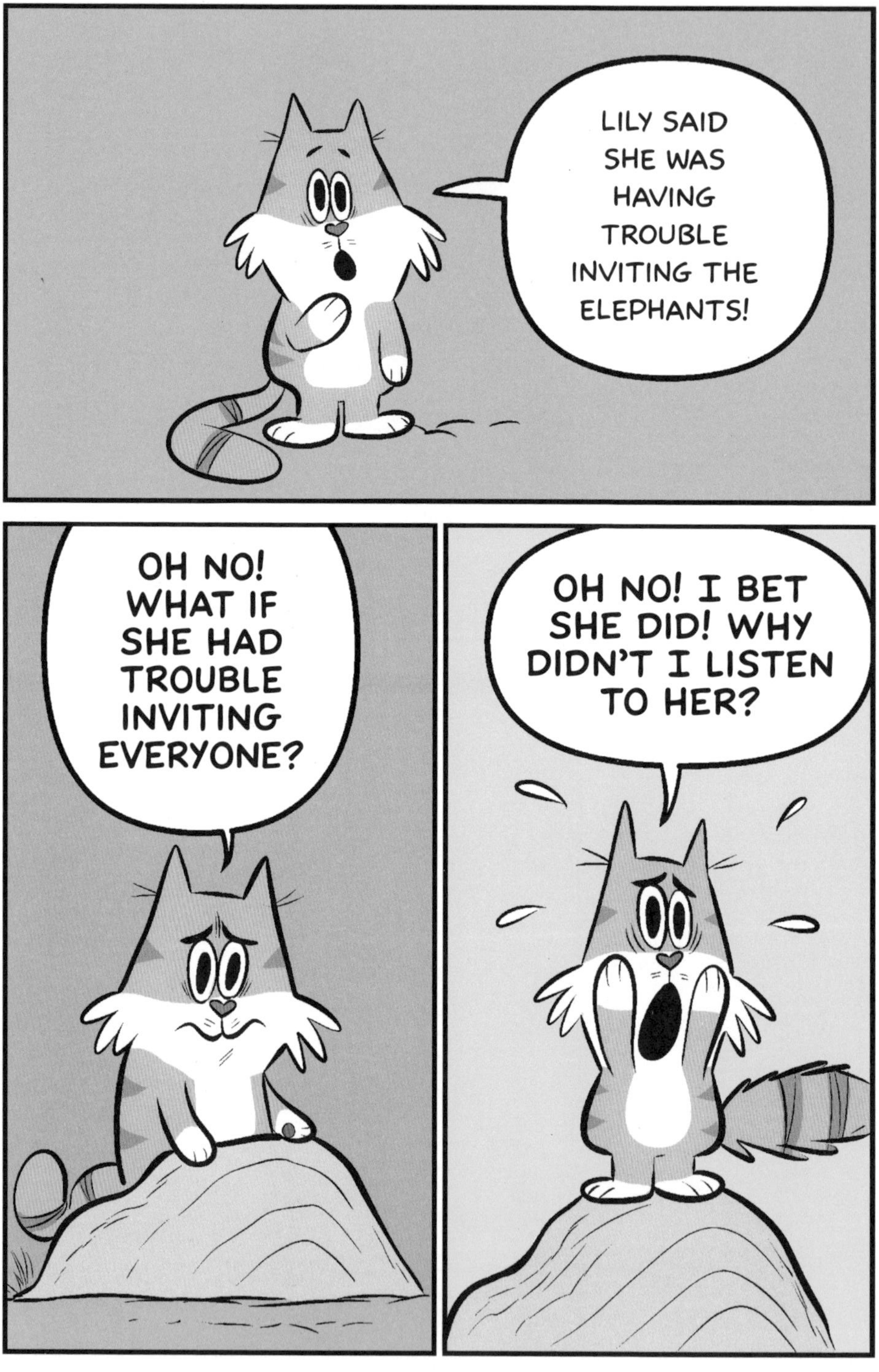
LILY SAID SHE WAS HAVING TROUBLE INVITING THE ELEPHANTS!
OH NO! WHAT IF SHE HAD TROUBLE INVITING EVERYONE?
OH NO! I BET SHE DID! WHY DIDN'T I LISTEN TO HER?

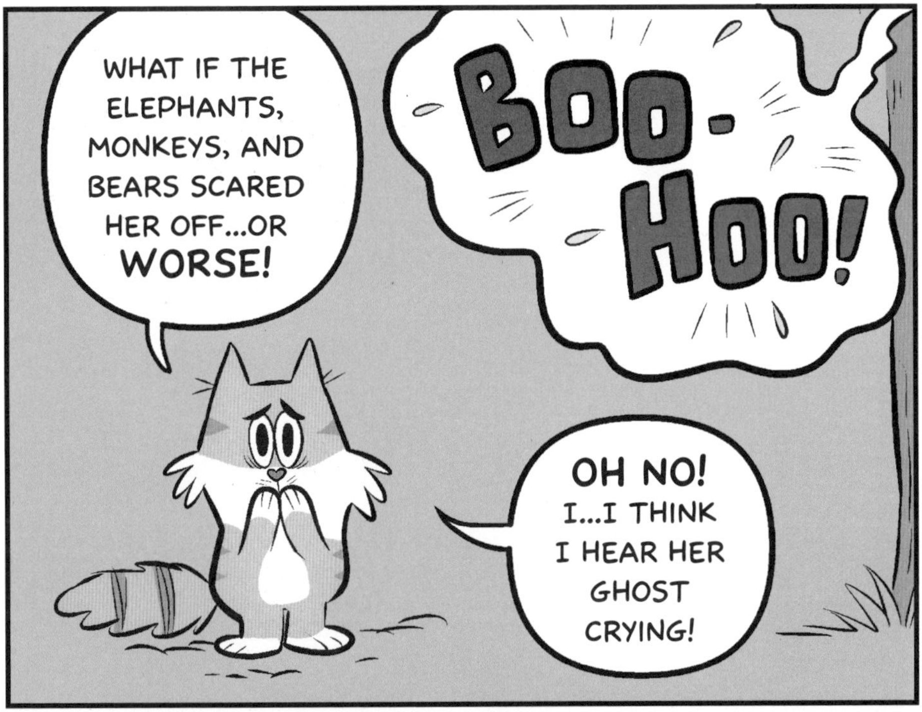
WHAT IF THE ELEPHANTS, MONKEYS, AND BEARS SCARED HER OFF...OR WORSE!
BOO-HOO!
OH NO! I...I THINK I HEAR HER GHOST CRYING!

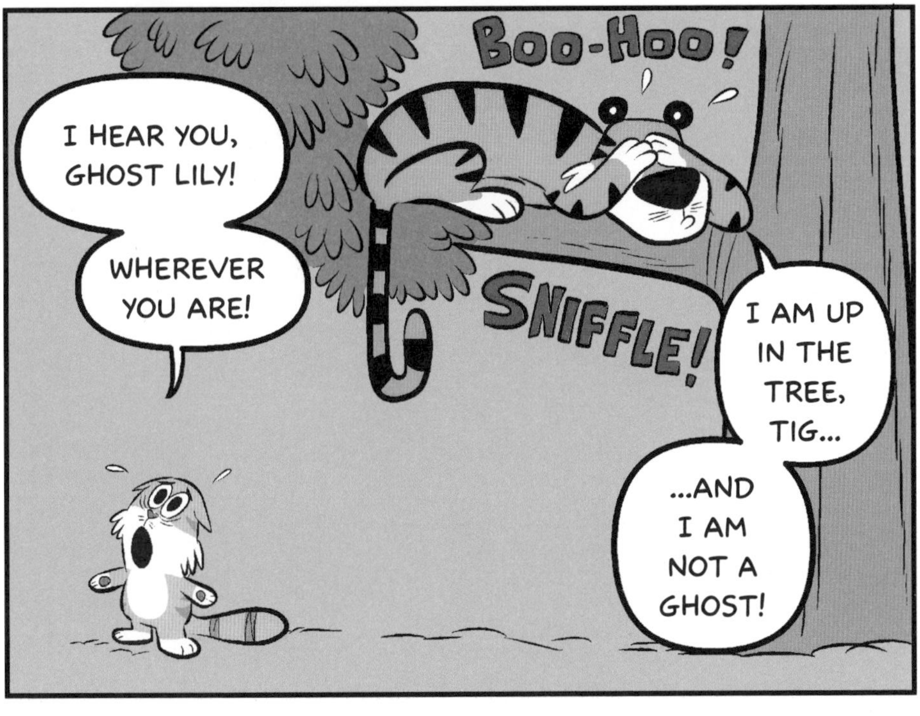
BOO-HOO!
I HEAR YOU, GHOST LILY!
WHEREVER YOU ARE!
SNIFFLE!
I AM UP IN THE TREE, TIG...
...AND I AM NOT A GHOST!

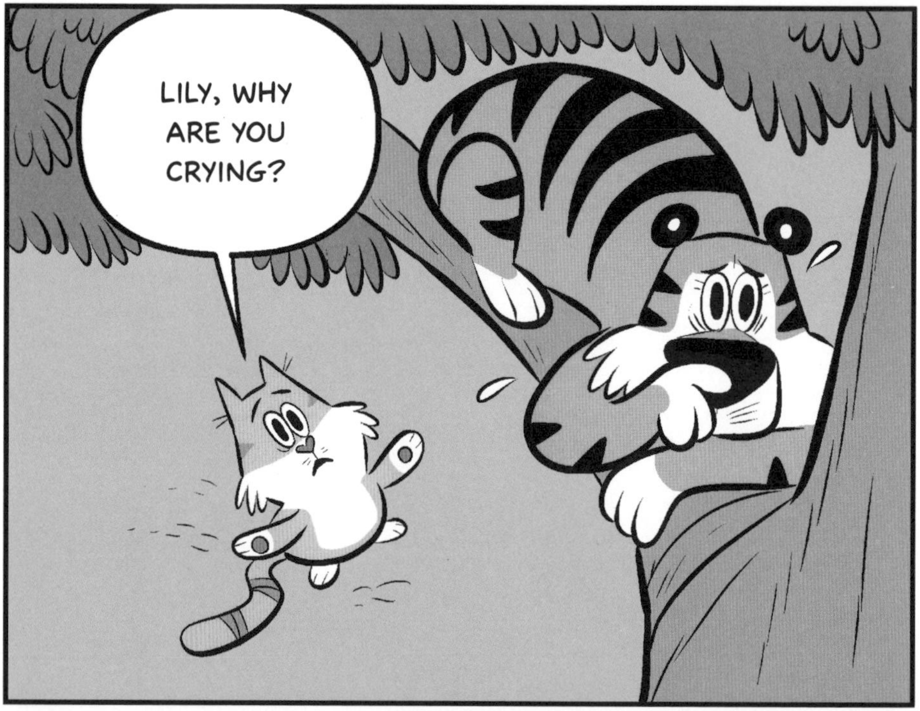
LILY, WHY ARE YOU CRYING?

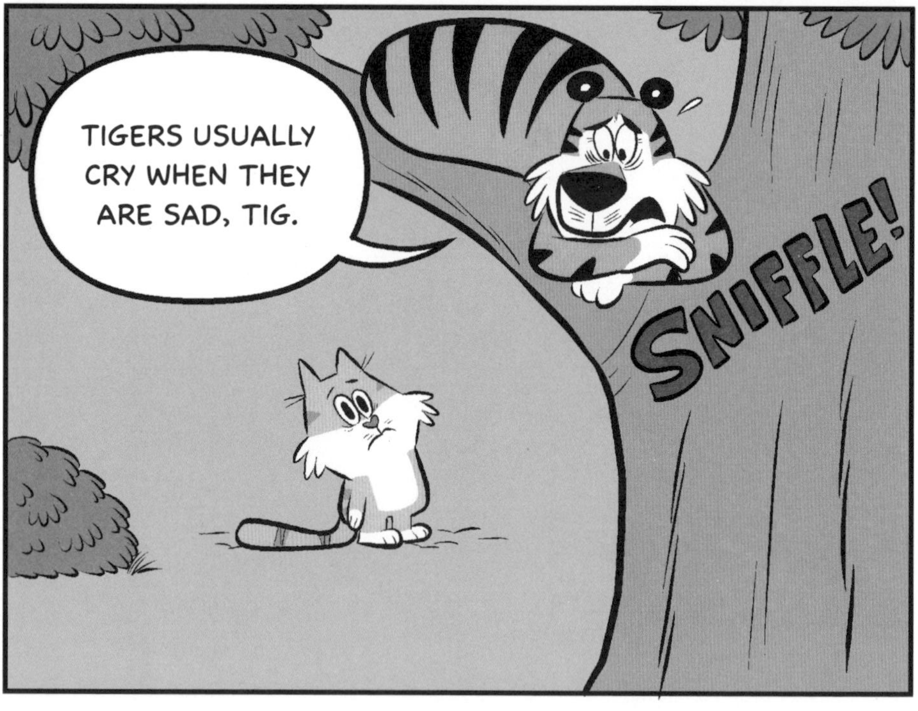
TIGERS USUALLY CRY WHEN THEY ARE SAD, TIG.
SNIFFLE!

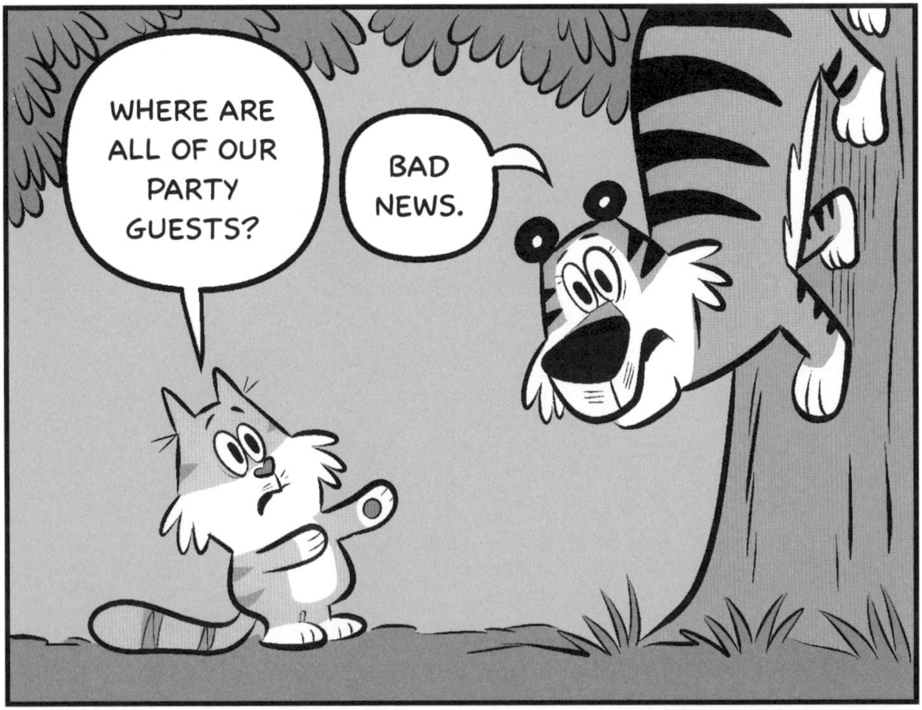
WHERE ARE ALL OF OUR PARTY GUESTS?
BAD NEWS.

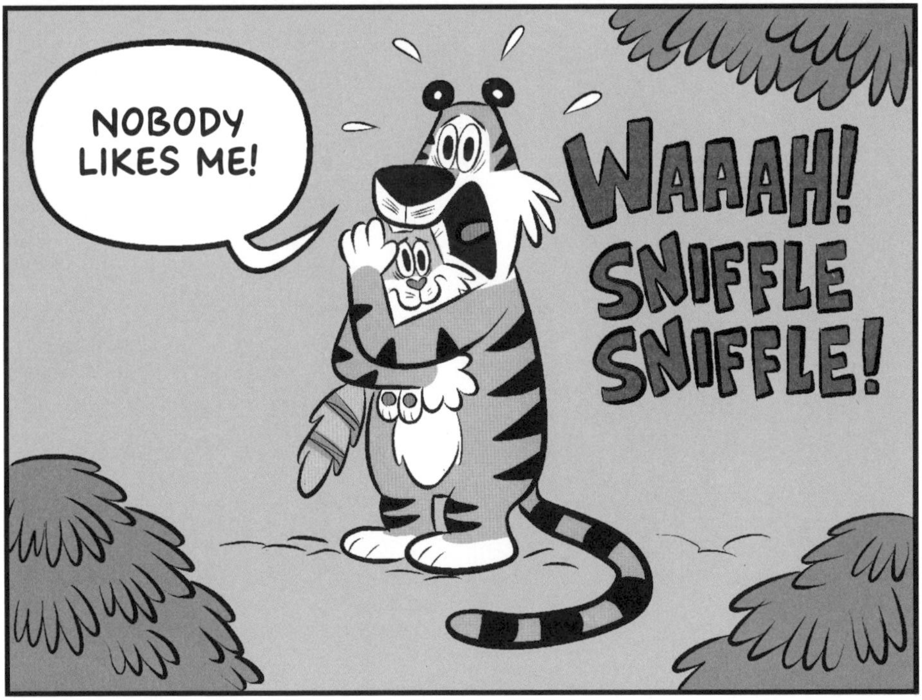
NOBODY LIKES ME!
WAAAH! SNIFFLE SNIFFLE!

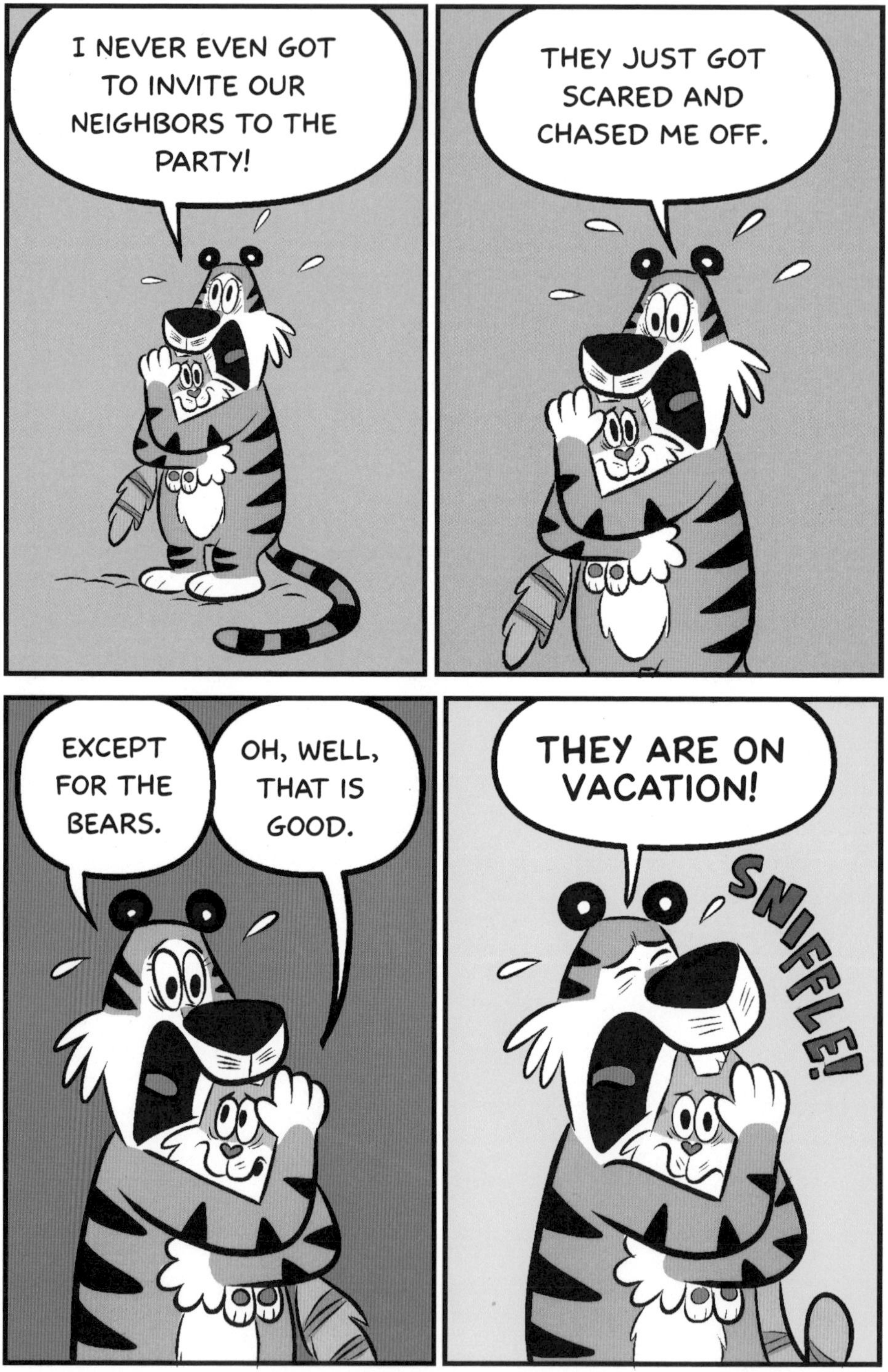
I NEVER EVEN GOT TO INVITE OUR NEIGHBORS TO THE PARTY!
THEY JUST GOT SCARED AND CHASED ME OFF.
EXCEPT FOR THE BEARS.
OH, WELL, THAT IS GOOD.
THEY ARE ON VACATION!
SNIFFLE!

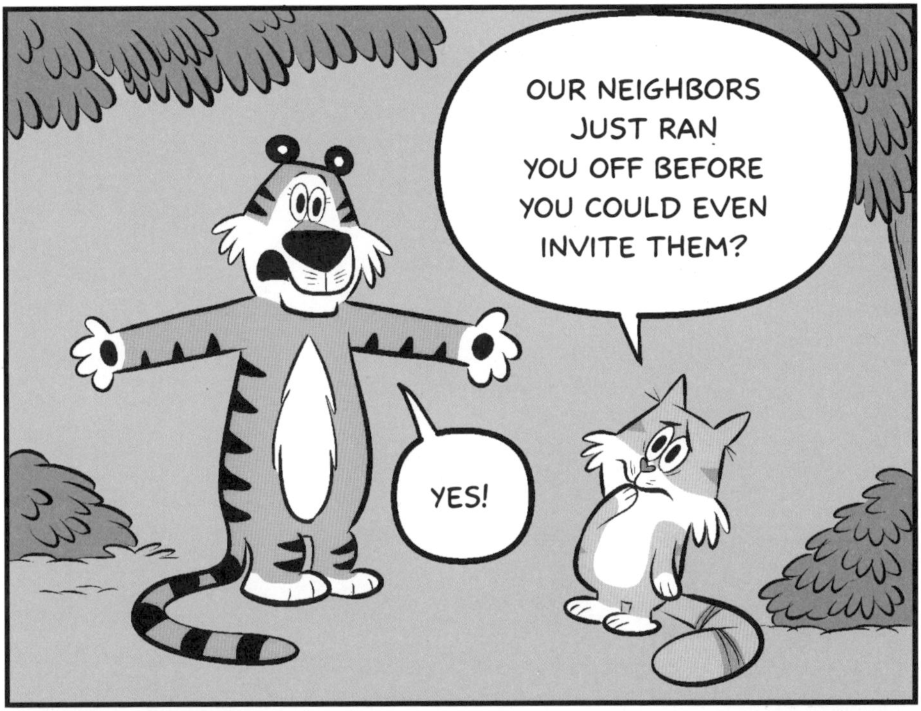
OUR NEIGHBORS JUST RAN YOU OFF BEFORE YOU COULD EVEN INVITE THEM?
YES!

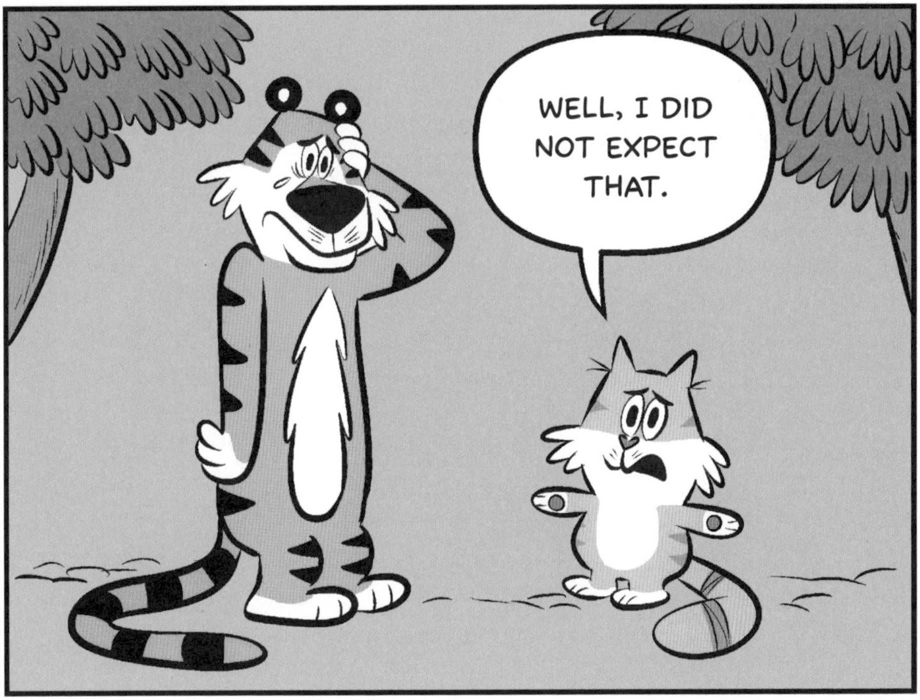
WELL, I DID NOT EXPECT THAT.

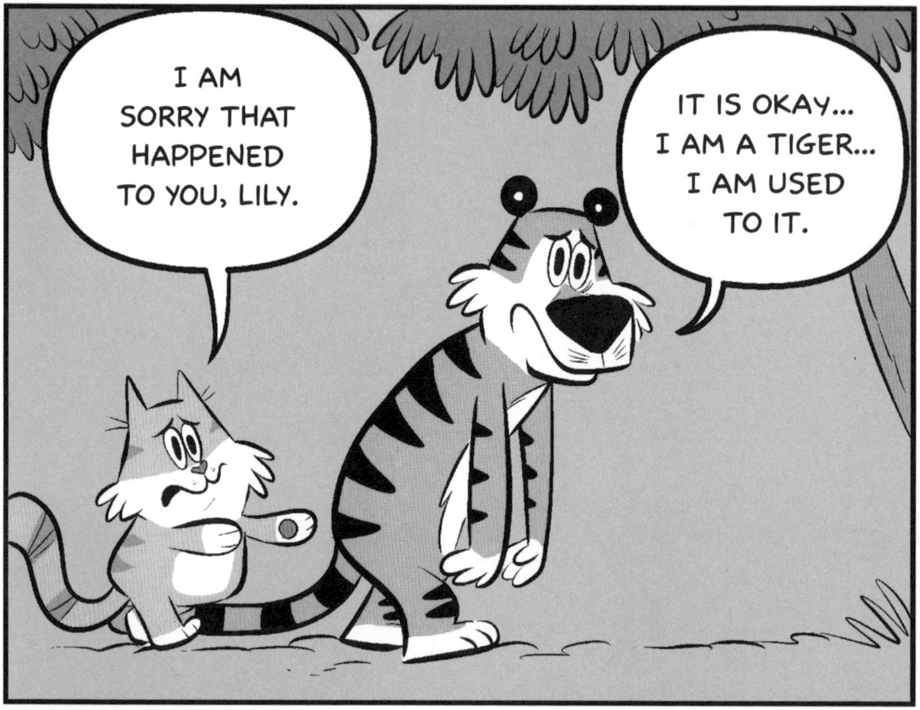
I AM SORRY THAT HAPPENED TO YOU, LILY.
IT IS OKAY... I AM A TIGER... I AM USED TO IT.

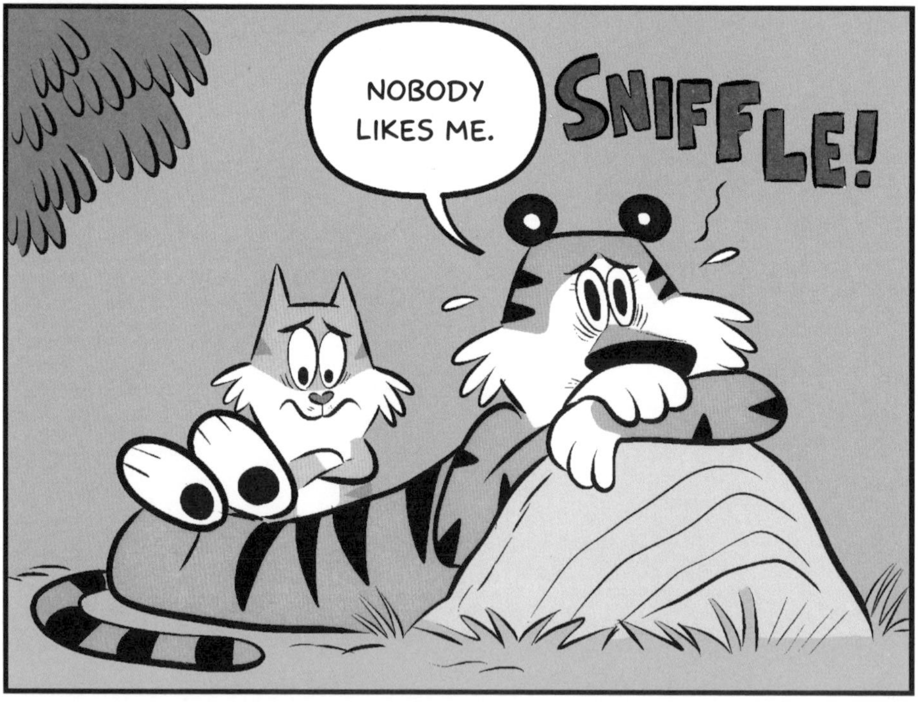
NOBODY LIKES ME.
SNIFFLE!

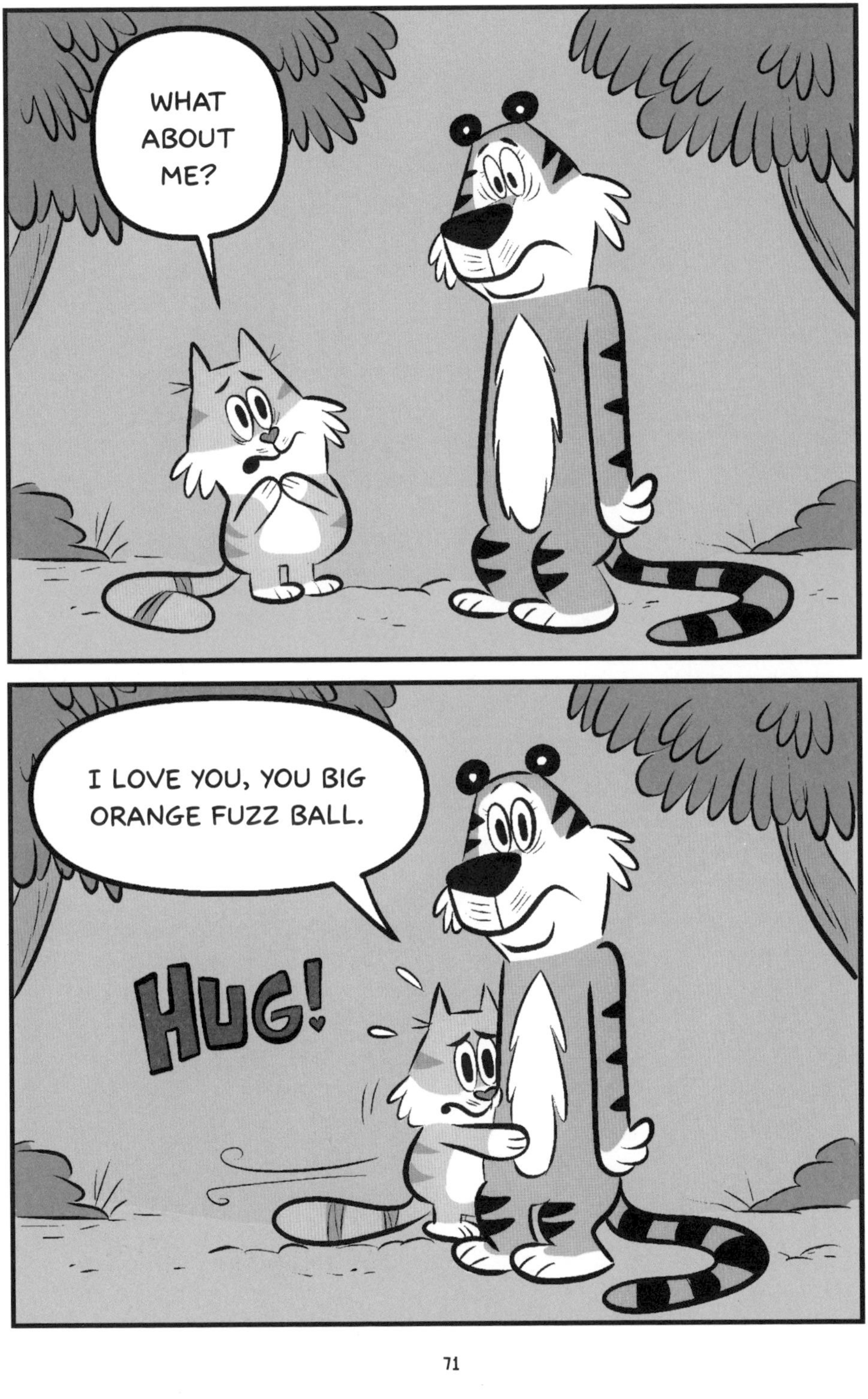
WHAT ABOUT ME?
I LOVE YOU, YOU BIG ORANGE FUZZ BALL.
HUG!

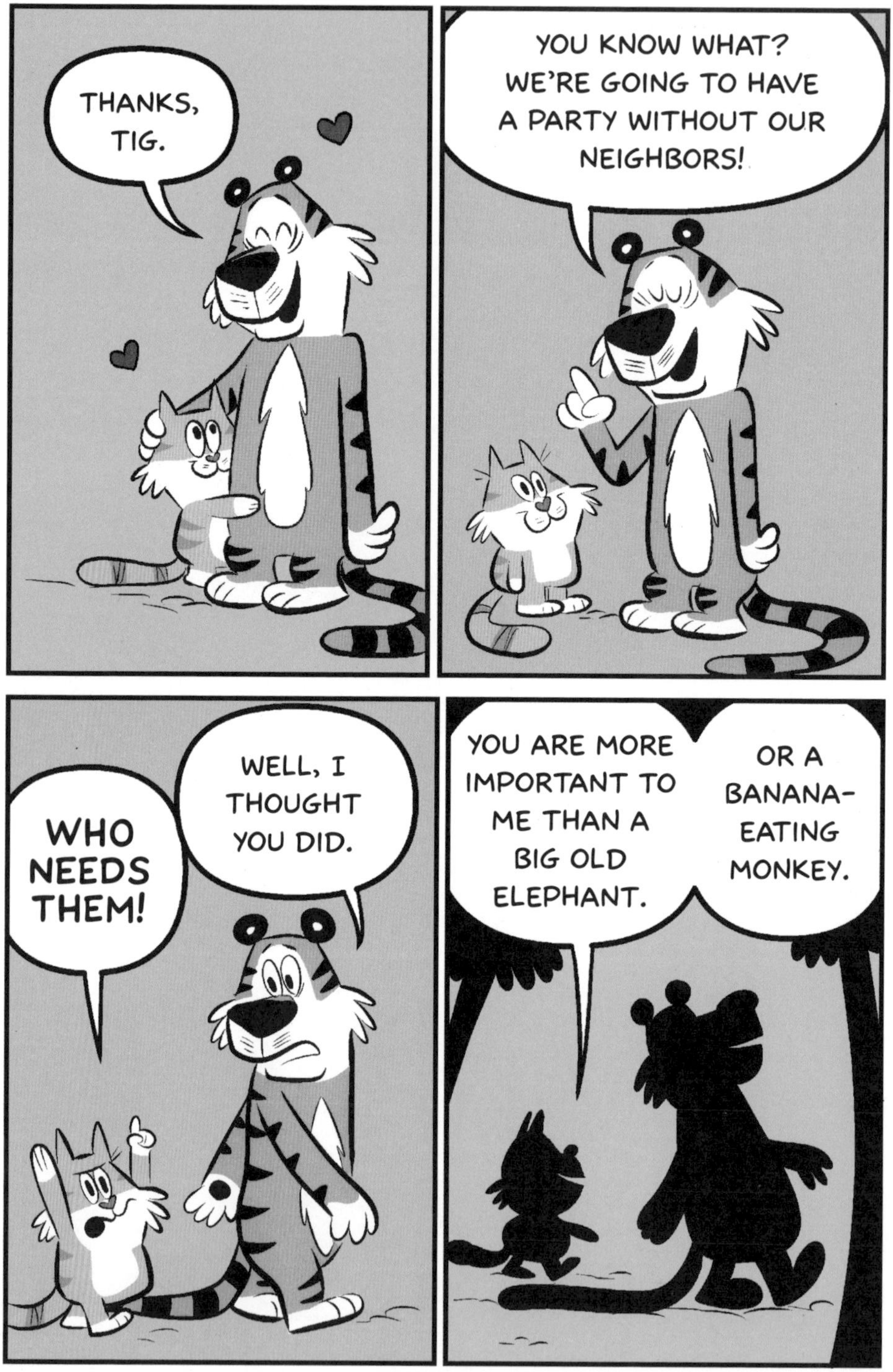
THANKS, TIG.
YOU KNOW WHAT? WE'RE GOING TO HAVE A PARTY WITHOUT OUR NEIGHBORS!
WHO NEEDS THEM!
WELL, I THOUGHT YOU DID.
YOU ARE MORE IMPORTANT TO ME THAN A BIG OLD ELEPHANT.
OR A BANANA-EATING MONKEY.

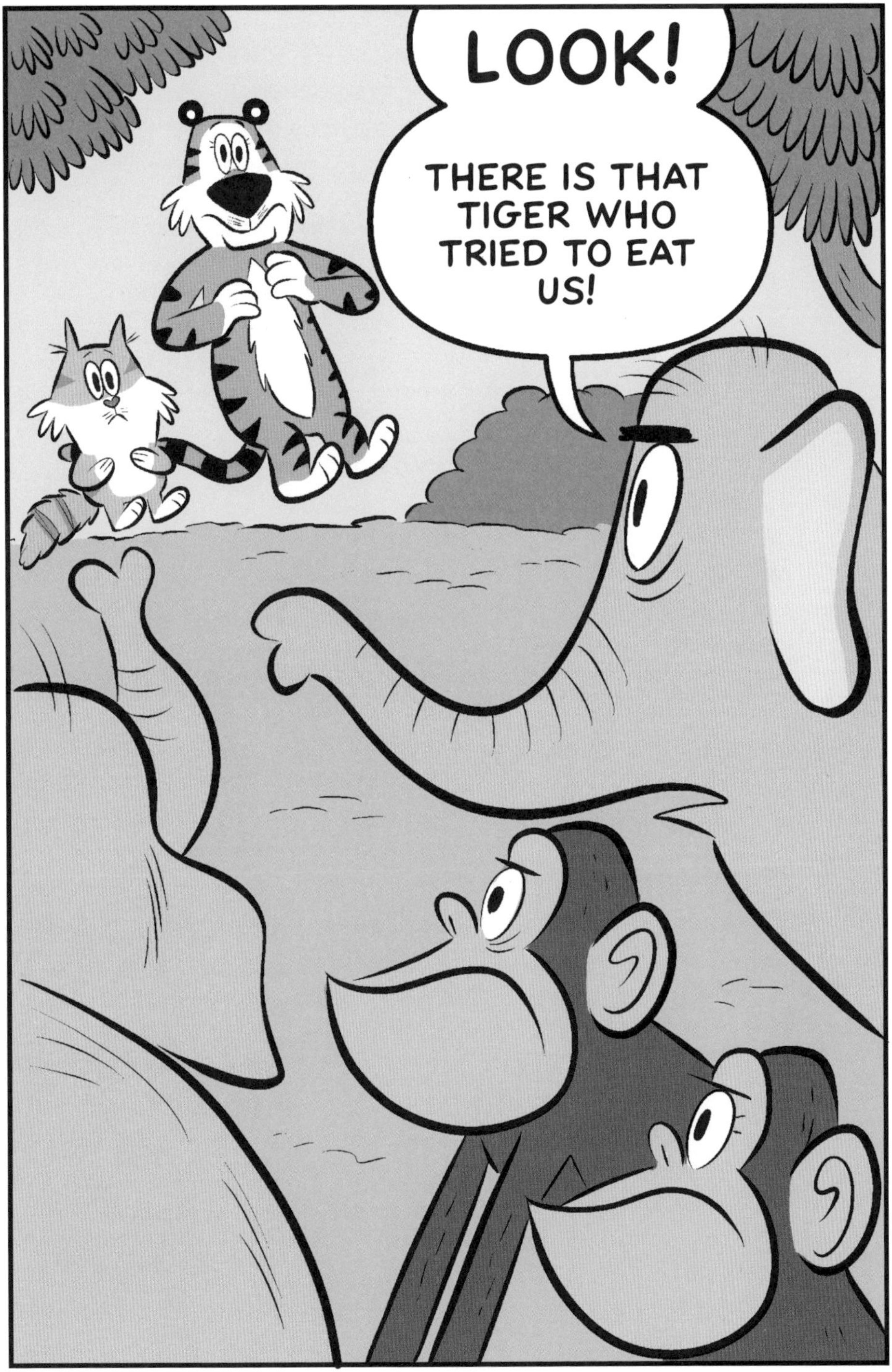
LOOK!
THERE IS THAT TIGER WHO TRIED TO EAT US!

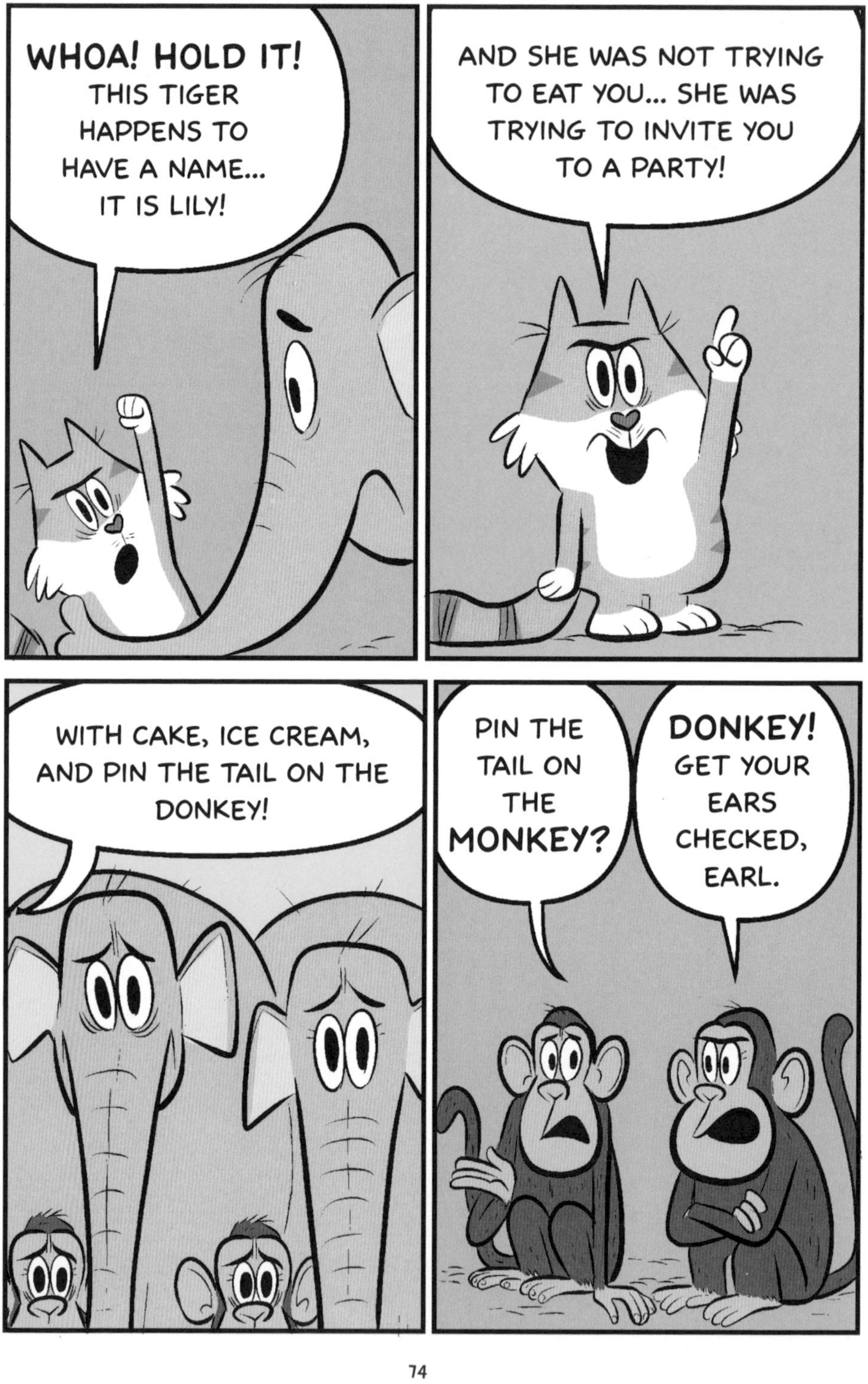
WHOA! HOLD IT! THIS TIGER HAPPENS TO HAVE A NAME... IT IS LILY!
AND SHE WAS NOT TRYING TO EAT YOU... SHE WAS TRYING TO INVITE YOU TO A PARTY!
WITH CAKE, ICE CREAM, AND PIN THE TAIL ON THE DONKEY!
PIN THE TAIL ON THE MONKEY?
DONKEY! GET YOUR EARS CHECKED, EARL.

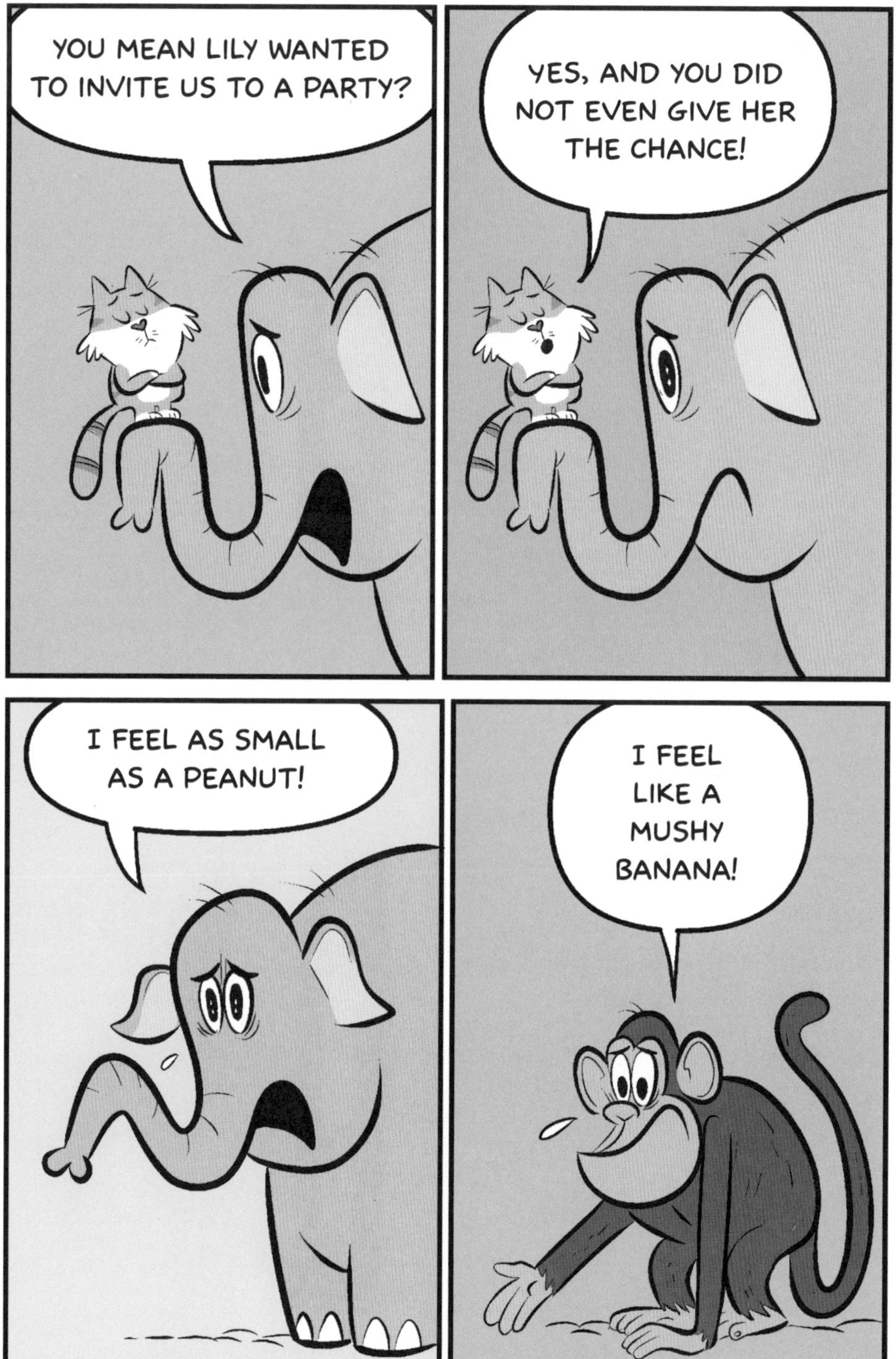
YOU MEAN LILY WANTED TO INVITE US TO A PARTY?
YES, AND YOU DID NOT EVEN GIVE HER THE CHANCE!
I FEEL AS SMALL AS A PEANUT!
I FEEL LIKE A MUSHY BANANA!

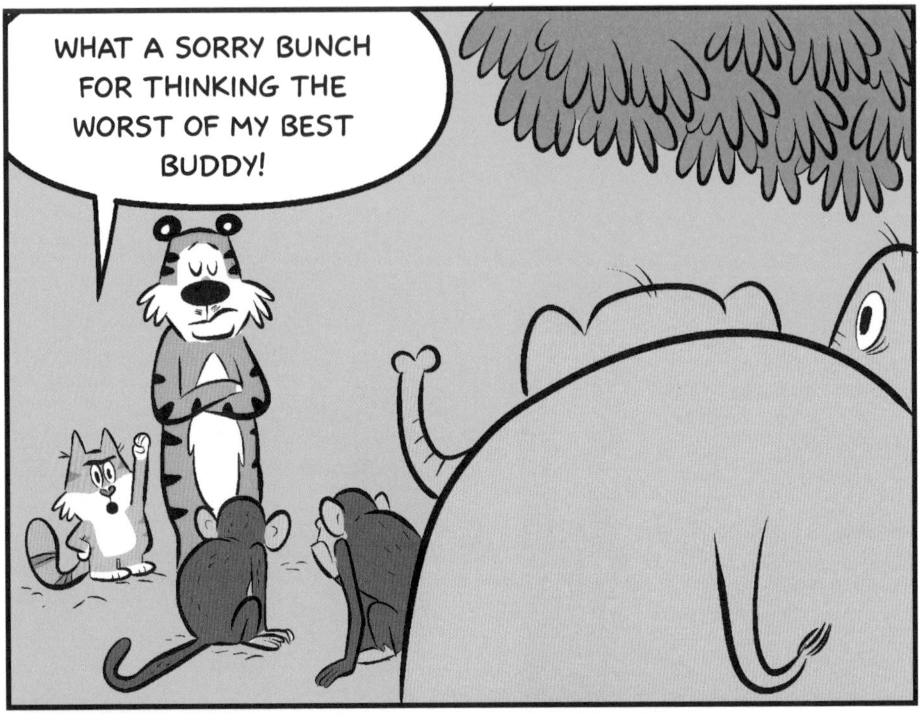
WHAT A SORRY BUNCH FOR THINKING THE WORST OF MY BEST BUDDY!

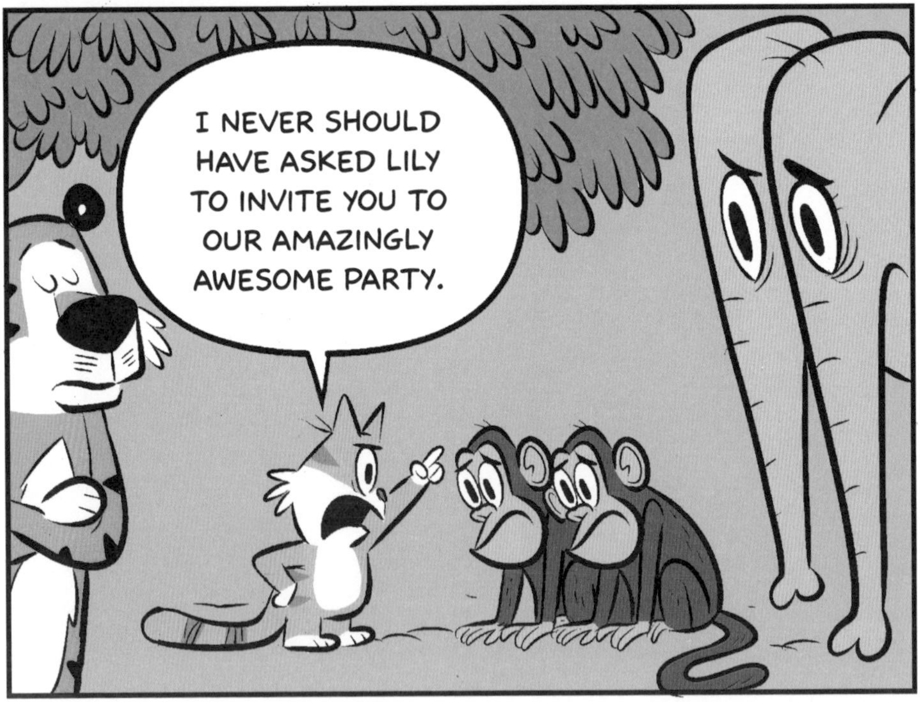
I NEVER SHOULD HAVE ASKED LILY TO INVITE YOU TO OUR AMAZINGLY AWESOME PARTY.

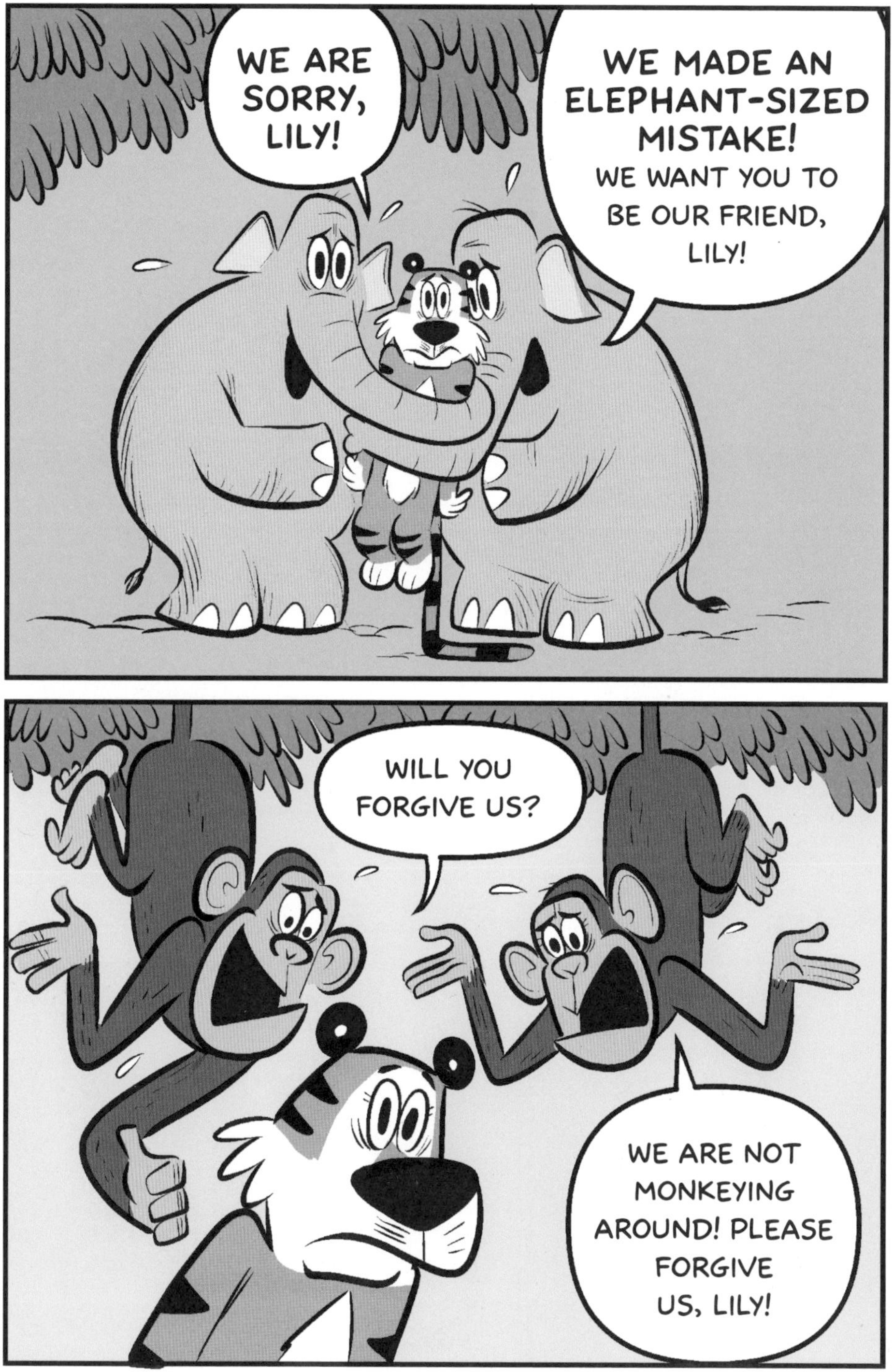
WE ARE SORRY, LILY!
WE MADE AN ELEPHANT-SIZED MISTAKE! WE WANT YOU TO BE OUR FRIEND, LILY!
WILL YOU FORGIVE US?
WE ARE NOT MONKEYING AROUND! PLEASE FORGIVE US, LILY!

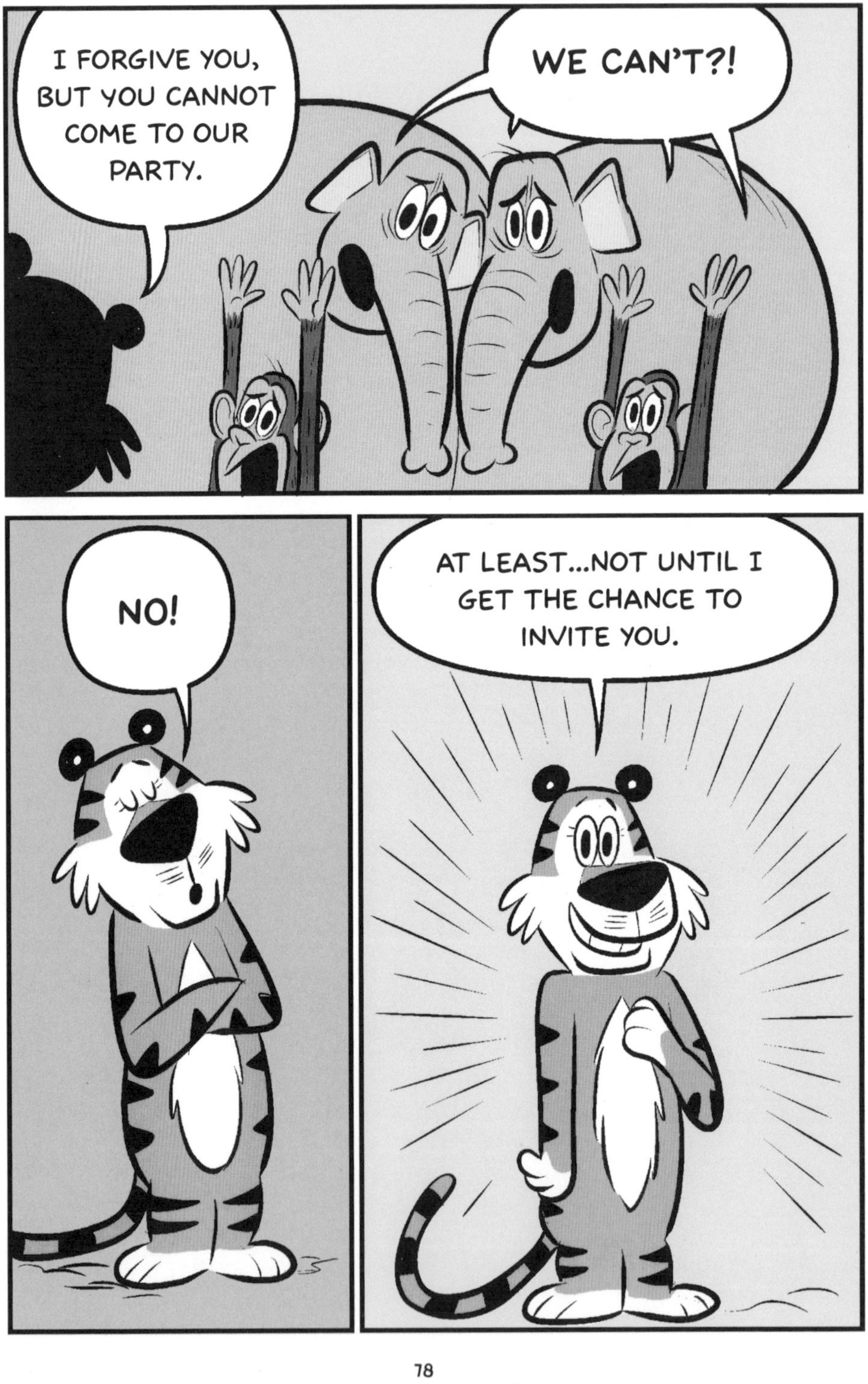
I FORGIVE YOU, BUT YOU CANNOT COME TO OUR PARTY.
WE CAN'T?!
NO!
AT LEAST...NOT UNTIL I GET THE CHANCE TO INVITE YOU.

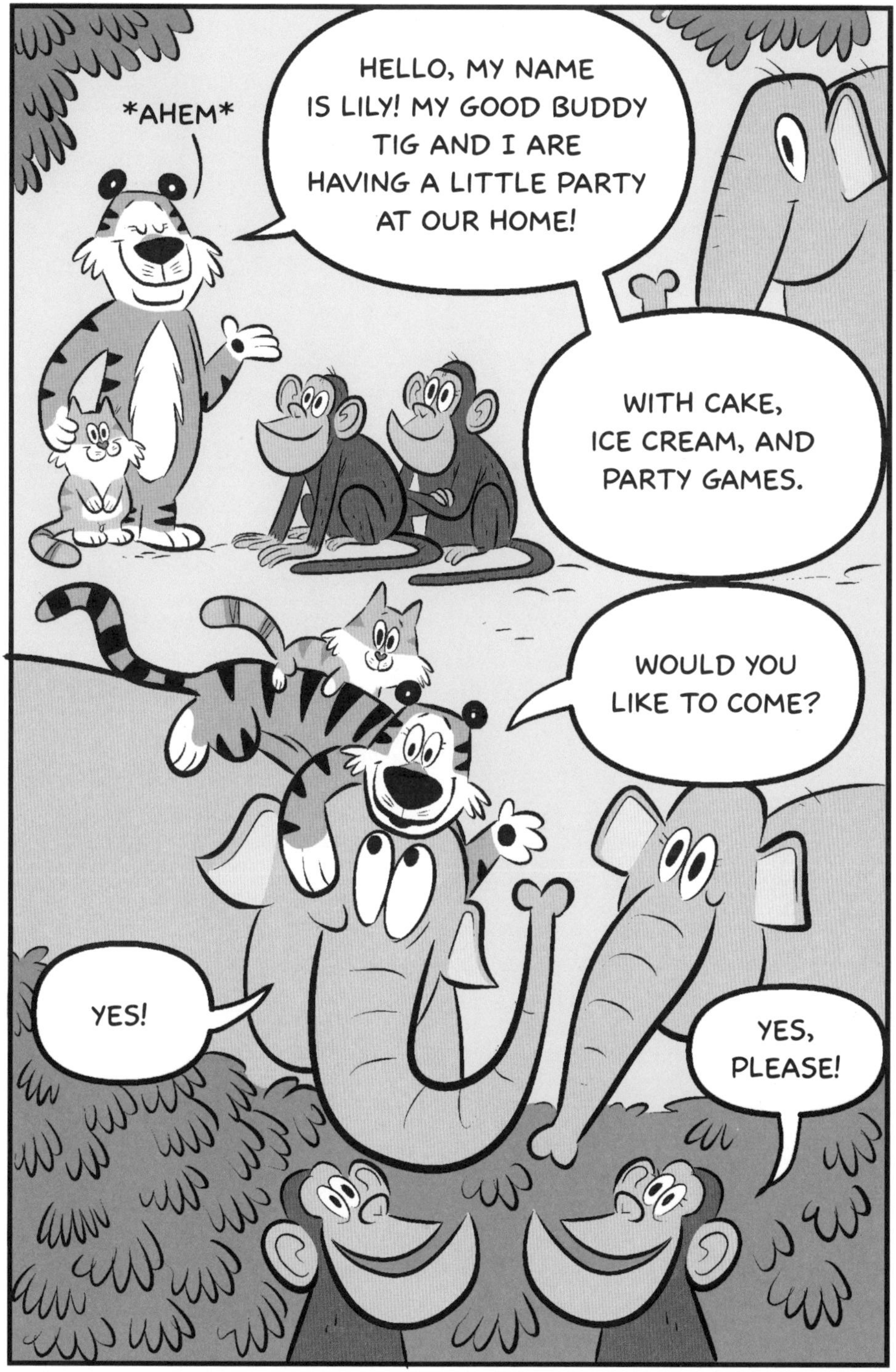
AHEM
HELLO, MY NAME IS LILY! MY GOOD BUDDY TIG AND I ARE HAVING A LITTLE PARTY AT OUR HOME!
WITH CAKE, ICE CREAM, AND PARTY GAMES.
WOULD YOU LIKE TO COME?
YES!
YES, PLEASE!

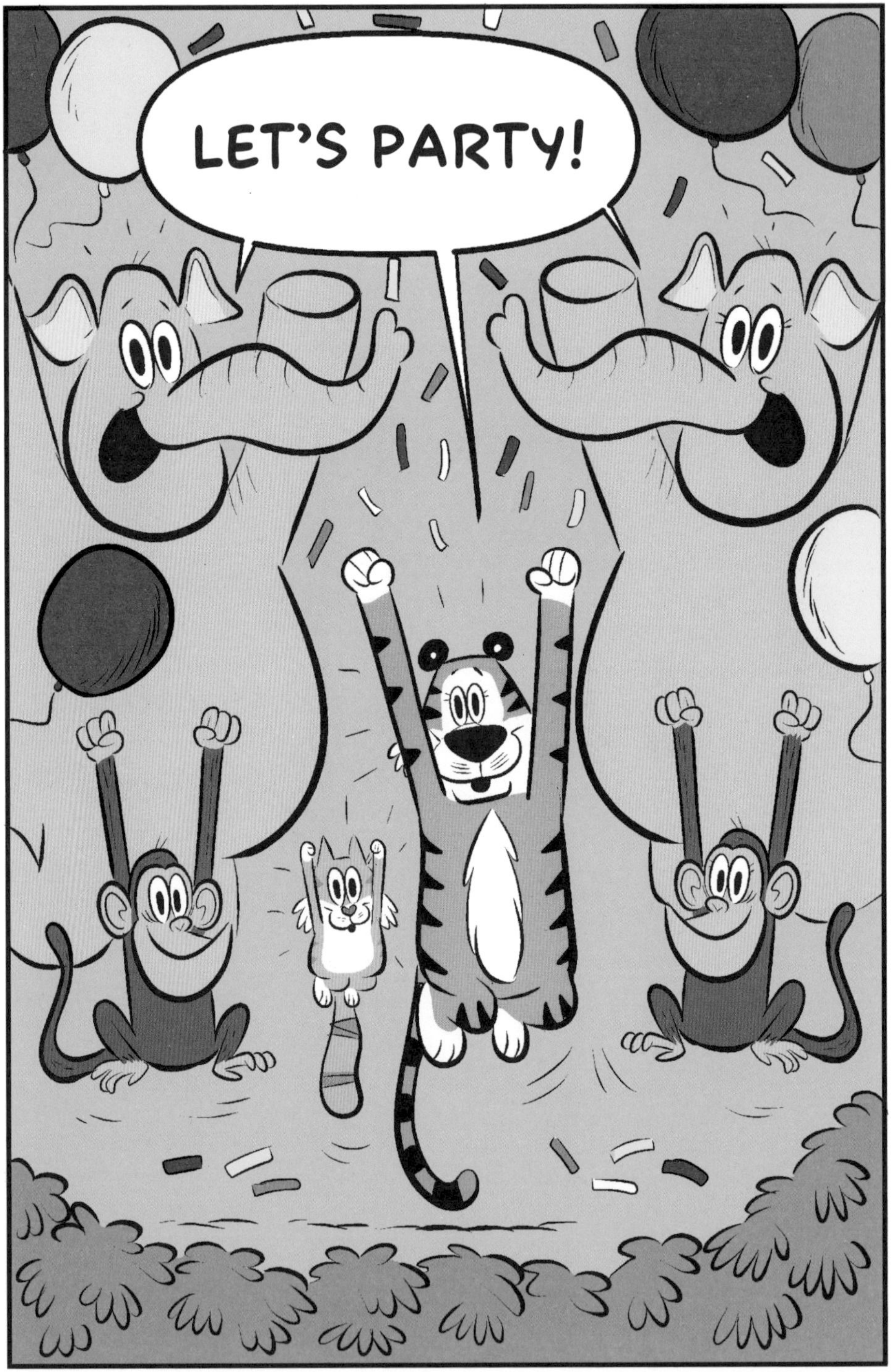
LET'S PARTY!

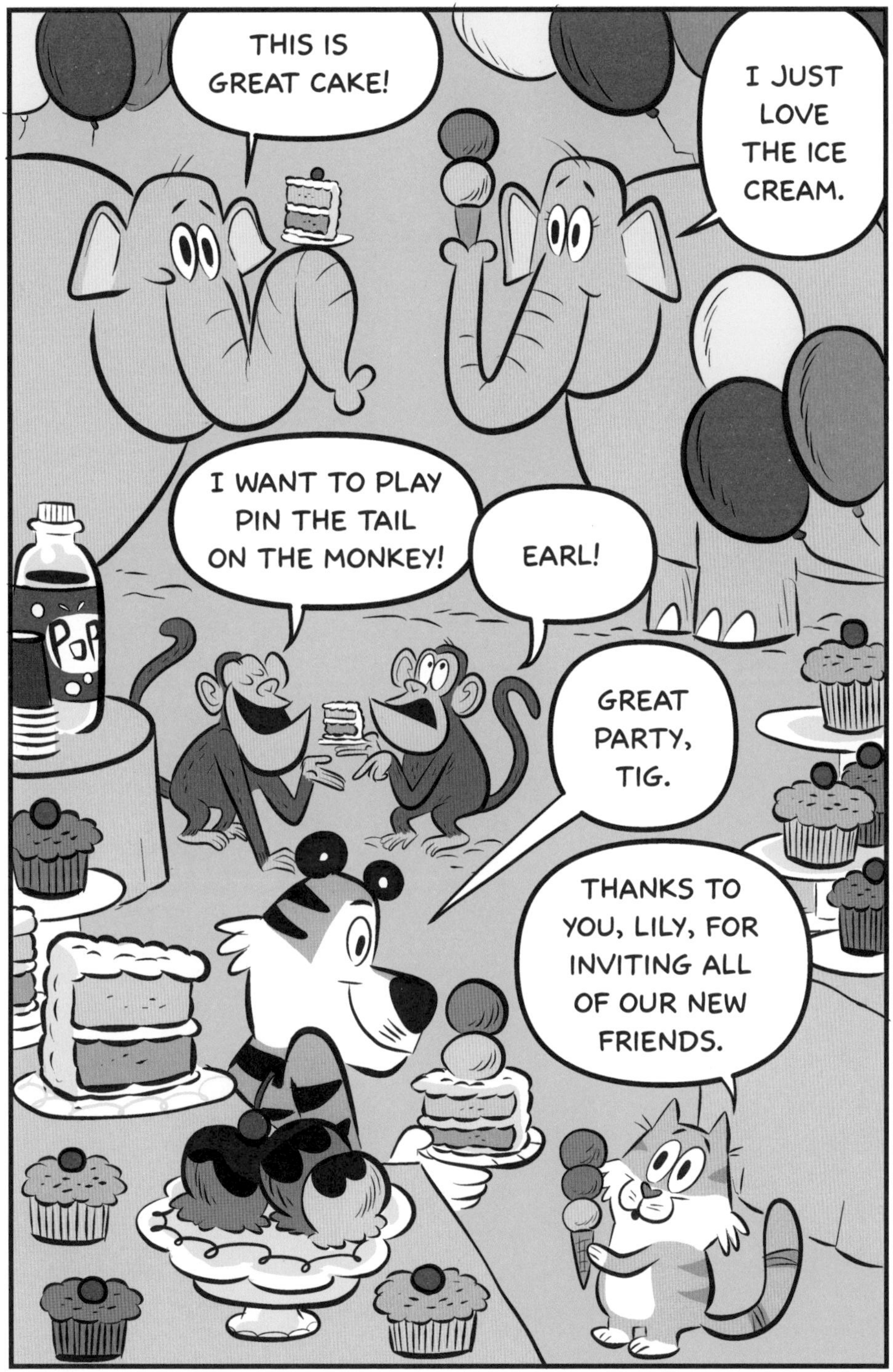
THIS IS GREAT CAKE!
I JUST LOVE THE ICE CREAM.
I WANT TO PLAY PIN THE TAIL ON THE MONKEY!
EARL!
POP
GREAT PARTY, TIG.
THANKS TO YOU, LILY, FOR INVITING ALL OF OUR NEW FRIENDS.

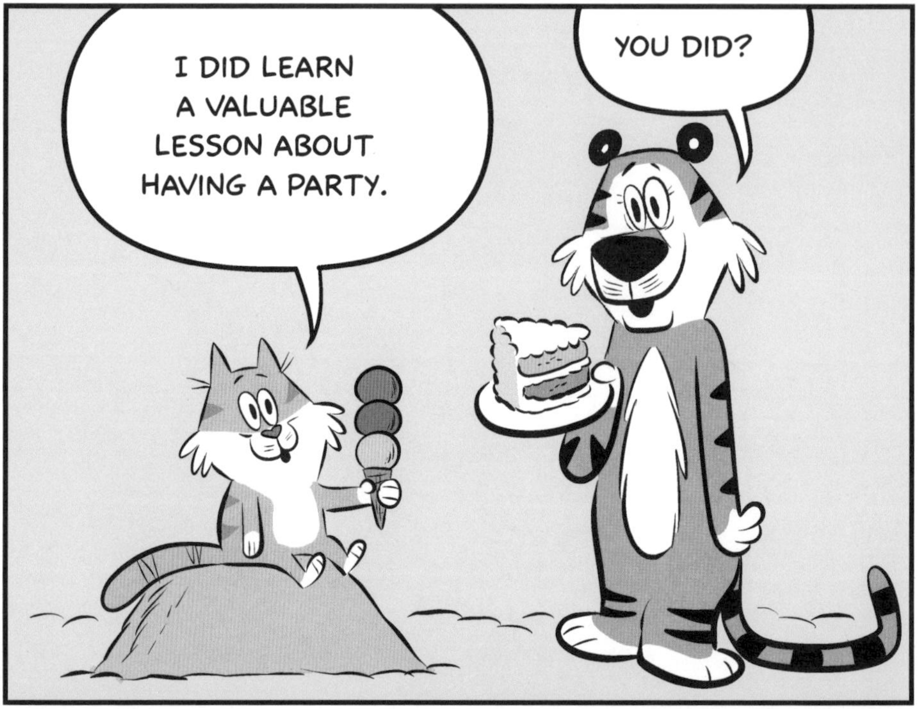
I DID LEARN A VALUABLE LESSON ABOUT HAVING A PARTY.
YOU DID?

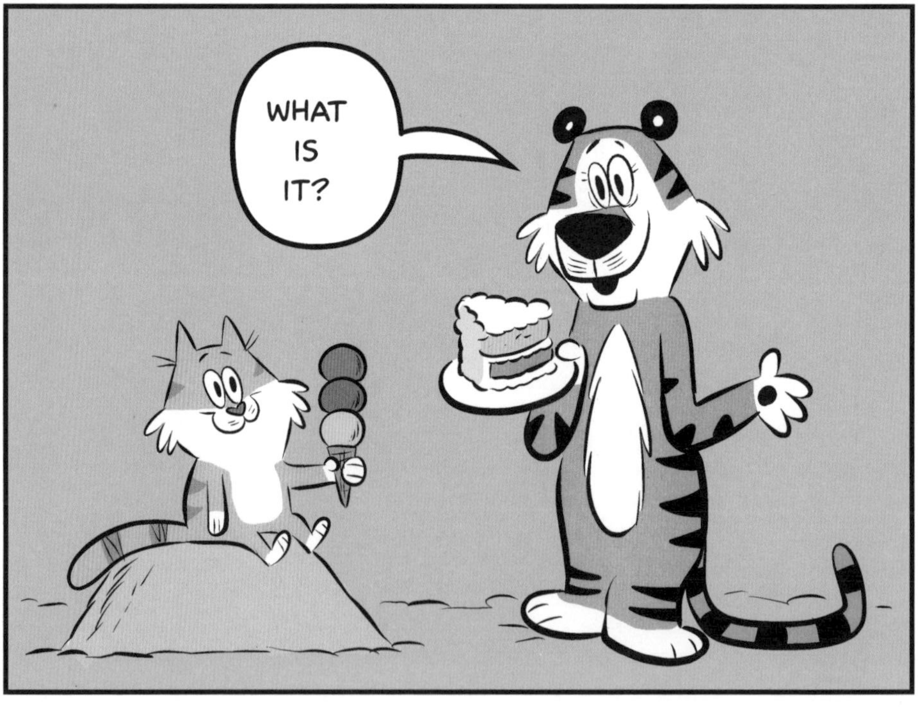
WHAT IS IT?

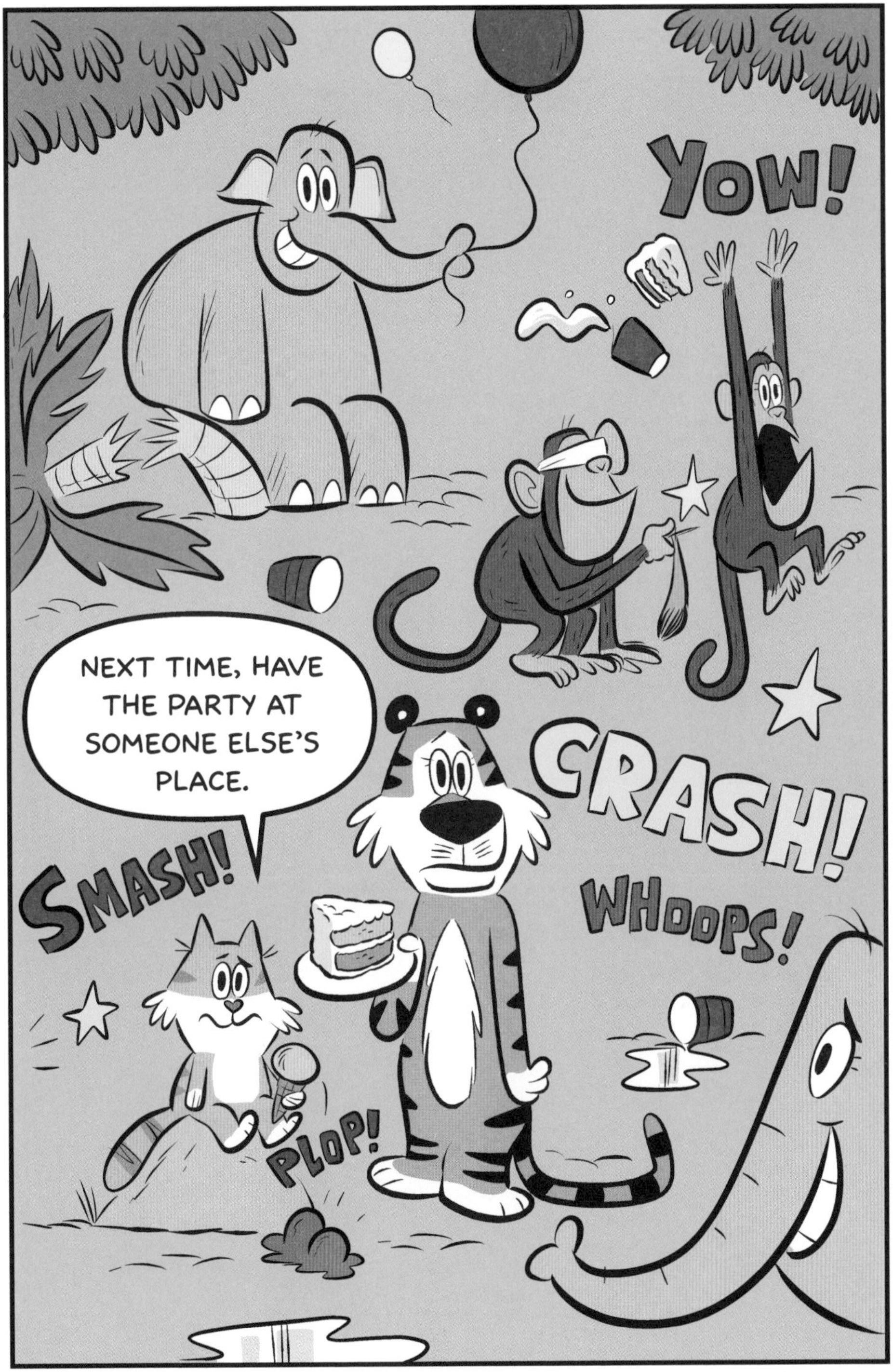
YOW!
NEXT TIME, HAVE THE PARTY AT SOMEONE ELSE'S PLACE.
CRASH!
SMASH!
WHOOPS!
PLOP!

BONUS COMIC!

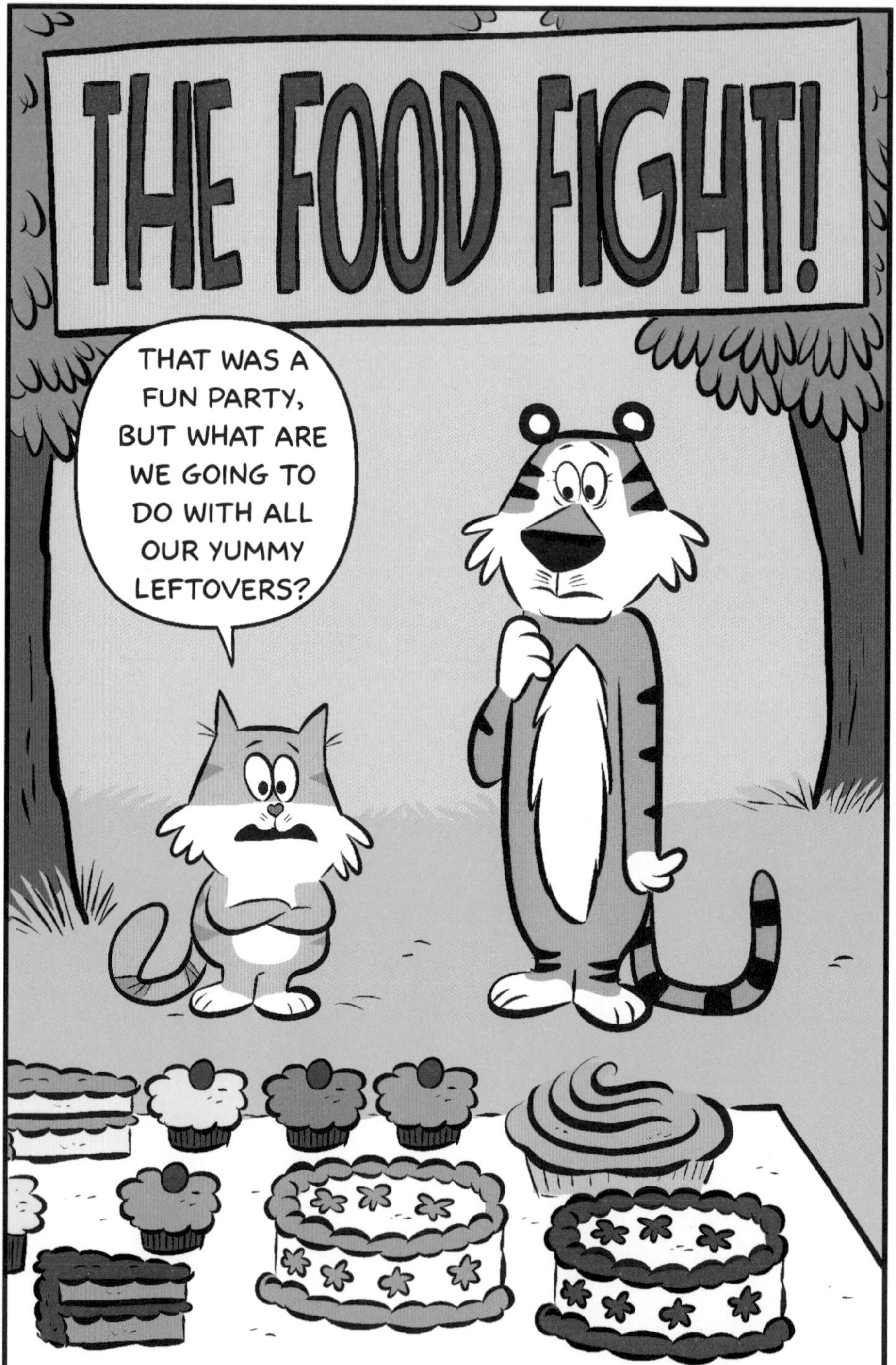
THE FOOD FIGHT!
THAT WAS A FUN PARTY, BUT WHAT ARE WE GOING TO DO WITH ALL OUR YUMMY LEFTOVERS?

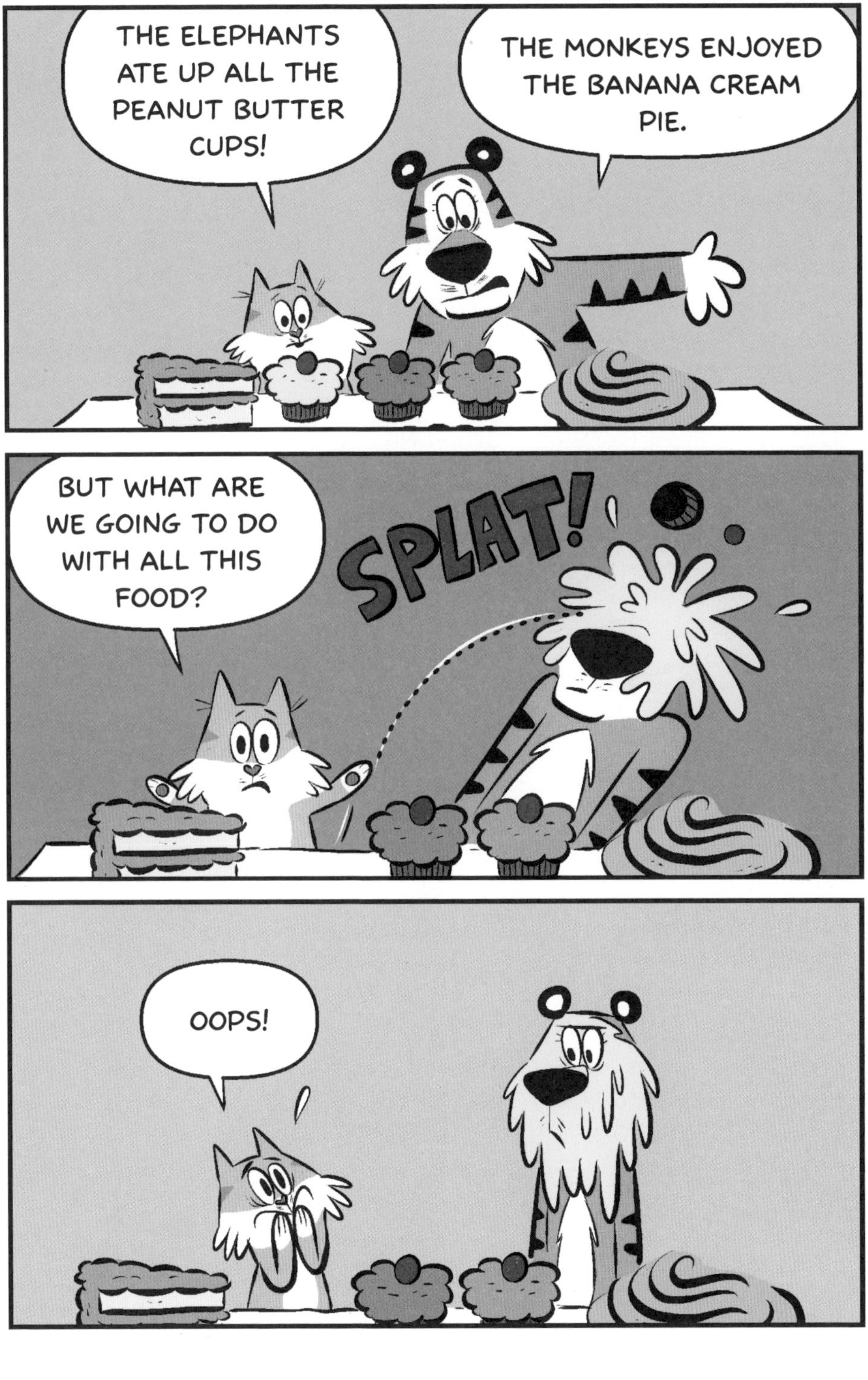
THE ELEPHANTS ATE UP ALL THE PEANUT BUTTER CUPS!
THE MONKEYS ENJOYED THE BANANA CREAM PIE.
BUT WHAT ARE WE GOING TO DO WITH ALL THIS FOOD?
SPLAT!
OOPS!

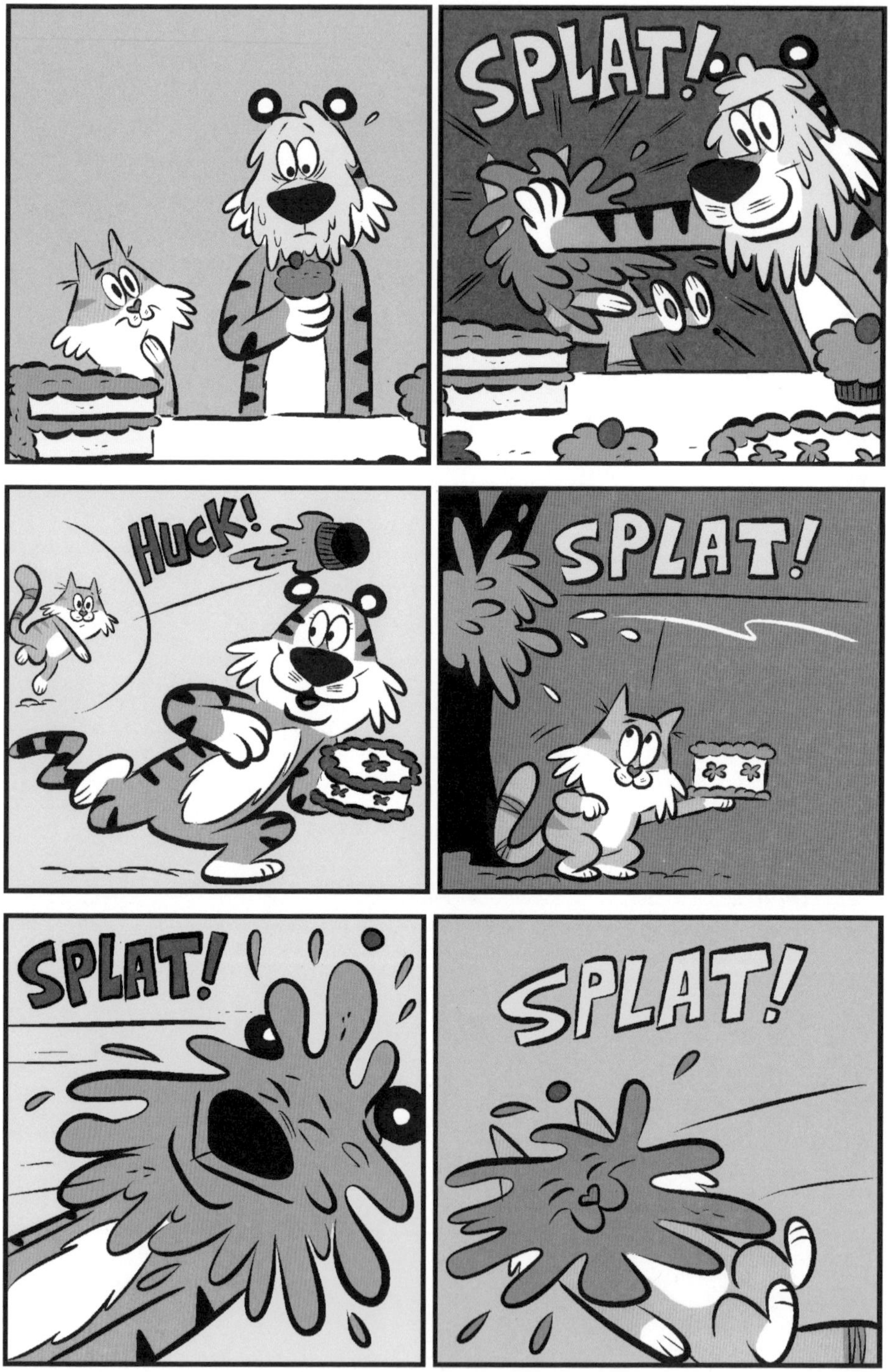
SPLAT!
HUCK!
SPLAT!
SPLAT!
SPLAT!

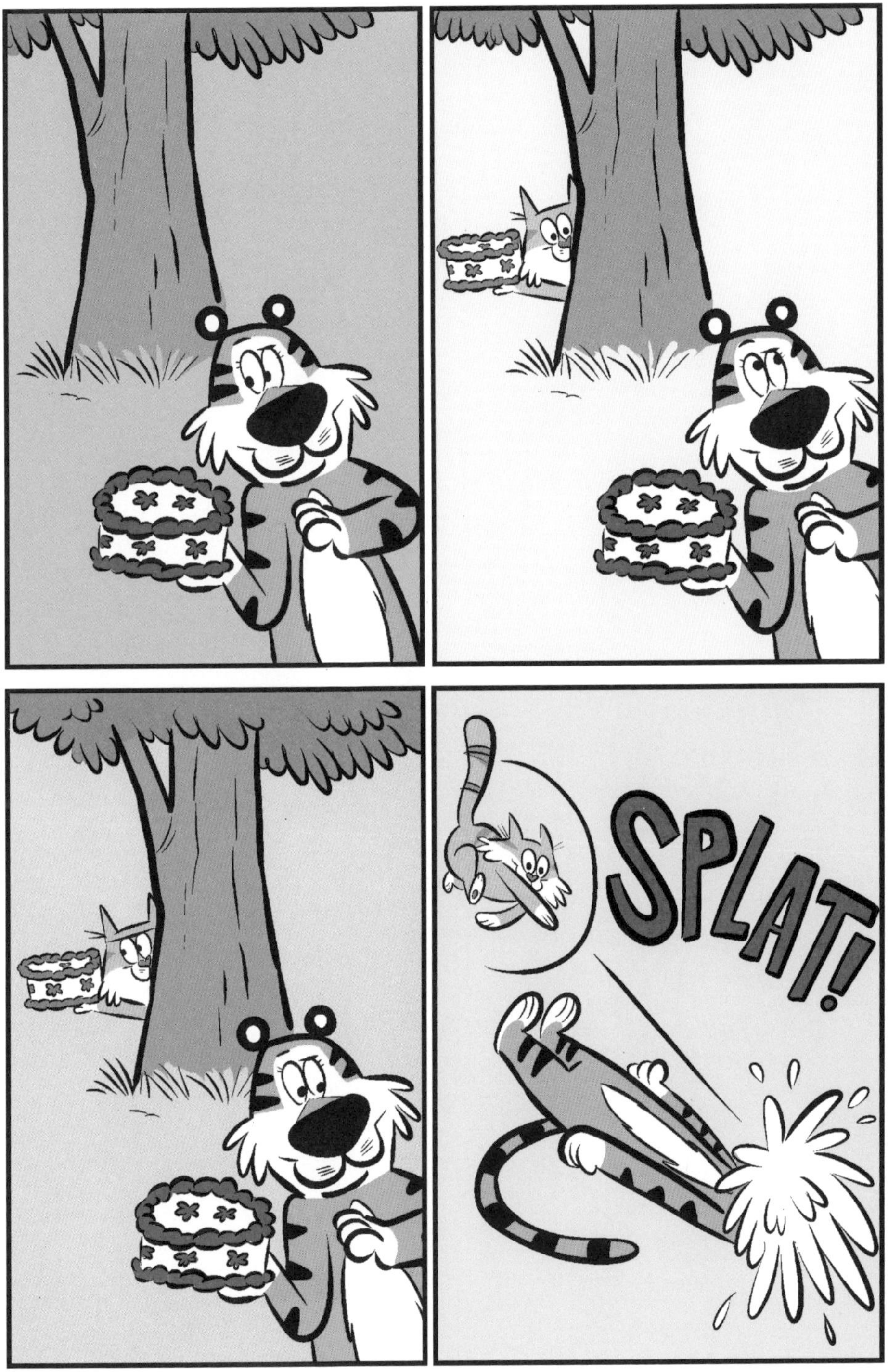
SPLAT!

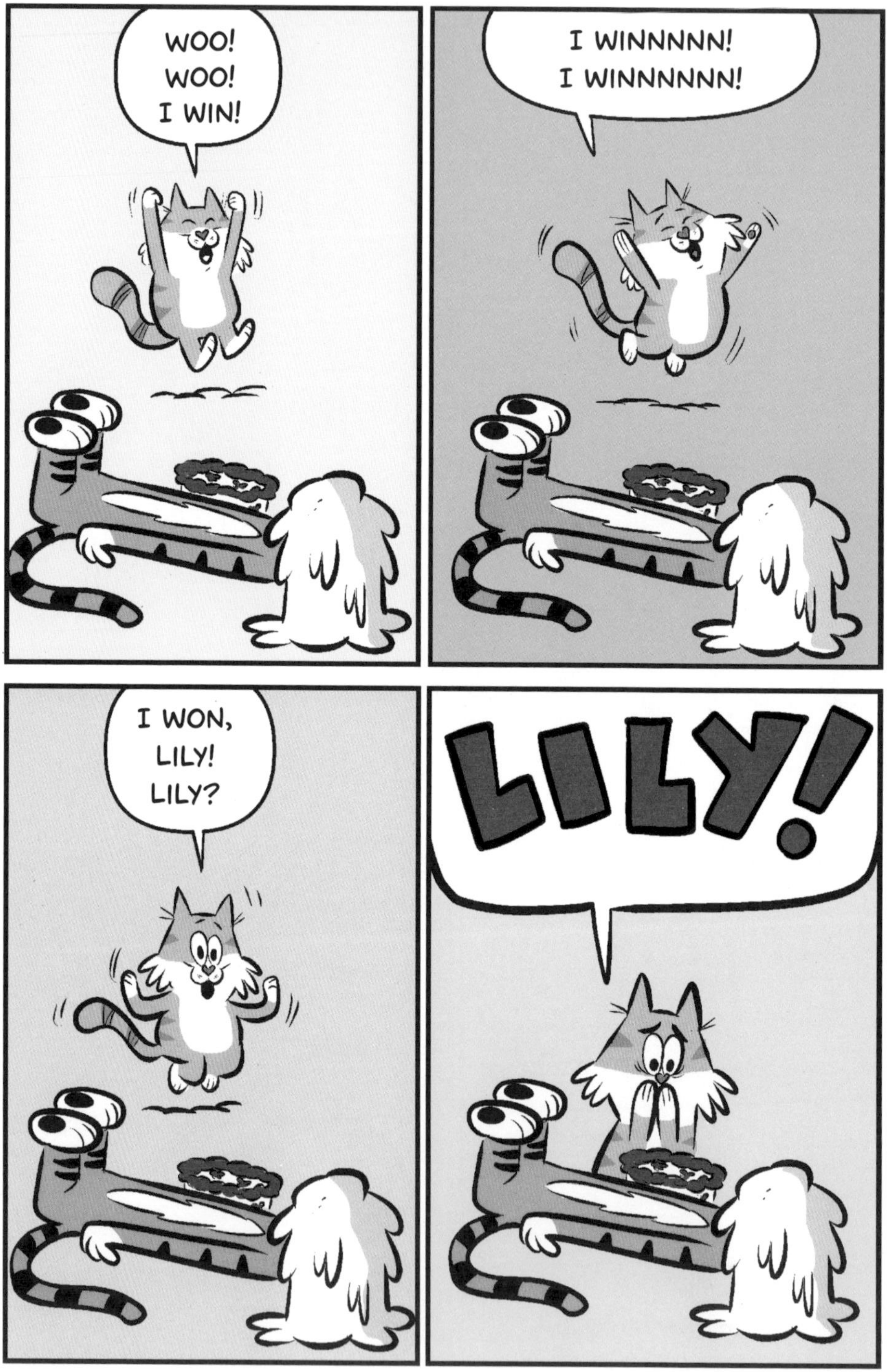
WOO! WOO! I WIN!
I WINNNNN! I WINNNNNN!
I WON, LILY! LILY! LILY?
LILY!

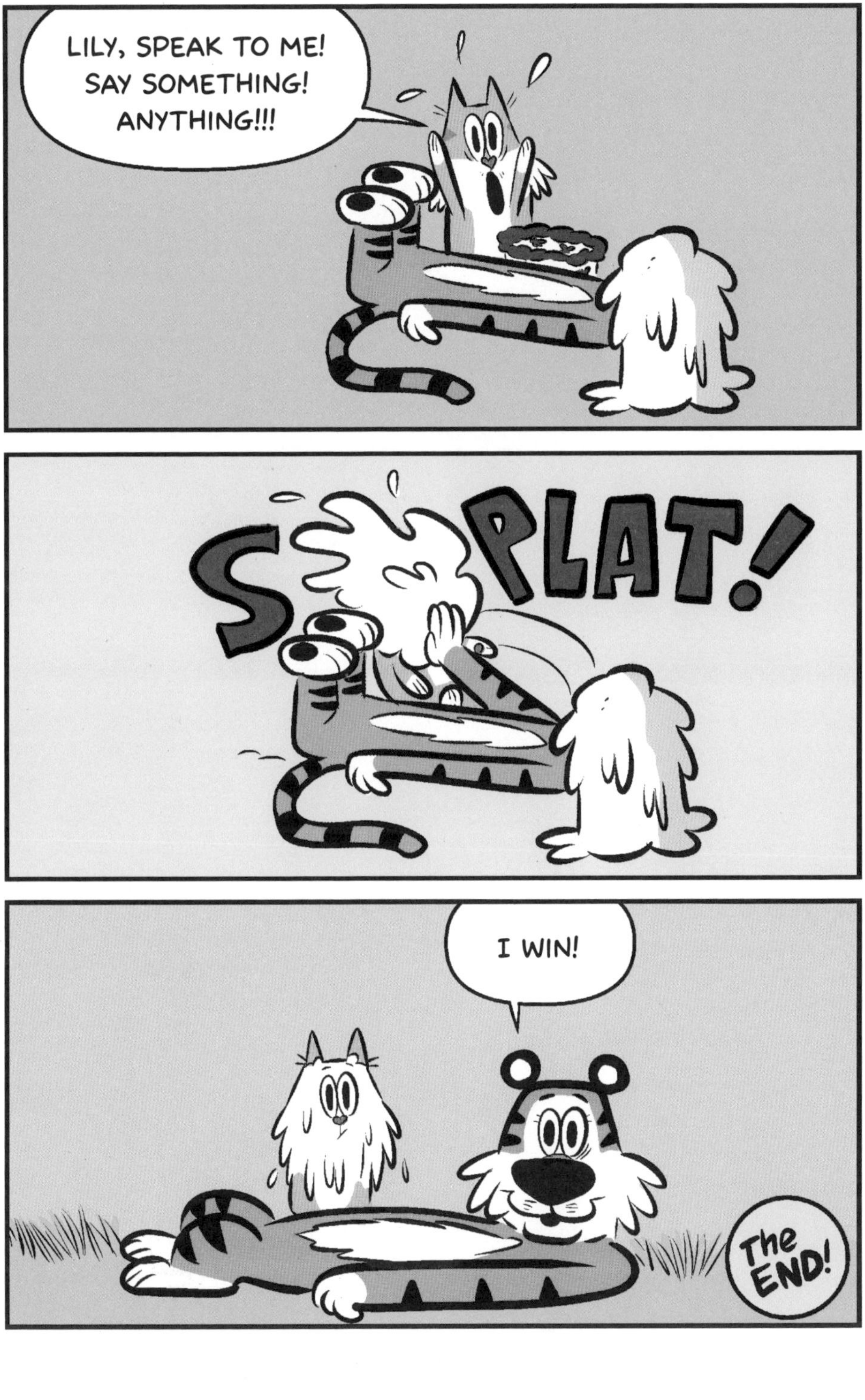
LILY, SPEAK TO ME! SAY SOMETHING! ANYTHING!!!
SPLAT!
I WIN!
The END!

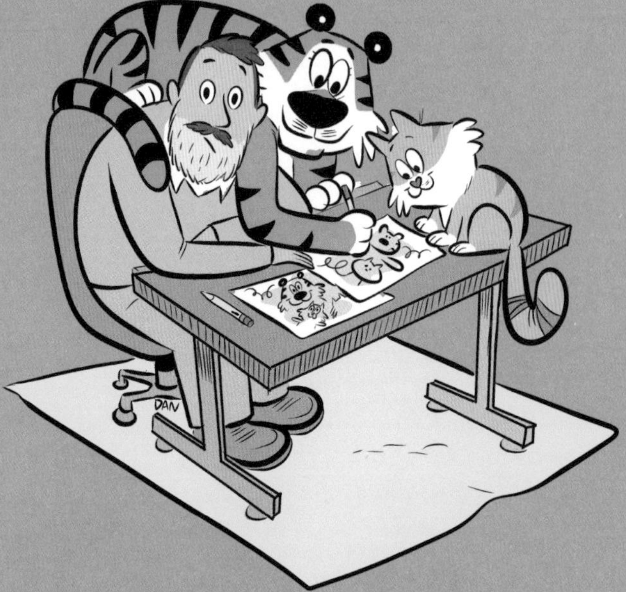
DAN

Dan Thompson began his professional career doing character design and animation for Funnybone Interactive, then moved into freelance cartoon illustration and gag cartooning. He writes and draws comic strips for Andrews McMeel Syndicate in Kansas City, Missouri, including *Rip Haywire*, a humorous adventure comic, and *Kidspot*, a daily children's puzzle. Thompson also draws for the *Brevity* comic panel. A New England native, Thompson was born and raised in Lowell, Massachusetts. He now lives in Graham, North Carolina, with his wife and two sons.

@Thompsoncomics